ABOUT

Alan Wilkinson is a British author with a lifelong interest in the American West. As a young man he worked as a factory hand, gardener, railroad brakeman and rat-catcher, racking up a total of over forty jobs. At the age of thirty-five he enrolled for a degree in American Studies and spent an exchange year in New Mexico. After graduating, he dedicated himself to writing.

In 2004 he was appointed Jack Kerouac Writer in Residence in Orlando, Florida. Seven years later, the receipt of a Wingate Fellowship allowed him to spend six months alone in the Nebraska Sandhills, where he absorbed the spirit of a place that had long fascinated him. In 2015 Alan won a Fellowship at the Wurlitzer Foundation in Taos, N.M., where he completed his first novel, Cody The Medicine Man and Me.

In between authoring ghosted biographies, corporate histories and similar commissions, Alan concentrates on creative work linked to his love of natural surroundings. He lives in Durham, a cathedral city in the north-east of England.

Visit his website at *http://alan-wilkinson.co.uk/*

ALSO BY ALAN WILKINSON

Non-fiction

The Red House on the Niobrara

There Used to Be a Guy… But He Died

Between the Rockies and a Hard Place

Fiction

Cody, The Medicine Man and Me

**all available from Amazon.com*

For Chris & Joan
so happy to have your
ongoing support
x

LOST AND FOUND IN NEBRASKA

ALAN WILKINSON

INJURY-TIME PUBLICATIONS

Injury-Time Publications

A CIP catalogue record for this book is available from the British Library

Cover design by Karri Klawitter

Print ISBN 978-0-9532629-5-3

AUTHOR'S NOTE

This book owes a lot to the generous and hospitable people of Nebraska, particularly those who inhabit the remote and beautiful Sandhills. It celebrates the memory of a truly great author, Mari Sandoz, born in that region and proud of its history.

There is one real-life character who consented to appear as herself within these pages. Jeannie Goetzinger at the Olde Main Street Inn, Chadron, has been a wonderful hostess and loyal friend for some twenty years now. I thank her for her gracious cooperation.

Warm thanks too to my dear friend and editorial adviser, Joan Deitch in London, and to Jamison Wyatt, of Lincoln, Nebraska, who gave me such useful advice on Mari Sandoz and corrected the 'Britishisms' in my original text.

However, the book is dedicated to my partner, Alyson Learmonth, whose astute reading of the text and observations on my story, not to mention her willingness to understand the subject-matter, helped me complete the task I set myself on our retreat in the Scottish Highlands two years ago.

1

Around ten o'clock on a sunny Monday morning in April 2011, in a small town in eastern Oregon, Steve Kaminski checked his watch, stowed his electric jig-saw in the back of the truck and strolled across the forecourt of the Thunderbird Motel, emerging onto Main Street. From there he walked three blocks to the Western Union office where he collected a large sum of cash. Sitting on a cheap plastic chair, he peeled off fifty twenty-dollar bills and tucked the rest down the front of his denim shirt. Back at the window he wired the thousand to an address in Portland. That would keep the vultures off his back for a few weeks.

Across the street he entered the family-run diner where he got breakfast most days. He ordered his usual eggs over easy, wheat toast (no butter) and bacon. He sat for some time over his coffee, absorbing the feeling of deep ease that had spread through his body. When the owner came by with the refill she asked him what his plans were for the week.

'Nothing much,' he said. 'Might take a little trip. Might not.'

'Sounds like a plan,' she said, and moved on to the next table. She knew better than to quiz him.

From the diner he made his way to the thrift store. By eleven o'clock he was back at the place he'd called home for longer than he cared to recall. Turning the key in the door marked 109, he entered a sparsely furnished room, approached the bed, moved the neatly folded Navajo rug to one side and sat down. He took out the money, four notes at a time, folding a fifth over each bundle, just the way they'd showed him when he worked at the race course all those years ago. He slipped two hundred into his billfold, the rest into the beige nylon fanny pack he'd just bought for a dollar fifty, previous owner a smoker by the smell of it. It felt odd when he fastened it around his waist. Reassuring, but odd. It wasn't a thing he'd ever used before. As to the sensation of closing his hands around the fat wad of bills, that would stay with him for some time. Four thousand bucks, near enough. He hadn't had his hands on so much cash in years.

He shifted the bulge round to the small of his back where his quilted jacket would hide it from view. Just to make sure, he stood up and twisted his neck to check in the mirror. Then he opened the door and stepped out into the yard, sliding a hip flask from his pocket and taking a quick nip. It was a chilly morning, despite the sunshine.

He walked across the gravel towards his truck, opened up the tailgate and took out a small, rectangular double-glazed panel. He held it against the matching hole he'd cut in the freshly painted plywood shell, and eased it into position. It fitted snugly. It took him but a couple of minutes to work the rubber seal into place around the edge. When it was done he stood back, squinted at it and nodded approvingly.

A few yards away Wayne was standing at the office door with a cup of coffee in his hand. 'Gotta say you're doing a hell of a job there,' he said.

Steve reached out and wiped a smear of dirt off the glass with his shirt cuff. 'Yeah.' He turned to face his employer. 'I've had a whole lot fancier campervans, but this one comes cheap. Got all my materials outta your dumpster there.'

'Is that a fact?' Wayne walked across and peered into the back of the truck. There was an old wooden tool-chest, a mattress and a pile of folded blankets, above them a set of little wooden drawers that Steve had fashioned out of reject lumber. A couple of cast-iron pans and a large enamelled mug hung from hooks set in the roof. 'Looks real cozy,' he said.

'Needs to be,' Steve said. Shielding his eyes against the sun, he looked at the snow-covered mountains, barely five miles distant. 'No telling what the weather's gonna do this time of year.'

Wayne paused, then asked, 'So, any chance you'll come back – after you've finished in . . . where'd you say, Nevada?'

'Nebraska. For chrissake.' Steve turned to look at him. How many times did he have to say it?

'Yeah. Well, the offer still stands.'

'Listen,' Steve said, 'I blew into your yard looking for a place to stay the night. The *night*. Remember?'

'Sure I do. Damned truck woke me up, coughing and barking like a sick dog.' Wayne waited a moment, then added, 'You weren't too clever yourself.'

'That was then.' Steve flicked a bug off his wrist. 'Hell, I ain't stayed this long in one place since . . .' He shook his head. He'd said enough.

Wayne wiped his lips with the back of his hand. 'What about Lois?'

Steve knew he didn't need to answer that. It was none of the guy's damned business. He picked up a second glazed panel and took it around the far side of the truck. Wayne followed, watching him as he slotted it into position.

'Woman like her,' Steve said as he worked his way around the seal, 'she can do better for herself than an ageing drifter.' He pulled out the flask, and tossed back another nip. 'And if she can't, why would I be interested in her?'

'So what am I gonna tell her when she gets back from the coast?' Wayne asked.

'No need to tell her a damned thing,' Steve said. 'I up and left, is all.' Things were quiet for a few moments, just a faint rustling sound as the breeze rolled a plastic bag across the yard. He thought for a moment, then said, 'Tell her my sister died. By the time I get to where I'm heading . . .' He didn't complete the sentence. He hadn't yet gotten used to the idea that it really would happen. Part of him hoped it might be over before he got there.

Wayne sipped at his coffee, pulled a face and threw the rest onto the ground. 'Well, me and Ellen are gonna miss you. Not many guys around these days fix things like you do.'

'We're a dying breed,' Steve said. 'And that is a fact.' He put away his tools, closed the lid of the box, and crossed the yard to his room.

Twenty minutes later he was packed and ready to go. Two duffels, the Navajo blanket and a Coleman stove, a couple of decks of cards, a supermarket 'bag for life' containing a few favorite books. That was it, apart from the bits and pieces that he kept in the truck. Tools, a mess kit, work-clothes, the harmonica he still hadn't learned to play. He paused briefly on the threshold, remembering what moving used to be like. The U-Haul truck, the trailer, the countless boxes, the tangle of kids' bikes and garden tools, the fights over antique furniture and framed photographs, the tears - and always someone's damned records. 'Jesus,' he murmured, slammed the door and went to the office with the keys.

'Well, I'm real sorry to lose you,' Wayne said. 'I've hired guys half your age who couldn't work like you.'

'I told you before,' Steve said. 'Hispanics. I worked with them down in New Mexico. Those guys are still hungry enough.'

Wayne took out a cigarette and lit up. 'So when you're done in Nebraska, where are you heading, long-term? Where's home gonna be?'

Steve pointed at the truck. 'You're looking right at it,' he said. He held out a hand to Wayne. They shook. He turned, and walked across the yard. Wayne stood at the door of the office and watched as the other man hesitated, felt around to the small of his back, then climbed into the cab. Before he slammed the door he raised a hand to Wayne. 'Take her easy now,' he said. The truck crunched over the gravel and onto the highway.

Steve's last sight of the Thunderbird Motel and RV Park was pretty much the same as his first, except that the large red sign on the roadside now hung straight on its tall post, and come sundown every one of the letters would light up and VACANCIES would flash, on off on. That was his first job, in exchange for his first night's lodging. And then there were other jobs and other nights, and before he knew it a year had gone by, near enough. Around a place like that there was always something for a handy guy like him to work on.

As he headed north a thought occurred to him that had him shaking his head. He wondered briefly what might have happened if the truck hadn't all but died, if he hadn't met Lois, if the bronchitis had really gotten hold of him. At one point he'd imagined he might die in that crummy little town. He shuddered. There was an upside to moving on, even if it did mean he was heading towards the past.

An hour or two later he'd crossed the Columbia River and was on I-90. Already his back was complaining, and the rhythmic pulse of pain in his right knee had started up again. He pulled off at Spokane and filled up with grease and caffeine. Hung around long enough over refills to let the pain-killers kick in.

Already he was resenting the effort this journey required of him. It hadn't been easy negotiating with his sister, and he hadn't exactly felt good about the way it went. But what was he to do? Sure, she was dying, but he hadn't shown up for the old man, nor Irena, so what made her think he would come to her bedside?

'You have to come,' she insisted. It was their longest phone conversation in years, and before she'd even asked how he was doing she was pressuring him. 'Get me out of this damned place and take me home.'

That was the problem. She really thought he would consent to take her to the old place, hang around until she died. 'And we got things to talk about,' she said.

'Like what?' he said. 'Like why you ended up living in clover?'

'Steve, there are things you need to understand.'

'Go right ahead. I'm listening.'

'Face to face, Steve. We need to talk face to face. This is your sister you're talking to. Your own flesh and blood. I'm sick, I'm looking at death, and I'm asking you to come home.'

'Ever occur to you I might be busy?' he said. 'Takes time to travel. Money too.'

'Is that it, Steve? Is it money that's worrying you?'

'Well, I sure can't afford a road trip right now, if that's what you mean. Truck's barely fit to get me to the grocery store. I'm hanging on here, minimum wage, debt collectors at my throat. I don't have ten thousand acres rented out. No damned house to sell either.'

'What'll it take, Steve?'

'Whaddaya mean?'

'How much? To fix your truck or – couldn't you rent something? Look, I'll send you some money. Just tell me what you need.'

'Let me think about it. I need to do some figuring.'

He was tempted to take his time over it. Last time they had a situation like this she'd pleaded with him, told him the old man was asking for him, daily. But he dragged his feet, and then it was too late. And he knew, deep down, that it suited him that way. Sure, he said how sorry he was that he'd missed the funeral, but she knew the truth. They'd hardly spoken in the twenty years since then.

Now, before he could even figure out what to ask for she called again. She'd had another dose of chemo, but the latest prognosis wasn't good. She wanted to give Steve power of attorney. That shook him up. Why him? He stalled. Told her he'd need a couple of grand to put the truck right, a few hundred for gas, and then accommodation on top. No, he wasn't going to stay at the old place. No way. Too many ghosts. As he mumbled his way through his protestations she cut him short. 'Five,' she told him. 'I'll send you five thousand. Will that be enough? To get you to your dying sister's bedside?' An hour later she called to say she'd wired it through.

Back in the truck he put the radio on, and settled into a travelling mindset, eyes fixed on the road ahead as the miles flickered by. If he had to drive on into the night at least the traffic would be lighter then. He was still thinking about Wanda. How had she managed all those years, stuck in the middle of nowhere? He remembered that last time she came to visit she'd said she needed a break. The old man was slipping away, and didn't like her to go to town. She was feeling stifled. Losing touch with any friends she'd ever had out there, too weary to make the effort, wondering what kind of life she would have when he finally went. She asked her brother to come and visit her, give her some relief. He told her his health wasn't so good. She told him he should quit the booze.

Steve cranked up the heat. The weather had deteriorated, and he was climbing. By the time he hit the western slopes of the Bitterroot Mountains the temperature had dipped below freezing. He made a rough calculation and decided he could get as far as Bozeman, possibly even Billings. That would leave him six or seven hundred miles next day. No big deal when he was in his prime; still manageable if he started early enough and took a couple of naps along the way.

Even at his age he still liked being out on the road. It reminded him of better times – or what seemed like better times. Once in a while he wondered just how much he had enjoyed those days, criss-crossing the Southern Plains from one site to the next and putting up in cheap motels. Maybe it was the telling of it, years later, in bars and diners. Maybe that was what persuaded him he had enjoyed it – the crazy little stories he liked to repeat, the characters he met, or heard about; the women.

He drove on. He was dimly aware of a weather warning. Snow coming in from the northwest, but not until tomorrow. The landscape he passed through was dramatic at first, but as the mountains closed in they started to look menacing. He remembered one of their neighbors in Sheridan County, way back when he was a kid. Took a honeymoon trip to the Black Hills, and Steve wanted to hear all about it. 'Sure it's pretty,' the guy told him. 'But you couldn't help feeling kinda hemmed in.' Steve was perplexed at the time. He'd seen the hills on TV and yearned to go there. They seemed so much more exciting than the eternal grasslands of Western Nebraska. Later, after he'd lived in cities and along the coast, he understood what the guy meant. He realized that he was never fully at ease any place where he couldn't see clearly from horizon to horizon.

He found a room in Billings and slept well, knowing he had a shade more than half the journey behind him. Entering the northwest corner of Wyoming next day he felt more relaxed. He tried to figure why that should be. Maybe it was the sun, still shining feebly through a thickening veil of cloud. Or maybe it was the memory of the spell he'd worked in Gillette, trucking supplies to the coal mines that had just opened up. Close to forty years ago now.

By mid-afternoon it was clear that the weather was changing. Casper was behind him, and as he approached Douglas County he could see the Laramie Mountains in the distance. He had camped there one summer, the year before he left home. Him and his buddy Luke. But they were a long way off, maybe forty or fifty miles. Right around him the land was flat, almost featureless, and the light was failing. Just enough to show up the ripples in a great sweep of grey cloud that was pressing down on him like a steel lid. The thermometer read twenty-six.

Half an hour later the truck was rocked by an unruly wind elbowing its way in from the north, shaking out flurries of dry snow that skittered across the highway, mingled with the dirt and formed grubby little drifts around the occasional shredded truck tire, the fence-posts, the bare stalks of last year's sunflowers.

The lack of traffic had been troubling him for some time. Maybe there was some kind of weather advisory in operation. He flicked the radio on. For the past hundred miles or so he'd driven in silence. There was a limit to the number of times he could listen to the Eagles' back catalogue. But he kept returning to the classic rock stations. Once in a while he'd find what he considered real music. The songs that had kept him halfway sane in Vietnam.

He pondered his options, humming along mindlessly to Creedence Clearwater. Shouldn't be more than an hour or two before he crossed the Nebraska line. He had imagined he would make it to Valentine tonight, get a room and call on Wanda's attorney next morning. She'd told him to go there and sign the papers that would allow him to access her bank account as her condition deteriorated. Then he could double back to Gordon and catch up with her in the care home.

He wondered what it would be like, seeing Wanda after all this time. Hell, last time they got together they were barely middle-aged. He was with Bonny. The kids were still around.

He turned off onto Highway 20. Christ, that road used to be so familiar. The times he'd shuttled up and down it with the old man, trying to close some deal or other, and later with his buddies, chasing tail. The radio told him that the highway was already closed behind him. A winter storm was bringing up to fifteen inches of snow to the Northwestern Great Plains, accompanied by winds gusting to fifty miles an hour.

Even as he absorbed what he was hearing, a white veil swept across the highway, wiping out most of his view. He dipped the headlights as a sign loomed out of the swirling flakes. Thirty miles now to the Nebraska line.

He passed through Lusk. He remembered standing somewhere around there, long ago on a summer night, a young guy in jeans and plaid shirt, hitching a ride west with a trucker out of Louisville, Kentucky. He grimaced as he recalled the guy giving him his first taste of chewing tobacco. And his last.

By the time he crossed the state line the wind was sweeping the snow into soft mounds. He was riding on a blanket of white, six inches, a foot, deeper in places. More than once he had to grip the wheel as the truck threatened to skid to right or left. It was some years since he'd driven in conditions like these. And of course he'd been younger then. Now, he reflected, he'd passed that moment where your growing experience makes up for your waning physical faculties. It was dark, his cell phone had died and he seemed to have mislaid the charger cord. Should he continue, and risk being stranded all night? Or turn off and hope he could find somewhere to stay?

Crawford advertised lodging, but he had no desire to stop there. He had a faint recollection of a grubby little town that bred troublemakers. Besides, Chadron wasn't so far now, and he could at least dredge up some kind of good feeling about the place. He and his buddies used to drive out there regularly in the old man's pick-up. In those days a sixteen year old could buy beer anywhere along Highway 20. Just thinking about that brought the flicker of a smile to his lips.

By the time he pulled into Chadron pretty much everything – the low walls around the parking lots, the dumpsters, the neat shrubs outside the First National Bank, the odd car abandoned to the weather – all were reduced to vague white humps tinted orange by the street-lights. One or two gas stations he passed appeared to be open, and the lights still shone in a couple of restaurants, but so far he hadn't spotted a living soul.

Turning into the parking lot of the Days Inn his front wheels started to spin. He just avoided colliding with one truck, but then, reversing, tapped the fender of another. It was a big old beast of a thing with a hydraulic hoist on the back. When he got out he could see no sign of damage. He went into the lobby and approached the front desk.

'I'm real sorry, sir. We don't have any vacancies.' The desk-clerk gestured towards the window, covered in snow. 'People hunkering down till this blows over.'

'Any idea where I could find a place?' he asked. 'I done enough driving for one day.'

She thought for a moment, then said, 'You might try the Olde Main Street Inn. Kinda funky, but they're friendly enough.'

'Olde Main Street?' Steve said. 'And that'll be . . .?'

'Right there on Main, I guess.' He raised a tired smile in response to her laugh. 'Back to the highway, up to the stop light, and take a left. It's right next to the police department.'

He drove slowly. Here in the heart of the town there were one or two vehicles out and about. He saw three youths pushing a car out of a driveway, knee-deep in snow. He was about to stop and lend a hand when they got it moving. As he approached the intersection he saw the stop light swinging crazily, the snow swirling in the wind. He turned onto Main and almost ran into a black sedan that braked suddenly and almost broadsided him. Crouched low over the steering wheel, he checked left and right through a blur of flakes.

The Olde Main Street Inn was a three-story affair built of brick. The ground floor appeared to be in darkness, just an illuminated drinks cabinet casting a warm light over a wooden bar. He parked the car, put on a baseball cap and got out, stepping into a pile of slush. He stumbled onto the sidewalk, reaching down to try and extricate the chunky crystals from his work-boot, but only succeeded in pushing them further in, where they started to melt.

He tried the big door at front. It was locked. He peered through the glass and saw a low light shining at one end of the bar. He banged on the door with his fist. Then again, this time turning his hand around so that the gold ring on his finger rapped against the glass. Nothing.

He went along the sidewalk, pausing to look in at each of the windows. There was no sign of life. Head down against the wind and cursing his sodden foot, he returned to the truck and paused for a moment, his hand on the open door. He had no idea what to do now. He looked up and down the street, then saw the sign in the next-door building, Police HQ. Maybe they would help. Just then, a car cruised slowly past. He recognised it as the one that had almost collided with him a few minutes ago. It was maybe twenty yards past him when the brake lights came on and it started backing up.

As it drew level the driver leaned out of the window. 'Hey, Oregon plates,' he said. 'You're a long way from home.' He was around fifty; wore glasses and had grey hair. 'Looking for a place to stay?'

Steve pointed to the hotel. 'Yeah, but it looks like it's closed.'

'Nah. She'll be around. Want me to call her?' The guy reached into the glovebox, pulled out a phone and said, 'Here, lemme call. You don't wanna be driving around in this shit.'

Steve hadn't realized just how tensed up he'd felt. Weary too. 'I'd really appreciate that,' he said. He approached the guy's car, turning up the collar of his coat.

'Jeannie? This is Joe. You gotta vacant room? There's a feller here looks fit to freeze. Just driven in from' – he looked up at Steve – 'where'd you come from?'

Steve didn't answer. He was not in the habit of trading personal information with strangers. The guy carried on. 'What the hell, he needs a room.' He nodded as he talked. 'That sounds great. What'll I do - send him round the . . . right, the other entrance. Okay, he's on his way.' The man called Joe threw the phone onto the seat beside him. 'Okay, my friend, you got yourself a room. Just go to the side door, right around the corner there.' Before he drove off he called out, 'Maybe catch you in the morning. Coffee time.'

Steve walked back to the truck, took his overnight bag from the front passenger seat and walked around to the side door. He stood there, shoulders hunched, for a minute or two before it was opened. Before him stood a woman - about his age, he guessed. Maybe a few years younger. She had luxuriant red hair, tied back with a purple chiffon scarf, and wore a thick, old-style plaid bathrobe. She ushered him in and locked the door behind him. A large tan dog ambled over and eyed Steve cautiously.

'Well,' the woman said, 'I reckon you got the last room in town. This weather . . .' She opened her hands, palm up and smiled. 'You'll excuse me. I don't usually dress this way nine-thirty in the evening, but I got a full house for breakfast. People who were going to move on but thought better of it.' She looked along the deserted bar. 'Thankfully my regulars all stayed home.' She reached under the counter and took out the register. 'So where have you blown in from this dark and stormy night?'

Steve placed his case on the floor. The dog came to investigate, and he stroked its head. 'Out west,' he said. 'Oregon. Been driving flat out for two days. I was trying to make Valentine, but . . .'

'Well, you're gonna struggle to get there tomorrow the way they're talking this storm up. Listen, the only thing I have is a suite. But I can give you single room price tonight. If you want to stay any longer, we can talk about that tomorrow.'

'That's fine,' Steve said. 'I need to be on my way first thing.' He gave a short laugh. 'Plan was to camp in the truck. Guess I need the weather to improve first.'

'Okay, if you can just sign in here – then I'll show you upstairs. My name's Jeannie, by the way. In the morning, well, just come down whenever you're ready. I have the coffee on around seven.'

Steve filled in the register, followed Jeannie round behind the bar and up a set of creaking wooden stairs. The landing was broad and low-ceilinged. More like an elongated lounge, with its antique love-seat, its piano and several bookcases, the magazines stacked up on an old laundry hamper. Jeannie unlocked the door for him and showed him into his suite.

'Named in honor of Mari Sandoz,' she said. He noticed that she seemed to hesitate, as if he was supposed to say something. Then she nodded to a door across the landing. 'And that's General Miles. He stayed here the time of the Wounded Knee . . .' She tailed off. 'Look, you just make yourself at home and I'll see you in the morning.'

'Thank you.'

'Sleep well,' she said.

Steve didn't bother to look around. Didn't see the sitting-room, the little kitchen with the fridge, the stove, the sink. Nor did he see the picture of the woman who gave her name to his rooms. It wouldn't have meant much in any case. Not yet. Exhausted, he crashed out in his underclothing.

2

He didn't sleep as well as he'd hoped, nor for as long. He was out of bed at midnight, and again at five, peering through the blinds to check the weather. The snow out there just kept accumulating. By six-thirty he'd given up and was looking around what was effectively an apartment. It reminded him of the kinds of joints he occasionally put up at when he was out on the Texas Plains, when the money was coming in. In the sitting-room he noticed there were shelves full of books. Nice touch, he thought.

In the shower his thoughts turned to his sister. He'd never considered the possibility that she could die before him. What was she now? Sixty-three. What kind of age was that? Perhaps it was a lack of imagination on his part, an inability to imagine such a thing. She'd always been the one with the healthy lifestyle. Never drank, only ever smoked as a kid. But maybe, he thought, living alone on the ranch all these years since the old man died - who knows what that would do to a person? From what he'd heard from her she didn't do too much socialising, hardly ever went anywhere. He and Bonny knew an old gal once. She'd been perfectly healthy when she lost her husband, but was dead within a few months. She just gave up the ghost. Never cooked, hardly left the house. Lived on a diet of chocolate and cheap sherry till her body couldn't take any more.

As he got dried and dressed, he started to wonder what the people around her might think, his turning up now like some predator. Then he dismissed the thought. Hadn't she told him one time that she hardly had any friends? Besides, he was family, and families instil patterns of behavior. Hierarchies. Wanda had got out before he did. Just turned sixteen and fixing to get married. But she was soon back, the baby adopted, her nineteen-year-old husband long gone. And soon after he left, Mom died, and Wanda stayed. Like him, she'd been in and out of a succession of jobs, always finding a way to fall out with someone. As he recalled, she'd worked with a livestock auctioneer till she called him out for cheating on some deal, then in real estate, was finally a grade-school teacher, before she got in a row over the way her principal applied the rules. Finally, she settled for running the house, helping the old man out on the ranch. Quite how she'd lived these past twenty years he didn't really know. After he'd hitched up with Bonny and moved out to the coast they'd barely exchanged more than a Christmas card. At first she used to call and remind him, time after time, that the old man was asking for him. Couldn't he change his mind? Find some kind of common ground? But intransigence was one of the many traits he'd got from the old bastard. And then he'd gone, and Wanda stopped calling. And now she was dying. Cancer with secondaries. People didn't recover from that, did they?

He tidied his bed, picked up the damp towel and hung it neatly over the shower-rail – an old bachelor habit that had always made Bonny laugh. Then he went downstairs.

The place was empty. He sat at the window, looking out

on a scene that reminded him of those long-ago days on the ranch when he'd trudge in from his morning chores, his face raw, his hands red and his feet frozen, to thaw out by the stove. The wind had dropped but the snow was still falling. The power-lines sagged under the weight of it. He looked outside for his truck, and couldn't see at first glance which of the five or six curbside mounds belonged to him.

'Guess Valentine's gonna have to wait, huh?' Jeannie said.

'You think so?'

Jeannie placed a coffee in front of him. 'I do,' she replied, then asked, 'How did you find the Mari Sandoz suite? Were you warm enough?

'Fine,' he said. Then, 'Sandoz? Do I know that name?'

'Our Panhandle secret,' Jeannie said. 'She was a writer. *Crazy Horse, Cheyenne Autumn*. A whole bunch of stuff. And *Old Jules*, of course.'

'Crazy Horse. Is that a fact?' Steve had an idea who the old Lakota chief was. 'Yeah, think I read a book about him – years ago. But what's the connection?'

'She grew up right out there in the Sandhills. We have a conference dedicated to her every year. Get a whole bunch of scholars come to stay with us. And fans. It takes place up at the college.' Steve looked blank, and blew on his coffee. 'They have a dedicated study center. If you got nothing better to do you should call in. They have all of her books up there. And some fancy artwork.'

'Yeah?' He was hardly listening now. His mind was elsewhere. 'You seen a forecast this morning?'

'Only last night's. They say it should moderate before noon. We'll most likely get the first plow through sometime this morning. They're pretty good at keeping 20 open. Then it's up to you if you want to risk it.' She turned to go. 'Listen, I've got hot cinnamon rolls out back if you'd like one?'

'That would be great, thanks.'

Two couples, both in their fifties by the look of them, had entered the bar from out back. They exchanged good mornings then went to the farthest table, in a poorly lit corner by a little stage. A moment later a younger couple joined them, pausing first to say a quick howdy.

Steve took out his flask and poured an ounce or so of bourbon into the coffee. He sat there, thinking. This place was pretty comfortable. Gordon was barely an hour's drive, and once the weather turned he could take the truck out to the State Park and camp there.

'Listen,' he said, when Jeannie returned with the cinnamon roll, 'I think I'll stay another night. And if I can keep the suite?'

'Why sure. Just let me check the bookings. Oh, excuse me.' Three more guests had come in and she went to see them into their seats.

The side door opened and Steve saw a tall man enter. Snow cascaded off his shoulders as he pushed back the hood of his parka, took a large Thermos from his pocket and placed it on the counter. Steve recognised him as the guy who'd helped him out the previous night.

'So, she didn't make you sleep out in the yard,' the man said, grinning. 'Guess you must've charmed her, 'cos she can be pretty hard to please.'

'Don't listen to him,' Jeannie called across from the other table. 'And Joe, try shaking that damned coat before you come in next time.' She addressed her guests generally. 'Just because I sell his CDs at the bar he thinks he can treat this place like he owns it.' She brought the coffee-pot to Steve's table.

The guy walked over, peeled off a huge glove and held out his right hand. 'Name's Glenn,' he said. Jeannie, at the counter now, was filling his flask from the coffee pot.

'Glenn? She just called you Joe.'

'That's my stage-name. You gonna be around for a spell, or just passing through?'

Steve dodged the question. Just shook his head and said, 'Thanks for helping me out last night. Appreciate it.'

'Small-town hospitality, my friend. We're a pretty strange breed out in the Panhandle, but that's what you get when you populate the howling wilderness with a bunch of freaks and deadbeats.' He paused and looked around. He had the attention of everyone in the place, and he seemed to like it. 'On the one hand, yeah, you get some cranky individuals doing weird stuff, but on the other, you get a lot of old-fashioned humanity. Okay, I got things to do.' He picked up the flask and moved towards the door. 'What did you say your name was?'

'Steve.'

'Okay. Maybe see you for a beer later. Wednesday's kind of our social night.'

Steve took a refill of coffee back to his room, and unpacked his case. There wasn't much in it, just a few clean clothes. His heavy anorak, gloves, boots and the like were still in the truck. For a while he lay on the bed, his head and shoulders propped up on the thick pillows. The mattress was firm. It sat high on a sturdy metal frame with brass rails at either end. It felt good.

When he'd finished the coffee he went through to the sitting-room to inspect the bookcase. Might as well entertain himself till that plow came through. The thought occurred to him that he should call Wanda, but the fact was he wasn't ready yet to fix a time when he'd show up. Part of him was still wriggling, looking for a way out of this.

There was a framed black and white photograph hanging on the wall. A woman, seated at a typewriter. She was handsome, fine-featured, apparently relaxed, as if this was her preferred posture – upright, at her work, yet in absolute repose. Her eyes were those of a woman who knew herself and had found her place in the world. There was a quiet intensity on display too. According to the title underneath she was Mari Sandoz.

Steve stood there for some while, studying her. Her clothes, her hat, the way she wore her hair, suggested that the picture dated from the 1940s, or maybe the late 1930s. He was struck by the self-confidence that shone through. Or self-possession: maybe that was the word. His eye lingered on the image.

On the adjacent shelf was a row of her books. There was *Crazy Horse,* and beside it *Cheyenne Autumn.* He had that halfway off the shelf when his eye was caught by *Old Jules,* and the picture on the cover of a crusty old man, bearded, with a piercing gaze. He pulled it down, opened it and flipped through a few pages. When he returned to the bedroom he took it with him.

As a child, Steve had always been the reader. For his sister, the passion had been music, but Steve had been all about books. If he cared to think about it, he would have admitted that he owed some of that to his father, who also read a lot, although it was mostly westerns, not what you'd call literature. Steve's tastes ran to some of the classics. His high school teacher had told him to go to college, study English or journalism, but by then all he wanted was to get away from home, live an independent life. The enjoyment of books, however, never really left him. Over the years he figured he must have devoured thousands. Mostly these were the sort of things he came across when he was on the road, living the bachelor life in cheap motels from Santa Rosa, New Mexico to Abilene, Texas, from Laredo to Dodge City – the slim, grubby paperbacks left on bedside tables by people who move on in a hurry and travel light. A bare evening's entertainment, most of them. But they satisfied his need to escape the realities of his life at the time; and among them he found occasional gems – one or two by Louis L'Amour, for example. Later he would read the man's autobiography and develop a high regard for someone who, like him, had drifted from job to job as a young man.

He well remembered too stumbling upon more serious books about the west. Somewhere he chanced upon *The Big Sky* and found himself perplexed that such a powerful story about the way a savage landscape can shape a man could have been translated into that grinning oaf of a movie he'd seen in a theater in Leakey, Texas. That story, about a man quite alienated from common humanity, had stayed with him, but by and large he had a very poor memory for the content of what he read, just whether he liked a book or didn't. Whenever he got deeply into one his mind would be triggered - by a setting, a character's behavior, even a turn of phrase - into distractions. In the same way, impressed as he was right now by the opening of *Old Jules* and the author's poetic evocation of the Panhandle landscape, he was soon imagining places from his own memory.

Within a dozen pages he was transported a few miles and several decades to those very Sandhills that lay south and east of town, to the land where his Polish grandfather had settled in the late 1800s, the land where he was born and raised. And as he read Sandoz' vivid descriptions of an area he once knew so well, he could hear, for the first time in many years, that wizened old man's fragmented memories, told partly in fractured English, partly in a language Steve had once spoken but now forgotten, about how he came to be there.

The eldest of eight children born in a village close to the German border, Andrzej Kaminski had left home alone to travel to the United States. At twenty-two, he told his family he would claim a plot of land and prepare a place for the rest of the family to follow. But for one reason or another his parents, his two brothers and five sisters all found reasons to delay, and delay and delay. The time never seemed quite ripe, and Andrzej, raised always to speak the truth, was never able to write and say that this truly was the promised land he had heard about. He had found it hard. He had seen more failure than success among the farmers he got to know in those early days. He had seen suicides, madness, hunger. He'd watched successive crops destroyed by drought or tempest or plagues of grasshoppers, lean cattle sold for next to nothing. So the time never seemed right to call for his family. Always it was next year, or the year after. Through the Depression years he even toyed with the idea of returning to the old country. By the time the Germans started rounding up the Poles for their labor camps – and worse - it was too late. He never heard from anyone after 1943.

Had he, as a young emigrant, been more aware of what was happening in the United States, he might have settled in one of the big cities like Chicago, or Cleveland, and sought work in the factories that were transforming the promised land into an industrial behemoth. But he was of peasant stock. The only wealth his people understood was land, and what the land produced. Corn, cabbages, potatoes and beets. A milk cow. A game-bird or rabbit if you were lucky. And timber, of course. So maybe he had gone west a decade or so too late.

As a boy, Steve loved to hear Grandpa talk of his young days. It seemed to bring the old man out of his solemn, pensive self and animate him in a way that little else did. And so Steve learned to prod him. *Tell me about the old times, Grandpa. Tell me about when you crossed the ocean. Tell me about riding the freight train. And the steam threshers.* Of course, he soon got to know all these stories by heart, but he was always ready to hear them again, the way they came out slightly different every time. It was a thrill to see this frail old man come alive once more, to sit at his knee and listen to the familiar tale of how he docked in New York on a sweltering day towards the end of June, how he rode the train west as far as his precious few dollars would take him, then traveled with hoboes, seeking work as a hired hand with the harvest crews. Sometimes Steve would even correct his grandfather on a point of detail – about precisely how long the voyage took, or how much money he had in that secret pocket in his pants, about the name of a particular river he forded with his bundle on his head, all of which might vary from one telling to the next. And then he would listen, again, to these tales of adventure in a new land, always secure in the knowledge that a satisfactory outcome awaited.

Grandpa was right to arrive in summer. At that time of year young men like Andrzej were in demand, and he always found work. Slowly he progressed westward, farm to farm across the Alleghenies, over the lush prairies of Ohio and Indiana, then on to Iowa and over the broad Missouri River into Eastern Nebraska, where they grew the crop they called Indian corn. He worked in the fields, cutting, threshing, binding, and sleeping under the stars. Along the way he marvelled at the fruitfulness of the rich soils, the feeling of freedom among the gangs of men who worked the snorting, steam-powered machinery and harnessed the teams of stout horses, and managed to make their voices heard in any of a dozen strange languages. He started to acquire a few English words and phrases. He learned to swear, Yankee-style. He learned too to carry a knife, and to use it. For the rest of his life he was never without one. He worked as if his life depended on it. Every time he had a few dollars in his pocket he moved on, heading for those free lands that always seemed to lie just over the western horizon.

It was late October 1887 when Andrzej found himself

leaving the rich farmlands of Nebraska's Lower Platte Valley and heading northwest towards the remote and forbidding Sandhills.

He didn't like what he saw there: high rolling dunes with a thin coating of bunch-grass that glowed pink in the fading autumn light, and rounded hills dotted with a plant that looked like a cluster of dark green daggers. People called it soapweed, for some reason he didn't yet understand. He promised to explain it to young Steve, yet again, in a later story. Underfoot – well, they called it soil, but to him it seemed more like the sand you'd find washed up beside a river. Whatever vegetation he saw looked dead, or desiccated. Just a few green patches around the scattered shallow lakes. People told him that these came and went with the seasons, that in a drought they could disappear underground for years at a time and then return with the rains. And yes, some of the local people did raise cattle that were sleek and healthy, but the trees - where were the trees? What did people build their homes with? What did people burn in their hearths when winter came, as come it must?

Steve learned that the answer to the first question was the dried cattle dung. And he always pulled a face when Grandad described how they gathered it, the women and girls in their aprons or skirts, although the old man insisted it burned with a sweet smell, like hay.

As Andrzej traveled across this strange land, he kept asking himself, had he made the right decision in following the advice of the railroad man in North Platte who told him to go to Alliance and head north? Everywhere he stopped he found that the good public lands had been taken, and the talk now was that if you wanted to claim your 160 acres you needed to go right up into the headwaters of a river called the Niobrara. He started asking people along the way whether this was true, and they all told him that they'd heard the same thing. They said the west was getting settled up, and mighty fast. Someone he met told him to contact a man up there who would help him find a plot, a guy from Switzerland, a French-speaker, and a cranky sonofabitch at that. He charged twenty-five dollars.

And as Steve reminisced, sitting on his bed there in the Olde Main Street Inn, as his memories intermingled with the text he was reading, a name, long forgotten, rose from deep in his memory, emerged from his grandfather's lips and met the name on the book's cover. The name was Old Jules Sandoz.

Steve sat bolt upright. It was as if he had awoken from a dream, and in a sense he had. From time to time, over the years, mostly when he was alone and thinking of nothing in particular, he would be surprised by such an echo of the distant past. It might be a long-forgotten rebuke from a school-teacher, the voice of his father nagging at him to clean and oil his tools after a day's work, the taste of a particular dish his mother would cook. It might be a former lover, tiptoeing into his head as he lay in the embrace of another woman, forcing her name from his lips in the throes of passion.

Right now it was his grandfather, Andrzej, who used to sit by the fire before they built the bungalow and moved out of the old home. In the middle of telling any particular story he would cough up random fragments from his past. Sometimes he'd speak of life in the Old Country, of his mother's beetroot soup, or the goose they killed at Christmas; of bidding his sisters farewell at the end of a dusty lane that May day when the lindens were coming into leaf; of the journey by cart to the railroad station; the long weeks crossing the Atlantic, wet, seasick and wondering what the future held. He'd talk too of passing through the immigration control and seeing some of the people he'd mixed with on the ship being turned away as diseased, or mentally feeble. He'd start to talk of the stories that came across about the horrors of the Nazi regime, and then he'd fall silent, sucking on his pipe and staring into the flames.

Other times he'd tell Steve about his early days in the Panhandle; of the bitter winter he spent, alone, in the dug-out he'd built under the banks of Leander Creek chopping ice to melt on his crude stove. He'd talk of his first attempt at homesteading on a claim down there and how he'd given it up when his first wife was bitten by a rattler and died. He'd tell of the new claim in Sheridan County, of the young woman Gabriela he met off the train at Rushville after he'd advertised in the Polish newspaper in Chicago, where she worked as a housekeeper to a doctor. He spoke but occasionally of the sod-house he built in preparation for her arrival, of the family they raised, so Steve knew little about them. He knew there were twin girls, Nadia and Mata, and three boys. Waldemar and Pavel had both gone to fight for their country in France in 1917, very much against Andrzej's wishes. Piotr would also have gone but Andrzej insisted that he should stay. No way he could run the place alone, especially now that their mother was dead. Pavel was buried in France, and Waldo had only passed through on his way to a new start in California. Steve thought he'd once met his Aunt Nadia, but he couldn't be sure. As to Mata, only once was she mentioned. It seemed she'd died young, a drowning accident of some kind. But nobody ever talked about that. There was a hint of suicide, an ill-fated love affair, but it was never openly discussed.

And now, sitting in his room deep in thought, Steve recalled that Grandpa did – yes, he really did, more than once, mention this man Old Jules, whose life story he was now reading.

The further he read, the more it all made sense. Jules

Sandoz, it seemed, was among the first to settle this far west. Fired with a missionary zeal to populate these bleak lands with a community of fellow Swiss, he promoted the area, wrote letters home in which he painted lurid pictures of a rich country, with huge potential. A visionary rather than a farmer, a 'bunch-quitter' rather than a mixer, more at ease with the Lakota men who called in to trade furs for the guns he repaired and rebuilt, he was an educated man who had studied medicine in Zurich until a family row ignited his fury. There was a rumour that he'd shot a man. Always impulsive, he packed his bags and set out for the States. There, he headed as far west as he could, past the farthest line of settlement to where there was no law, no restraint on the one thing he needed above all: freedom to conduct his life on his own terms.

Old Jules was a man of unbridled passions. He was also a man of many skills, with an enquiring mind. As well as collecting stamps he would dispense medicines, build guns, mold his own bullets. A crack shot, he could shoot a bird in flight from two hundred yards. His family would never want for fresh meat, or garden produce, since he knew how to grow fruit and vegetables, but of course he was too well-bred for manual labor and left the hoeing and digging to his wife. He knew how to operate a compass and theodolite, how to survey land; and so he earned money by locating unclaimed quarter-sections for newcomers - just so long as they would settle, marry, raise families and develop the land. With his knowledge of law he would lead them through the process of registering a claim under the Homestead Act of 1862, register them as citizens if required, sometimes find them a wife.

And it was this man Sandoz, Steve now realized, who had persuaded his grandfather, still grieving over the loss of his first wife, to settle on that harsh yet beautiful land that Steve too once called home, to the west of his first claim and far from any creek.

Steve put the book to one side and went to look out of the window. The snow was easing up. One or two vehicles were slip-sliding along the street below. Some way away he saw an orange flashing light, the first plow approaching town from across the railroad tracks. He closed the book, put on a jacket and went down to the bar. Jeannie was there, maneuvering a step-ladder into place under a light that hung from the ceiling.

'Here,' he said, walking over and taking hold of the thing, 'let me do that.'

'I can manage,' she said, looking him up and down. He was barely a couple of inches taller than her. 'It's only a bulb needs changing.'

'Sure,' he said. Then, 'Force of habit, I guess.'

'You were raised a gentleman, that what you mean?'

He shrugged off the remark. 'No, I used to earn my corn doing that.'

Jeannie was up the steps now, deftly screwing the bulb into the socket. 'What were you, some kind of a handyman? No, don't tell me – stage electrician. A rigger in the movies.'

'Me?' He reached out a hand to hold the steps steady as she climbed down. 'Yeah, I've been a handyman. But back in the day I was the guy they sent for when the light at the top of a radio tower went pop.'

Jeannie folded the steps and leant them against the wall. 'Those great tall things? Wow, if that don't beat all.'

'Someone has to do it.'

'Well, I guess they do,' she said. 'Not a job I ever thought about though.' She went to the counter, picked up the coffee pot and held it up, questioning him with her eyes.

'Sure,' he said.

She grabbed a mug and poured. 'Ever get stuck?' she

asked. 'Way up the top?'

'Couple of times.'

'And?'

'Mostly you make sure you know what the weather is doing, but once in a while you're a hundred feet up and a hailstorm roars in outa nowhere.'

'So what do you do?'

'Hold tight till it blows over.'

'Ever drop the bulb?' she asked, grinning.

'You learn to carry a spare.' Steve paused as Jeannie handed him his coffee. He smelled it and sipped. 'Yeah, it was a good job for a footloose young guy. And then . . .' He checked himself, saying, 'I saw a plow go by just now.'

'You thinking about getting to Valentine?'

'That's what I had in mind. Or Gordon would do.'

'Well, someone just called from Crawford and said they got a plow heading east along the highway. That was a good half-hour ago.' She glanced out through the window. 'Forecast says we've had all the snow we're getting for now. What are you driving?'

'Truck. It's a big old Dodge Durango. 'Ninety-eight.'

'Still going strong?' Jeannie asked.

'Oh yeah, that mother was built to last. 5.2 liter, V8 engine.'

'Sounds like you're good to go. And what about tonight – you coming back to us?'

He paused before answering. 'If my room's still available.' Fact was, Wanda wanted him to put up at her house, and he resisted the idea. The last time he'd slept there was the night before he lit out.

'I'll have to charge you the full rate.'

'Comes a time of life when comfort is what counts.' He looked at his watch. 'Okay. I'll maybe grab a bite in town, and follow that plow when it comes through.'

3

It was almost two o'clock. The skies had cleared, the temperature was in the upper thirties, and patches of dun-colored grass were visible amongst the drifts that shone a brilliant white under the April sun. He nodded in recognition of what used to be such a familiar pattern, winter giving way to spring in a heartbeat, the thirsty Sandhills gratefully lapping up the melt-water. And who ever knew what tomorrow would bring?

To his surprise, he was almost enjoying the ride. He'd had the road more or less to himself, and was able to relax and take note of the towns he passed through, all of them throwing up memories from his boyhood. Hay Springs, Rushville, Gordon – his father had done the rounds of all of these places in his pursuit of a bargain, haggling over a beat-up old truck or checking out some prize bull whose services he might want, admiring a young horse and then looking to find fault with it to keep the price down. And often he'd take Steve with him. Livestock auctions, fire sales, now and then an old-timers' picnic: they were, for a few short years, a team. Sometimes the old man would explain that this was an important part of Steve's education. 'You're gonna need to know how to do all this,' he said, more than once. 'I mean when you take the place over. Because one day it'll come to you, the whole caboodle. Father to son, right?' It was the central feature of the landscape that constituted young Steve's world view. It was his future. As real and immutable as the hills that surrounded him.

Damn. It pained him to admit it to his adult self, but Steve and the old man were like buddies back then. Two guys on the road together. Even those tiny little places he was passing through - Merriman, Cody, Nenzel (*pop.* 13) - triggered recollections of their visits to isolated farms to look over a possible bargain amongst a clutter of used machinery. There was always someone selling up and moving out. Old folk dying, and no family around to pick up the reins. And Dad always looking to increase his holding if he got the chance. At that age Steve was outgrowing his earlier self-consciousness about having a father who sported a black patch over one eye and was starting to consider it – not cool, that wasn't a word they used back then; maybe piratical.

He found himself easing his foot off the gas, lost in thought, re-acquainting himself with the sensation of driving in that wide, empty landscape. He was reminded of those long days when he worked down south, in the Texas Panhandle, the way it sometimes seemed that the truck was stationary and the great empty plains were rolling past him. And then he remembered how the first seed of doubt had been sown in his young mind. Some old bastard had been rummaging through a stack of lumber to haul out a couple of beams his father wanted, and for no clear reason he turned to Pete and said, 'This your son, ya say?'

'Yeah. Name's Steve.' Once in a while, Dad introduced him to strangers as Stefan, his proper Polish name – until Steve asked him not to.

This guy looked the boy up and down and laughed an old man's laugh, wheezy, inward-turning, as if he knew something the others didn't. 'Guess he favors his mother, huh?'

Steve shoved the memory to one side, like he had done to so many that pained him. Bonny and her kids, his mother's death, Vietnam. He had plenty to worry about now, without dredging up those particular corpses. Wanda looked like Mom, for sure. Tall, with thick brown hair. At thirteen she was equal in height to her brother, and constantly teasing him about it.

As he approached the seat of Cherry County he realized just how deep his feelings were about the task ahead. Not the attorney. That was just a matter of signing a bunch of papers. But seeing Wanda. He'd always shrunk away from sickness. Hated hospitals. He was already swimming in a sea of emotional fatigue. Just what do you talk about when you have all that unfinished business, but you know the other person's going to die?

He pulled in at a diner next to Valentine's one and only stop light – the first he'd seen along that two hundred-mile stretch of Highway 20. He treated himself to a slice of cherry pie with ice-cream. Sat there listening to the farmers, mostly old guys, their jeans held up by suspenders, their huge hands cupped around steaming mugs of coffee. They talked about the weather, the cost of feed, the lousy prices their cattle were fetching at market - the eternal concerns of people who work the land.

He finished his pie, and went to the counter to pay. With his stomach full and his right leg threatening to seize up, he decided to take a little stroll. His appointment was twenty minutes away yet. After paying, he went outside and crossed the highway. The day had warmed up nicely. He walked towards the bank, a long low building whose front was adorned with a spectacular relief carving in red brick, depicting the history of the area. There was a herd of buffalo, a bunch of longhorn cattle, a man on horseback, an old-style steam loco which looked ready to leap out of the wall. He paused to take it in, then spotted a bookstore, and on impulse decided to see whether he could get a copy of *Old Jules*. He already knew he was going to read the entire damned thing, chunky as it was. The idea that this man had known his grandad, most likely shaken his hand, intrigued and excited him, and he tended not to get excited about much these days.

In the store he approached the counter. A woman was standing there with a handful of books, settling her bill. She was tall, slim, with a fine head of wavy dark hair. He guessed she was about fifty. She was dressed in city clothes – charcoal-grey slacks and black patent leather shoes. Her coat was a long, quilted thing with a fake fur collar. Beside her on the counter was a large blue hat. If he'd been asked to describe it he would most likely have said it was a city hat, broad-brimmed, light, with a couple of feathers that quivered as she threw a pair of black leather gloves onto the counter. Not a damned lot of use, but pretty to look at.

As the woman started to write out a check, the proprietor glanced up and addressed Steve. 'Looking for anything special, young man?'

'Sure,' he said, 'I'm after a book.'

'Well, my friend, I'd say you're on the right trail. This being a bookstore an' all.'

Steve nodded his head. He remembered how much he'd missed that dry western humour when he first moved out to the coast. 'Yeah, I get your point,' he said. 'It's called *Old Jules*.' He hesitated. 'By Mari Sandoz?'

'Just behind you,' the proprietor said. 'On the far wall there. We stock most everything she wrote.'

The woman had finished making out the check. She handed it over, snapped her purse shut. 'So, a fellow enthusiast?' she said. The questioning tone only seemed to kick in as an after-thought.

Steve looked at her, noting her eager smile, her slender aquiline nose. 'Not really,' he said.

'Oh, she's such a wonderful author,' the woman said. 'But just be careful. People get hooked,' she added, with a little laugh. She lifted the pile of books she'd bought and turned towards him. 'I'm always adding to my collection.' For a moment he thought she was about to show them to him one by one. 'But *Old Jules*,' she said, 'that's definitely the place to start.'

'Right.' Steve took a step back. He wasn't crazy about enthusiasts. They always seemed like they were selling you something.

However, she didn't push it, just smiled and turned to exchange a few words with the proprietor. By the time Steve had found the book and taken it to the counter she was on her way, pausing at the door to call out, 'Happy reading!'

The proprietor told Steve she was a professor of literature. 'We get quite a few of them, summertime mostly. Some of our best customers. She's on a research trip.'

Steve didn't say anything. He'd never ventured into the academic world. Should've done, he occasionally thought, but didn't. In his mind research was what guys in white coats did in laboratories. He handed over a twenty-dollar bill, took the change, and made his way to the attorney's office.

The business with Wanda's lawyer was easier than he'd expected. He was well prepared. He'd brought along his birth certificate for ID. The guy outlined the terms of the arrangement – how he would access his sister's bank account if required, and so on - and handed him a bunch of documents to sign. 'And there's a set of keys,' he said. 'For the home place.'

Along with the keys came a slim envelope. Inside was a letter headed *To Whom It May Concern*, stating that he had right of access to the property. 'Just in case the neighbors start getting nosy,' the lawyer said.

'That wouldn't surprise me,' Steve said. He knew he should leave now, but he recognised in himself a certain reluctance. He deliberately extended the interview, talking like a farmer about the climate on the west coast, the weather, the price of beef - as if he gave a good goddam about any of the above. But it really was time to leave. It would take him an hour and a half to get to Gordon. Then there would be no further excuse for delaying. He was already wishing he'd stayed in Oregon.

4

Merilyn Collier was almost hugging herself as she placed her new books on the front passenger seat of her sedan. The charm of this little town where she'd sought shelter the previous night after driving across Iowa, the treasure trove of Sandoz-related works she'd uncovered at the bookstore, the friendliness of the owner, this glorious sunshine after the blizzard, the vast sky . . . it was all so wonderful. For close to twenty years she'd dreamed of coming back to Nebraska, but had never had either the time or the money – leastwise, not concurrently. It was a single, brief visit, back in the early nineties, that made her decide to concentrate on Sandoz' work, and narrow down the focus of a PhD thesis that was threatening to embrace a whole raft of western authors.

Year after year she'd hoped, one day, to come back and pick up the pieces of a project that had hit a brick wall during that first visit. And now, here she was, on a fully funded sabbatical, with a copy of the publishing contract tucked away among her papers. She'd packed that for the simple purpose of being able to remind herself, any day when she felt the doubts creeping in, that she was no longer shooting in the dark, that both as a scholar and a writer, she was about to arrive. Not for the first time over these last few weeks, she felt like giving out a whoop of pure joy. Wow. Just . . . wow.

This was the first time she'd been to Valentine, and she would have liked to look around, but it was already past lunchtime and she wanted to call in at the library and make personal contact with the woman she'd communicated with by email about their newspaper archive. She would arrange a time and date to start her researches in that area, then she could continue on her way. Sitting in the car, however, she allowed herself a couple of minutes to take another look at her purchases. There was just the one by Mari Sandoz, a slim little thing entitled *These Were the Sioux*. It was one of the very few books by her heroine that she hadn't read. A contact at the University of Nebraska had recommended it. She said it was written for younger readers but had taught her more about Native Americans on the Great Plains than any other book she'd read.

With this were three equally slight volumes published privately by Mari's sister Caroline. Looking at them in her hand, Lyn sighed, remembering the time she visited the old lady in her home, back in 1993. It seemed like a dream now. It had been arranged on the spur of the moment and had yielded so much more than she could have hoped for. From a research point of view, she appeared to have uncovered pure gold, but the thrill of that discovery had been squashed flat by the news of her husband's betrayal.

The trauma of the break-up not only derailed her academic plans. It cost her years of nagging depression, anxiety, and a subtle kind of self-harm – the neglect of this research project, which was so dear to her heart. But she was over that now. At least, that is what she told herself. She was single, focussed, and had at last some degree of professional security, this bolstered by the contract with a major academic publisher.

So there was unfinished business in this part of the world. She'd cleared the decks in preparation for the work at hand. If things went to plan on this trip, she should be able to go back to Madison in a few weeks' time and start putting it all together. She had already drafted several chapters of her book. She had seen two of them appear in academic journals over the past year, and that had been enough to persuade the university press to go with it. And . . . if the good Lord willed it, and the creeks didn't rise, as her old grandmother used to say, she could be delivering a finished manuscript to them before she resumed teaching at the start of the fall semester. Fall: it sounded such a long way away, and that added to her feelings of delight, of freedom, of joyous anticipation.

Right now it felt like she was swimming in an ocean of time. She was time rich. If she wanted to - and she did - she could afford to spend the next few days sitting in her hotel room devouring her new acquisitions, preparing herself for the completion of the work she had started thirty years previously as a doctoral candidate in Boston. The thesis she had picked at, sporadically, over the last twenty years as she moved from city to city on one short-term contract after another. What with having to teach summer school year after year so that she could help her daughter through college, there simply had never been enough time. Until the miracle of the publishing contract, she had been telling those friends who still asked about it that she had abandoned her project. Or that it was on ice - anything to avoid further discussion. In her head, of course, it had always lived on, but explaining that was just too much hard work. It was easier to stifle such conversations before they grew into an interrogation of her failure to complete.

Now though, now it seemed that what Grandma had told her might be true, after all: that good things come to those who wait. If she'd imagined, back then as a young postgraduate, that she would still be striving to complete her PhD project all these years later, she would have buckled. But that, she mused, was the way of the young. Everything had to be immediate. The very idea of being fifty-three years old was simply unimaginable then. Just that thought made her grin as she sat there. Older in years she might be, but she was far richer in experience, in her understanding of what drives people to do the things they do. Didn't she always say that she loved having the older students in her literature classes, because they brought something to the discussion of books that the twenty year olds rarely could? They were people who had had careers, been married, had kids, got divorced, lost parents, sold up and started again . . . They saw things in the literature they studied that were out of reach for the youngsters. In the same way, she would surely now bring her mature insights to all the stories she had gathered on her subject's life, raw material which she would interpret with her deepened sensibilities, and finally shape to fit her thesis.

She unzipped a small document case and put the books away. Then she unfolded her AAA map of Nebraska. Ever since that first, brief visit she had been fascinated by the geography of this western half of the state. She'd never been anywhere with so much empty space. Cherry County, she'd read, covered 5000 square miles, and was home to barely that number of people. And the emptiness made travel so simple. Out here you could time your journey almost to the minute. Just stick your car in cruise control, 60 mph, and do the math. It wasn't like the East Coast, not at all.

Unable to suppress the smile on her lips, she started up the engine, and headed for the library.

5

Driving west, Steve continued to fret about what lay ahead. The last person he could recall seeing on the brink of death was Grandpa. The decline had started when Steve was twelve years old. Until that point, Grandpa had been active - always in the yard or the barn, occasionally riding the fence-line. Now he stayed around the old house, keeping himself apart from the family. At first the boy had called in on the old man daily, right after he got home from school. Dad was always out on the range, and soon as Wanda came in she went straight to her room to play records and read her magazines. Mom was rarely home before six. In time, she took to staying out later, so it was often just the two of them. Steve soon learned to fix a cup of milky sweet coffee the way Grandpa liked it and take it over to the old house where he preferred to live. The man had built it, after all, with his own hands. Sometimes they would just sit and talk. Sometimes Steve would read to him from the *Omaha World-Herald*.

Grandpa was a keen follower of international news. He liked to know what was happening in Europe. He always told

Steve they had to be on the watch for the next dictator. He spoke of Fascism, not that Steve really understood what that meant. He talked of demagogues and democracy, and for years Steve got the two words confused. Later, as the old fellow faded and his stories became less coherent, Steve didn't stay with him so long during those after-school visits. He found it painful to see the old guy shrink as he ate smaller and smaller meals, and also shrink in terms of his presence, which, in young Steve's life, had been substantial. He was talking less and less, and what he said didn't always make sense. From time to time he'd lapse into German, the language he'd been forced to learn during his own schooldays, or a Polish dialect which Steve could barely follow.

Grandpa had always talked to the boy, tried to tell him what was important, how precious life itself was, a gift to be enjoyed to the full. Freedom was a word he used frequently. You had to grasp life by the throat, was his message. In his teenage years, after the old fellow died, Steve embraced the idea with gusto. Hence the beer parties, the girls, the rows with his father, his eventual departure, and the twenty years of reckless wandering that followed. Damned if he was going to end up like his old man, tied to the land, to a life he'd always sworn he didn't want but had, finally, become accustomed to. At times, looking back, Steve was tempted to compare his family history to the shenanigans in the soap operas Bonny liked to watch on the TV, but then he had seen enough of life to know that few families were much better.

He pulled up in the nursing home parking lot and sat for a moment, musing. How the passions ebb and flow. Love, and hating. Desire, and repugnance. Hope, and disappointment. And all of it, finally, meaning so little when death comes into play. The great leveller.

He was met at reception by a woman with Slavic good

looks, a sweet-looking woman of about thirty. She wore a badge with her name on it. Lejla. Her parents, she told him, had brought her to the United States from Kosovo – or was it Bosnia? – in her teens. By the time she had led him down the corridor towards Wanda's room Steve was barely listening, although he remained aware of her slim body rustling against her scrubs. Some things, he thought, some things never will change so long as there's a pulse running through my veins.

'Have you come a long way?' the young woman asked.

'Right now? From Valentine.'

'Oh.'

They were in Wanda's room. His sister was sitting in a winged armchair, next to a window that looked out onto a small formal garden, and beyond that a large lawn, streaked with the remnant drifts of yesterday's storm. Her head lay to one side, and she was snoring gently. She'd aged, of course. The long, wavy hair that had been her trade-mark look as far back as as he could remember was gone. It was gray now, and cut short. But her eyes, those vivid blue eyes that had attracted so many men, the eyes she'd inherited from their mother, they hadn't changed. And still she wore the gold earrings she'd bought after Grandpa died and left them both a share of his savings.

'She usually sleeps in the afternoon,' Lejla said. Then she gave a short laugh. 'Everybody does, except the staff. Are you staying long?'

'I'll be here as long as it takes,' he said, then he caught the look in her face. 'I mean as long as she needs me. Listen,' he said, 'I can call back here any day.'

'I see. Morning's usually a good time, around eleven. Or later on in the afternoon.' She paused, then asked, 'But maybe you want a coffee. Sit with her a while. See if she wakes up?

But don't be surprised if she's . . . sort of drowsy. She's on heavy meds.'

'Sure.' He looked around. 'Is there a bathroom I can use?'

By the time he was done Wanda had woken up. He saw her struggling to get upright and went to help her. At first she gave no sign that she knew who he was. Beside her was an oxygen tank, and a table cluttered with drinks containers, an empty coffee mug, and an appliance that fed a tube inserted in her right arm. When she seemed comfortable he waited for her to show some sign that his presence had registered. She just stared towards the window.

'It's me,' he said, after a while. 'Your brother Steve.'

'Steve,' she repeated, then gave a short laugh and uttered a phrase he hadn't heard in years. 'The cuckoo in the nest.'

Even now, from the mouth of a dying woman, that stung. He looked at his sister, but she was smiling at her carer, who had reappeared with a tray of drinks and cookies. Lejla gave Steve his coffee, placed a mug beside Wanda, then reached out and stroked her forehead. It seemed to Steve that her touch was as light as a lover's caress, her voice the voice a mother might use to soothe a baby.

'You feeling better for your little nap, I think. Does you good, in the afternoon. Maybe I should have a little sleep too. We girls need our beauty sleep, don't we?' Without taking her eyes off Wanda's she reached out and patted Steve's hand, the light contact sending a little shiver up his arm. 'You must be happy to have your brother here. Come a long way to see you.'

'Who did you say? Brother?' Wanda looked at her. She seemed puzzled, almost vexed.

'It's me, Steve,' Steve repeated, bracing himself for whatever might follow.

'What are you doing here?' his sister asked, then turned to Lejla. 'Why's he here?'

Lejla smiled at her. 'He's come to visit you, Wanda. Aren't you pleased to see him?'

Wanda didn't answer. She sipped her drink and turned away to face the window. For some time she stared out at the garden, the sky. Lejla nodded at Steve, and whispered, 'She'll be with us in a little while. Takes time. You know she had chemo yesterday?'

'I didn't, no.'

'All the way to Rapid City and back. So she's very tired.' Lejla made to leave and Steve stood up.

'Can I have a word?' he asked.

'Sure. You want to come to the office?'

He sat at her desk and watched her lower herself onto her seat, back straight, head held erect above the bare nape of her neck. Jesus, he thought. Then dragged his mind back to the here and now. 'Am I going to get any sense out of her, you think?'

'You just need to be patient. She's very lucid most of the time.'

'What are you saying? She's not - she hasn't got dementia, has she?'

Lejla shook her head. 'No, not at all, but like I said she's on heavy medication – for pain. You cannot predict. Sometimes she's fine. She tells me stories, about the old days. You'll see – if you stay. But never for long.'

'Say what?'

'You shouldn't stay too long. She soon gets tired. Then the pain, and then the medication again. And she will sleep.'

Steve looked at his watch. Maybe this was the excuse he had hoped for, to duck out. Regroup.

'Okay,' he said. 'Listen, I need to get my head around this. I think I'm gonna take a little drive. I haven't been in these parts for a long time. Why don't I call in later – or tomorrow morning. Eleven o'clock, you say?'

'That's a good time. Mostly. Or maybe about three.'

Steve went to say goodbye before he left. But his sister was asleep again, her drink half-finished beside her. He reached out, ran the back of his hand down her cheek, and left.

6

Merilyn's visit to the library went well. The staff were helpful, and she learned that a number of the local newspapers were archived there. A much larger collection was housed at the State Historical Society in Lincoln. And of course there was the dedicated Sandoz archive there, at the University. She'd only ever been to the capital city one time, and that fleetingly. That was 1993, the time when she went to the Willa Cather conference at Hastings, and she'd barely had time to get more than a vague sense of a spacious, quiet city with a striking capitol building at its heart. She was looking forward to spending time there.

Outside, the sun was still shining brightly. When she got in the car and turned it around to face west, she immediately had to reach into the glovebox to take out her shades. The weather had lifted her spirits yet further. Even the carcass of a deer, lying beside the road just outside town didn't faze her. When she was a kid, sometimes as an adult, such a sight would bring tears to her eyes. But out here it didn't seem quite such a big deal. She remembered that when she visited her grandparents' place, out in the country, they would often eat a deer that Grandad had shot.

Away from town, she relaxed at the wheel. It occurred to her that it was still only mid-afternoon. She had more than enough time to reach her destination. Maybe she could take a little detour to see Sandoz' grave. She knew more or less where it was, a turning off Highway 27, south of Gordon. The sky was still mostly blue. Out in the fields the drifts were shrinking rapidly. Yes, why not?

It took her an hour to reach Gordon, by which time there were only a few patches of snow by the side of the road, and they were melting fast, despite the fact that the sun was now playing hide-and-seek with a few ragged clouds. Highway 27 was mostly clear too, just a ridge of grubby slush down the center line, although she saw a number of huge drifts rising above the embankments, the tops curled over like waves frozen in time.

When she found the gravel road that led to the valley where Sandoz was buried, she turned off, then stopped the car immediately. Was this really wise? Most of it was covered in a layer of snow. But it was clear that there had been traffic along there, and the wheel-ruts were no more than a few inches deep. She nosed her way carefully along it for a hundred yards or so. As far as she recalled from the map she'd seen earlier, the gravesite was less than a mile away. When she hit a deeper patch and felt it brush along the car's belly she braked carefully and slowed to a crawl. The next time it happened, barely fifty yards further along, she stopped.

She sat there for a minute or so, with the engine idling. Ahead, the landscape was almost all white. When the sun slid behind a cloud, the sudden dimming of the light rendered the outlook bleak, almost menacing. She realized, quite suddenly, that this was a mistake. My goodness, what could she have been thinking, to set off down a gravel road, just hours after a snowstorm, in a sedan? Okay, she told herself, take it steady; no sudden movements. All I need is to get this thing turned round and everything'll be fine.

Taking a deep breath, she selected Reverse. She took it very slow, very careful, easing the car back in a gentle arc across the creaking snow. There seemed plenty of room. It was a wide road, that shelved gently to either side. Now she was in Drive, creeping forward, turning the wheel very slowly. Nice and easy, she told herself. No rush. She reversed a second time, and this, she felt sure, ought to do it. Perhaps that thought was what prompted her to go that extra yard, which brought her to a gully gouged in the gravel but obscured by the soft blanket of white. There was a dull thump as her right rear wheel sank a foot or so into the rut and the car came to an abrupt halt.

She didn't panic. She'd been in this sort of situation before and managed to extricate herself. But then, as the thought entered her mind, she remembered that she'd been in her ex's 4x4 with him screaming at her, telling her what a fucking useless driver she was; and she'd shouted back, that if he wasn't so damned drunk he could have been driving. She sat still, hands firmly gripping the wheel, and told herself: Okay now, whatever you do, do it slowly – and easy on the gas.

The front wheels were spinning, the rev count rising. Nothing. She tried it again. The car seemed to tease her, straining forward a few inches, then slipping back as she let up on the gas. She decided to take a look. She climbed out and immediately sank in the snow, stumbling, losing one flimsy shoe as she fell onto her butt.

Back in the car she reached into her purse and took out her cell-phone. No network. She looked around. Whoever had made the tracks in the snow would return soon enough, surely. People went to work, and they came back; took a trip to town, and returned home. It was just a matter of waiting. Sit tight, keep the motor running and stay warm. That was when she checked the fuel gauge, and swore – a thing she rarely did. Thirty-eight miles to zero. She switched off the ignition and huddled down into her coat. Sooner or later someone would come by. Surely.

7

Steve thought about hanging around in town for a while. Maybe stopping in for a beer some place and calling in later. Then he discarded the idea. Just that brief outburst of antagonism had reminded him how fragile he was around her. Back where he'd lived with Bonny, around her daughters, even with Wayne at the motel who had been his employer this past year or so, he was considered quite the tough guy. And he knew it. People approached him warily. They seemed to be extra polite with him. Maybe Bonny was right, that he'd cultivated some posture, some demeanour over the years that made people think before they challenged him. He remembered how she once laid it out for him, talking about the way he seemed to somehow avoid the everyday confrontations that other people got into as a matter of routine – with traffic cops, barkeeps, any kind of authority figure. She said, 'People see it in your eyes, Steve. That don't-fuck-with-me look, and they give you that extra bit of space.' He let out a quiet snort. Wouldn't Bonny have loved to see him with his sister. One word, one little phrase, and he was in full retreat. No, he would come back next day. And he would prepare himself.

He didn't head straight back to Chadron but turned south at Hay Springs. He was acting on an impulse, which he recognised was unlike him. But any suggestion that it was a nostalgic longing of some kind that sent him down this once-familiar highway would have had him screwing up that lined old face and shaking his head. However, the fact remained that he did feel an urge to sniff around in those hills. As to going by the old place, right now? No, that would be plain dumb in these conditions. There'd be plenty of time for that when the weather cleared up. Even so, the idea kept tugging at a corner of his mind. But no, forget it. The road up to the house – hell, nobody but the odd hunter ever used that these days. Wanda had told him as much the last time they spoke. Once in a while the UPS guy might visit. The mail had been dropped on the county road for many years. The isolation hadn't seemed to bother her. And now she was pleading with him to take her back, let her live out her remaining time in familiar surroundings.

He drove on. There was still plenty of daylight left, and he was enjoying the ride down Highway 87, the way the hills moved past him, opening and closing the vistas in a rhythm of their own making. For a few miles he gave in to the feeling that he was being enfolded in a series of gentle embraces and was struck by the sense of comfort that came over him – a sensation that was at odds with the memory of the way he'd turned his back on this monochrome, empty landscape, in a rage, and sworn never to return. And yet how could he deny the consolation he had found, as a youngster, in the very solitude that later oppressed him as a young man, restless, angry, bursting with energy and a breathless desire to see the wider world?

Driving through Alliance he was no more than mildly curious. Of course he remembered the place. The old man had done business there, had met friends there, had even dragged young Steve along to a couple of Elks Club meetings. But now the town meant nothing to him. He drove right on through, then slowed to pass the remains of Antioch. Even when he was a kid the old potash works had been in ruins and his father had told him how the tiny settlement had turned into a frontier-style boomtown overnight. For a year or two during the Great War it was the only place that was hiring as the demand for fertiliser pushed prices through the roof. Grandpa himself had gone to work there, briefly. All that was left now were the skeletal remains of a concrete-block building, a collapsed telephone pole, and weeds.

Then he saw the sign, *Ellsworth 8 miles*. That was where he'd driven, the very first time he was let out at night in his old man's pick-up, him and his buddies, singing along to the radio as he swerved this way and that across the center line, leaning on the horn as the boys all boasted about their conquests. That must have been when he first heard the Beatles, Steve thought. 1964. He was eighteen years old.

Ellsworth proved a wretched disappointment. Despite slowing to a crawl, he was through the place in seconds. His memory insisted it was a town, but here it was - nothing more than a general store surrounded by rolling grasslands. Had he imagined the crowded bar, the plates of burger and fries, the milk-shakes, the country music coming from the juke-box? Maybe he was mixing it up with some other place. But the beer, that was real enough. It was he who had to clear out the cab where Clyde had thrown up all over the seat. Clyde. Christ, he'd held that guy's memory at bay a good few years.

He was still trying to unscramble his thoughts as he headed north, back towards Gordon, along Highway 27. The sun was lower in the sky now, but the clouds he'd seen earlier were melting away. The temperature was dropping steadily. It was going to be a cold one all right.

At first he mistook her for a mail-box, the way she was standing there, still, erect, with that great big blue hat. Then she stepped out into the road and waved both arms above her head.

'Jesus Christ!' He braked hard, stopping a few yards past her. Then he backed up, opening the passenger-side window as he did so.

'Oh, God bless you. Thank you.' She was trembling, she was crying. She stumbled towards the truck as he swung the door open for her.

'Hey, get in the cab, 'fore you damn well freeze to death.' He reached across to help her inside; she barely had the strength to grab his arm. Then he saw the strands of dark hair that hung down one side of her face. The woman from the bookstore.

'Oh, my Lord!' She recognised him too. 'The Mari Sandoz fan.' She wiped a sleeve across her nose. 'Listen, my car . . .' she began, then surrendered to a violent shivering.

'Yeah, where the hell is your car? You have a wreck or what?' He was looking around. He knew he hadn't passed anything on the roadside. He fiddled with the controls on the dash, cranking the heat up to max. At the third attempt, she had managed to close the door. 'Here,' he said, handing her a red cotton handkerchief from his pocket.

She wiped her eyes, her mouth, her nose. 'My car's back there. Just down that turning.'

'What sort of a car?' He was looking over his shoulder. 'How far?'

'It's just a little sedan. I –I'll show you.'

He backed up past the junction, then turned down the snow-covered road. 'And you came down this in a sedan?' he said. 'What made you do a dumb thing like that?'

'I know it was stupid but the sun was out, the highway was clear.'

'Because it's been plowed, that's why,' he started. Then he stopped. He didn't need to tell her what she already knew, and she was plainly distressed.

'Well yes, that's why I stopped. As soon as I realized. It's just . . .' She pointed to her car through the windscreen. 'There it is.'

'How long you been stuck out here?'

'I don't know. Couple of hours. I – I got cold and decided to come out on the highway. You're the first vehicle I've seen.'

They had reached the car, slewed at an angle, its front end pointing at the sky.

'I was trying to turn around,' she said. 'Guess I screwed up.'

'Okay.' Steve stopped the truck, but left the engine running. He opened the door. 'You stay where you are,' he called out as his feet hit the ground. 'Get yourself warmed up. I'll shout when I need ya.'

He went around to the rear of the Durango, pulled out a pair of work gloves, a thick hat and a shovel. If he couldn't dig the wheel clear and get her out, he had a tow-rope.

He soon had the snow scooped away, and managed to scrape up a few loose stones to throw under the front wheels. Maybe that would give him enough traction. He took the keys off the woman, got into the driver's seat and switched on. He saw immediately the red warning light: she was almost out of gas. Jesus, this one really wasn't fit to be let out alone.

He fired it up, put it in Drive and gave it a bit of gas. He got it partway out, but no further. Tried again, same result, except that the front wheels had scattered the rocks and were now spinning on ice. Damn. That was the last thing he needed, down on his knees in this crap trying to tie the rope on it. But . . . it was a job that had to be done.

He was back at the tailgate, rummaging in the shallow storage compartment he'd built under the mattress. He pulled out a rope, found an anchor point under her car, looped the rope through it, then maneuvered the Durango into position.

'Okay,' he said, when he'd got everything set up. 'Do you wanna get in your car and we'll see if we can haul her out?'

'Yes,' she said quietly. Then she added, 'Look, I feel like a total idiot telling you this, but I'm almost out of gas.'

'I noticed,' he said. 'Any idea how many miles you got left?'

'It said thirty-eight.'

'Okay, that'll get you to Gordon easy enough. I'll follow you as far as the first gas station, just to be sure. But let's get you outa that ditch first. Then I'll drag you to the highway.'

The job was meat and drink to his vehicle. At the junction he got out and unhitched the rope. 'Okay,' he said, 'you'll wanna test your brakes. Could have fractured a pipe back there.'

'I'll do that. And here . . .' She tried to press a couple of twenties into his hand. He held his hands up. He didn't want her money. 'It would've cost me a lot more if I'd had to call for help,' she said. 'Not that the phone's working.'

'Thanks, but there's no need for that,' he said. 'Someone once told me, when someone does you a good turn you got a duty to pass it on to the next person in line.' He watched her get into the car. 'Okay, like I said, I'll be right behind you.'

He watched her drive away, then followed. She got a

hundred yards or so before the brake lights came on. Then she was away, giving a double toot on the horn, and he followed, all the way to town. As he watched her turn in at the gas station he nodded to himself. He remembered now who it was that first told him that pious little piece of homespun. His father.

8

By the time he got back to Chadron it was almost dark. He drove along the main drag until he found a place to eat, and treated himself to a steak dinner and a few beers.

At the hotel Jeannie was behind the bar, talking with a couple of what he assumed were regulars. She smiled at him and took a glass down from the shelf. 'You know, I always offer my guests a complimentary beer when they arrive,' she said, 'but that was pretty late last night - and me in my dressing-gown. What can I get you?'

Despite the fatigue that had washed through him, he accepted. Chose a wheat beer, bought a bourbon chaser, and sat at the bar, leaving a couple of empty seats between himself and a woman with dyed blonde hair who was talking to a much younger guy. It wasn't more than a minute or so before the blonde woman turned and asked him, 'Just passing through?'

'Yeah,' he said.

'Got a room here?'

'Yeah.' He decided to steer her away from wherever she

might be heading. She seemed the curious type. 'And you – you a visitor?'

'No, I live here. Born and raised. Name's Tina.' Before he could ask about the guy with her she introduced him. 'And Seb here, he's my nephew.'

'I'm Steve.' He shook hands with her, then Seb, who looked to be in his early twenties. Had quite a bit of the boy about him. He didn't say anything, just nodded at Steve, plunged his hand into a large bag of potato chips and chomped noisily.

Jeannie brought his beer across. 'So you made it to Valentine okay?' she asked.

'Sure. Road was fine. Near enough empty.'

'Lucky you,' Tina said. 'A storm like that, you coulda been following a whole convoy of recovery trucks. Damned ditches choked with wrecks.'

'You'd think people would learn,' Jeannie said.

Steve sipped his beer. 'Yeah, pulled one out myself, matter of fact.'

'You did? Here on Highway 20?'

'No, south of here, off of 27. Dumb woman decided to go exploring down a county road. In a little two-door Focus.' He took a mouthful of beer. 'She got about two hundred yards.'

'Shee-it.' It was the first word Seb had said. 'And then what? She roll it?'

'No. Just put her rear wheels into the ditch.'

'But you rescued her,' Tina said.

'Towed her to the highway and turned her loose. She was pretty well shook up.'

'Sounds like she was one lucky gal. I mean, county road - she could've been there yet.'

'Luckier than she had any right to be,' Steve said. 'Damned near flat out of gas as well.'

'Man, how dumb is that?' Tina drained her beer. 'Me, I get to half a tank I fill right up. Every time. Man, that is stupid.'

'You said it.'

'Okay, people.' Nobody had seen Merilyn enter from the darkened, far end of the bar. She walked towards them, holding her hands up. 'Might as well fess up. It was me. I was that dummy.' She addressed Steve directly. 'But I did thank you for your help. And if you recall,' she turned to address Tina, 'I offered to pay him too.'

Steve shifted in his seat so that he was facing her. 'Just telling it like it was. But it's done now. Let me buy you a drink, huh?'

Merilyn nodded and smiled. She wasn't the frightened, shivering creature she'd been last time he saw her. At all. 'Sure,' she said. 'I'll take that. Thanks.'

'What'll it be?' Jeannie asked. 'I have a nice wheat beer here, plus the usuals. Bud, Miller . . . or would you rather a glass of wine?' She grinned. 'It's your call. And he's buying.'

'I'll take the zero alcohol thing you have in the cabinet,' she said. Then to Steve, 'Thank you.' She looked at him for a moment, then added, 'Christmas and Thanksgiving I relent. Otherwise I abstain.'

Before Steve could answer Tina dived in. 'You staying here too?'

'Yup.'

'How ya feeling? Must've been pretty darned scared, out there on your own.'

'Till this guy showed up, sure I was.'

'Those county roads get kinda lonesome when the sun goes down.'

Merilyn nodded. 'I wasn't feeling too chipper. Especially knowing it was my own stupid fault.'

Seb spoke, through a mouthful of chips. 'Where you from?'

'Madison, Wisconsin,' she said, then added, 'For now at least.'

'What are you, planning on moving?'

'Who knows? College professors live pretty much from one contract to the next.'

'Whoa, college professor!' Seb whistled and shook his hand as if he'd touched something hot.

'Is that a fact?' Tina said. 'I always figured it was a pretty secure line of work.'

'Not in my experience.'

'You should check out the college here in town,' Tina said. 'People get hired and boy, they hang on like a sandbur. Price of houses in Chadron, they can live pretty well.'

'So how much do they make?' Steve asked. Then he glanced at Merilyn. 'Y'know, I never even asked your name. I'm Steve.'

'Merilyn,' she said, 'but I mostly go by Lyn.'

'And this is Tina,' Seb said.

'Hi, Tina. And you?'

'Seb.'

'Okay, pleased to meet you all.' She raised her glass. 'Well, here's to good Samaritans.' She aimed the next one at Steve. 'However rude they may be.'

Tina threw her head back and laughed. 'Boom! Round one to the lady.'

The door swung open and Glenn came in. 'Hey, the gang's all here,' he said, and glanced around the bar. 'Well, some of them.'

'The A team,' Tina said. 'The diehards. The ones who always show, rain or shine. Those other guys – a few flakes of snow and they wimp out.'

'Right.' Glenn took off his glasses. 'And look, we have the man from Oregon. The mysterious stranger.' He walked over to Steve and held out his hand. 'Boy, you looked like you were at the end of your rope last night. Standing there on Main in a foot of snow with that pleading look in your eye.' He was still shaking Steve's hand. 'How ya doing, pal?'

Lyn looked at Glenn, then at Steve. 'You mean you had to rescue him?'

Steve acknowledged her with a faint smile. 'Sure, I was pretty near beat after driving all day.' He took out his wallet. 'Guess I still owe you one for finding me a room. I could've ended up sleeping in the car. What'll it be?'

Glenn held up a hand and shouted across to Jeannie, 'Make that a double of your finest bourbon.'

'You're joking, of course,' Jeannie said.

'You called it. I'm joking.'

'So we'll make that a Bud, shall we?'

'If we must, boss lady.' He turned to Steve and said, 'Used to work for her and she never lets me forget it.' Then he saw Lyn. 'Aha, a new face. And what part of our great country are you from, madam?' He made a stab at bowing, theatrically. 'Or shall I call thee mademoiselle?'

'Christ's sake, Joe.' Seb threw his empty bag of chips at him and turned to Lyn. 'Always talking like a damned book, that guy. Hey, speak English will ya?'

'I'll rephrase the question,' Glenn said. 'What's going down, babe?'

Lyn laughed. 'It's a working trip. I'm doing some research.'

'Is that right?' Glenn leaned towards her, an exaggerated expression of interest on his face. Lyn didn't respond. She couldn't tell whether he was just play-acting. 'Well go ahead,' he said. 'Say more.'

'It's for a book I'm writing.'

'I like this more and more. Is it a novel, or what? No, don't tell me. A mystery thriller set in a small town in

Nebraska. Bunch of strangers thrown together by a spring blizzard . . .'

'Sorry,' Lyn said. 'Nothing so entertaining. It'll be a literary study. One of Nebraska's finest writers.'

'Oh yeah? And who's that?'

'Mari Sandoz.'

'Okay. This a biography? I'm all ears.' He took his beer from Jeannie and sat down on a vacant stool next to Lyn.

'You really want to know?' she asked, glancing at Steve as well. 'Cos I can spiel for hours on this subject.'

'Go ahead,' Steve said. 'I was reading *Old Jules* last night.'

'That old sonofabitch?' Tina pulled a face. 'Y'know, I never did get what she was about with that book. He beats on his wife, beats on his daughter, and then she winds up writing his life story. Can you figure that out?'

Lyn was about to reply, but Jeannie got in first. 'I guess this dates me, but I remember speaking to a few old-timers who actually knew him.'

'That a fact?' Glenn said.

'Sure. Folk who used to come here when Mom had the place. I'm going back forty years and more. You'd remember one or two of them, Tina.'

Tina nodded. 'I do. Horny old codgers, most of them.'

'Well, they always said Old Jules wasn't that different from a lot of men back then.'

'What are you saying?' Tina said. 'They were horny too, or it was okay to go around beating up on women and kids?'

Jeannie seemed surprised by the remark. 'No, but – '

'I mean, just 'cos everyone else did it, don't make it right.'

'No,' Lyn said, 'but you can't always judge an earlier generation by our modern standards.' She picked up her drink and raised it to her lips.

'Those were violent times,' Steve said. 'A man had to know how to defend himself.'

'What?' Tina turned to face him. 'Against a helpless child?'

'What I'm saying is, people were quicker to resort to violence. Not saying it's right.'

'But I take your point, Tina,' Lyn said. 'That's one of the things that drew me to Mari. I mean, why? After the way she was treated, why write up her father's life as if he was some kind of hero figure?'

'Well, yeah,' Tina replied. 'My point exactly. Good luck with that. 'Cos I still say the old guy was a stinker.'

Glenn had kept quiet through this exchange. Now he spoke. 'I knew his youngest. Caroline?'

'You did?' Lyn looked at him eagerly.

'Sure. I used to cut her grass for her, right up until she moved out of her home. That'd be ten years ago now, maybe more.'

'Wow. You ever talk with her - I mean about her dad?'

'For sure.'

'Well, go on.'

'I asked her what it was like growing up with a monster.'

'Wow, that was a pretty bold move. What did she say?'

'She near bit my head off. Told me not to believe everything I read. Course, I backed off. When she calmed down, she said Old Jules was a lot easier to deal with when she was growing up. Said the fire had died down.'

The place was quiet for a moment. Then Lyn said, 'I met Caroline too. Just once.'

'So you've been this way before?' Tina asked.

'It was a long time ago.'

'Was she still in her house?'

'Up at the ranch? Yeah. I spent a day with her. Matter of fact, I put up here that night.' She looked at Jeannie, 'But I don't recall seeing you here. Was someone else running it?'

'That would be my mom,' Jeannie said. 'This place used to be hers, until I took over. She still spends the summers here.'

'She'll be here any time soon, won't she?' Glenn said. 'End of April?' He didn't wait for an answer, but addressed Lyn. 'Now there's a character. She can tell a few stories about the old days. Same as Caroline Sandoz. Like I say, I was only there to cut the grass, sometimes haul trash. If I'd had my wits about me I would've asked her a few more questions. Believe it or not, I was a shy kid back then. Tried to write a song about her old man one time, but . . .' Glenn broke off. He was looking past Steve, toward the far end of the bar. 'Here comes trouble,' he said.

Steve looked up. The door had opened and a cop was standing on the threshold. 'Somebody own a white Focus?' he said. He was holding the door ajar, allowing a cold breeze to whistle in.

'Oh shoot,' Lyn said, dropping off her stool. 'What've I done this time?'

'You're parked in front of a hydrant, lady. You wanna just step outside?'

Everyone fell silent, straining their ears to hear what was going on. Then Tina said, 'They sure got a way of making a stranger feel welcome, don't they?'

'Shouldn't park on a hydrant, should she?' Seb said.

Jeannie gave him a hard stare. 'One day, young man, you may decide to leave this town and venture out into the big wide world. Before you go I'd suggest you take a lesson in empathy. Or maybe read a few books.'

Lyn wasn't gone long. When she reappeared she was grinning from ear to ear.

'What happened?' Tina looked seriously concerned. 'You okay?'

'I sweet-talked my way out of it,' she told them. 'I played the innocent abroad. Explained I'd had an accident.' She turned towards Steve. 'Said I'd been rescued by a cowboy hero. Told him what amazing folk you are in this great state.'

'You did?' Tina laughed. 'You really said that? 'Cos some of those guys next door, they can be meaner than a rattlesnake.'

'Yeah, he was going to cite me till I told him what a great impression you were all making. How the cops back home never cut you any slack. Time I'd finished he was asking me what I'm doing tomorrow night.'

'No way!' Tina raised her glass and turned to the others. 'Gotta hand it to her, she knows how to deal with them.'

'Well,' Lyn said, 'that's not my usual style, full-on bullshit, but I'm on a kind of a high right now and I guess something just came over me.'

'So,' Glenn said, 'no ticket?'

'No. In the end he was wagging his finger at me like he was my elementary school principal. "Don't do it again and drive careful, young lady." That was the best part: "young lady".'

'All right.' Glenn raised his empty glass. 'We celebrating?'

'I reckon so,' said Tina, and looked enquiringly at Steve.

'Tempting,' he said, 'but I think I'll pass.' He checked his watch. 'Got another heavy day tomorrow.' He drained his glass and went upstairs.

9

Back in his room, Steve took out his new copy of *Old Jules* and settled into the armchair. He was wide awake now after the conversation in the bar, and needed to wind down again.

Rather than pick up where he'd left off the previous night, he turned to the introductory material and read it carefully. It told, in brief, of the author's life, the hardships she had endured on the road to getting this story out. It was her first book, and it was a spectacular breakthrough for her. She'd been revising it for years, more or less rewriting it each time it was rejected. Fourteen times in all. She was living in the capital city, on the breadline. Later, Steve would learn how she'd take any job she could find, stay at it till she'd saved fifty dollars, then quit in order to go back to her writing and research. For years she struggled with bitter disappointment and frustration, several times getting to the point of giving it all up. But in 1934 she submitted yet another revised version for the *Atlantic Monthly* non-fiction award and, one June day in 1935, received a telegram to say that she'd won. An immediate prize of five thousand dollars freed her, at last, from the tyranny of ill-paid, meaningless work. Publication, and the attention it brought her, launched what the back-cover blurb declared was a significant literary career.

This woman, Steve thought as he went back to the bookshelf and picked up a copy of her biography, she really was something. He wondered why he'd never heard of her. Why wasn't her name better known?

He read for thirty minutes or so, then got ready for bed. If the weather tomorrow was fine he would take the trip out to the old place, then call on Wanda.

HE AWOKE to a sparkling spring day, the sun shining from a clear blue sky. The forecast was fair: temperatures up to fifty, light wind out of the southwest, likelihood of rain 10 per cent. Before he went down to the bar he slipped out the side entrance and walked the couple of blocks to the supermarket. There he bought a sandwich and cookies and a pint of bourbon. Who knew how long he might be out there? You got to be prepared.

Back at the hotel, when Jeannie served him his breakfast he mentioned that he was heading out into the hills. She was curious, but tried not to make it obvious. 'Pretty country out there,' she said.

Steve was warming to Jeannie. He liked the way she ran the place. He liked the fact that she had a spinning wheel in the corner and occasionally sat there with a new skein of wool and worked at various patterns that lay on a stool beside her. How incongruous it seemed to him, yet how charming, that above the bar was a photograph of her younger self astride a big beast of a motorbike. She possessed a calm sort of authority, and he found it easy to open up to her.

'I grew up out there,' he said. 'The place still belongs to the family – to my sister, in fact. She's been running it on her own for years. Rented out the grazing, of course. Now she's being treated for cancer and . . .'

'Oh dear.'

Steve didn't say anything for a few moments, and when he spoke he was looking out the window. 'Ain't nothing to be done. It's gonna kill her, and she knows it.'

'I'm sorry,' Jeannie said. 'Must be tough on you.'

'We aren't close,' he said. 'And I haven't been back to the old place since I left. That was, hell, over forty years ago.'

'Ooh,' Jeannie said, 'that is a long time. I guess you'd better brace yourself.'

The remark puzzled Steve. 'What are you saying?'

'Thinking about the impact, I guess. In my experience, when you visit old haunts you never know what your memory's gonna throw up at you.'

Steve didn't answer right away. Then he said, 'Guess you're right. Just driving to Valentine I found I was remembering things from way back. So yeah, point taken.' He rose from his seat. 'I got a feeling all this may take a little while. I mean, I could be around here longer than I planned. Soon as the weather settles I'm fixing to camp out in my truck – maybe at the State Park. It open yet?'

'Should be.'

'Okay. Meantime you better tell me when you need that suite.'

THE OLD PLACE was little more than thirty miles away, but it took him over an hour to get there. As on the long drive through Wyoming and into Nebraska, the nearer he got to his destination, the slower he wanted to drive. One sight after another, none of them unfamiliar but many of them unseen these several decades, arrested his gaze, causing him to ease off the gas. Here and there it was a ruined wooden home, or a schoolhouse with a tree poking through its skeletal roof. Occasionally it would be one of the windmills he passed. Not that they weren't common enough in other places he'd lived, rather that he never took much note of them. But here, in this landscape, their mere presence made him notice things as if for the first time: their almost stately outline, the way their vanes turned so slowly this mild spring day. Some of them even had wooden towers. All of them had that familiar circle of bare earth around the galvanised steel tank, newly trodden by sleek black Angus heifers.

When he came across one close to the side of the road he stopped the car, switched off the engine and opened the window, just in order to listen to the once-familiar clanking of rods, the slight groan of cogs turning with the wind, the rhythm of the water as it spurted into the tank in short, eager bursts. Here was a musicality that he had so often heard but never before appreciated, and the pleasant feeling it evoked took him by surprise. He even caught himself smiling. There was too the general shape and look of the landscape: the familiar, sensual curve of their slopes, poignantly reminiscent of a young woman's breasts; the blow-outs where the wind had found a bare patch of sand and worked on it, unrelentingly, gouging out wide, pale scars, occasionally scouring out a deep hollow which exposed the roots of the thirsty bunch-grass that held this soil together through drought, fire and blizzard. He saw too the familiar dry stalks of mullein, of last season's sunflowers, the clusters of soapweed with their previous year's seed-heads rattling in the breeze; and down by the road that ubiquitous memento of cowboy country – the upturned leather boot stuck on a fence-post.

When he got to the dirt road that led to the ranch he stopped to check the mailbox, an old, deeply rooted habit. He found that his hand was shaking and he had some difficulty in opening it. It was half full. Ninety per cent junk, of course, but one or two pieces that looked as though they might require his attention. Or Wanda's. Who knew what she would be capable of?

He put the lot on the seat beside him, rattled across the cattle-gate and headed up what was now little more than a dusty two-track curving towards the old house. He tried to remember whether it was always that way. Surely it used to be more like a road. He had a vague recollection of his father tipping crushed rocks in the hollows that appeared every spring. To either side there still lay a few drifts of snow, one or two of which sprawled across his path, but nothing deep enough to impede him. One thing about this country, he reminded himself, was the way the sand drinks up the snow-melt as fast as the sun can produce it. Only his own growing trepidation, and a trembling deep within him now slowed his progress towards the place where he'd left his past.

The trees were a shock. When he was a kid he could look out on miles of this country and see little more than the gray wooden fence-posts that marked the boundary between properties, the roof of an abandoned dwelling collapsing under the weight of its own shingles, and of course the cattle. Then he recalled that his sister had fenced off those last few acres close to the house, after she'd rented out the expanse of grazing that surrounded it. She'd written to tell him about the planting: cottonwoods, mostly, in the sloughs, but now, of course, the cedars had gotten in and taken over large swaths of what had been open ground. What would Grandpa have said to see that? He'd surely have some choice Polish profanity reserved for such slovenly practice. Steve remembered now seeing a photograph his sister had sent him, of the time they put the little cottonwood slips in the ground. Her and Dad. So the land close to the old house was altered almost beyond recognition. But what now knocked him sideways as he drove on, almost at a walking pace, was the new house, set back a little way to the right. Somehow, even though he'd lived in it for the last few years before he took off, all his memories were of the old place.

He stared at this new one, built in the early 1960s and perfectly reflecting the functionality of that time. To his mother it had been the fulfilment of a dream, but somehow he'd wiped it from his memory. Even the rows with Dad that precipitated his exit, when he replayed them in his mind, seemed to him to have erupted in the place Grandpa always called home. That was where he had the final bust-up. Of that he was certain. But why? What were they doing there on a summer evening, the four of them, with Grandpa dead and buried?

When Andrzej built the family's first proper house in 1909, on the back of a brief boom in cattle prices, he didn't cut any corners. He had had all he could take of the low-roofed soddy. Sure, it had its virtues. It was, he liked to remind Steve, warmer in the depths of winter, cool in the summer heat, but he always swore it accounted for the cold that turned to pneumonia and saw Grandma off around Christmas-time, even as he was building its replacement. No, the sod house had its plus points, but it was cramped, attractive to vermin and leaky. In his mind the place was never more than a temporary fix, albeit one that lasted fifteen years, during which time he had dreamed of a house like this.

And not just dreamed. Hadn't he once taken Steve to the old bureau and pulled out the sketches he'd made and constantly revised until the cash was there for all this fine timber he had shipped in on the Burlington and hauled from the depot at Ellsworth? When he finally built his house, he meant for it to see the family through several generations. The idea that his own son Pete would move his wife and children out before he died would never have entered his head. The fact that they could throw up this drab, featureless bungalow that sat like a great toad between the old place and the driveway that led to its front door, maybe that was what finally killed him off, Steve thought.

When Pete erected this monstrosity it was as if he was following so many of their neighbors in affirming his modernity, declaring his independence from his Old Country roots and maybe from his old man too. He was also making a final desperate attempt to appease his young wife, with the huge windows, the air conditioning and central heating system, but Steve didn't really understand that, certainly as a youngster.

And so that elegant, proud two-story house, with its attic windows breaking the roof-line, its stout carved pillars standing guard on either side of the front door, its porch running the full width of the house, its quite unnecessary but rather lovely turret room on the southeast corner, this fulfilment of Grandpa's dream had become home to sacks of feedstuff, items of unwanted furniture, old tools and various parts of the cars Pete was always fixing up. But oddly, it seemed as though Pete himself was reluctant to give the old place up entirely. He used it as a workshop, the downstairs part at least. He kept a kind of office in Grandpa's old bedroom, up in the turret there. According to Wanda, even in his old age he would go back there for hours on end, although she never really saw that he achieved a great deal. Sometimes he'd fix a washing machine or a radio, or tinker with an old TV he'd picked up, a gramophone. That kind of thing interested him. Occasionally he would sleep there, especially in hot weather. He preferred the draughts allowed by open windows to the hum and rattle of an air conditioner.

Now though, with Pete and Irena long gone, the land rented out, and the calving shed no more than a memory, the old house was home to armies of mice, any number of snakes, these mostly in the cellar, and had provided winter quarters for a several generations of skunks. His sister had written to Steve that she'd hardly been in there since their father Pete had died. She'd seen enough of the trash strewn around his makeshift workshop to know there was nothing of interest to her.

Steve knew he was going to explore the old house, but reminded himself he was here to check over the other one. He left the car, fished out the keys and entered the place his sister called home, wondering what he'd find. He hoped it would at least be clean. He'd known people who'd had to clear up an unholy mess where a person had been ill, or died. Once or twice he'd been hired to renovate such a place, replacing piss-soaked floorboards and ripping out rotten kitchen closets. But this ought to be okay, he told himself. It was only two or three weeks since Wanda had been taken to Rapid City for treatment, thence to Gordon – to rest, and eventually die.

He was surprised, as he pushed the front door open, to find the place as warm as it was and made a mental note to check the thermostat, also the levels in the propane tank out back. The living room was tidy enough, with cushions placed neatly on the chairs and sofas. True, there was a vase of flowers that had withered on a sunny windowsill, but otherwise the place seemed well cared for. The kitchen was clean, although on opening the fridge, he saw evidence of his sister's pared-down lifestyle: processed cheese in a plastic tub; a carton of milk which had separated out; a plate of cooked sausage, desiccated; a couple of rubbery carrots in the vegetable trays. He closed the door. He would empty that later. Mostly, it seemed that she lived out of cans – of soup, hash, beans and the like. There was a whole shelf of cookies. In a plastic bin on the counter he found the remains of a wrapped sliced loaf dusted blue with mildew. Finding the trash, he bundled that up and placed it outside the door.

He glanced at his sister's room. The bed had been stripped, and everything seemed as it should be. Going back into the lounge, he supposed he should check the large oak bureau that had been a part of their furniture ever since he could remember. It was the one piece from the old house that Dad had held on to against Irena's craving for modernity. Otherwise, there was little in the place to suggest that anyone with any history had lived there. No photograph of Grandpa and the family lined up at the door of the soddy, with chickens on the roof. Where the hell was that, he wondered. No portrait of the old guy in his collar and tie, hair plastered down for a trip to the County Fair, no proud owner of a prize-winning team of horses grinning at the photographer. Why? he asked himself. Why no mementoes? What had happened to all those pictures that had formed the backdrop to his early life? They used to be fixtures around the place.

Bonny had always insisted on having photos everywhere, even ridiculously out-of-date high-school formals of her kids. Never listened to him when he suggested they might be better in an album. He sighed as he remembered. What did it really matter, in the end? It had made her happy, and now she was no longer there. And, to be fair, she'd never asked him to remove that dark, water-stained thing Grandpa had bequeathed him: a picture of his family back in the Old Country, taken at a christening, and everyone's name written on the back, in a shaky old man's hand, with the dates of birth. All of them wiped out under the Nazis. But here - he looked around once more - here there was nothing.

He went to the bureau. Above it and to one side he spotted the thermostat and turned it down to fifty. Hell, it was nearly May. No point in wasting fuel. Opening the bureau, he found a pack of Christmas cards, one or two utility bills, a bunch of check-stubs, one current check-book, and little else save a pad of writing paper and a bundle of white, self-adhesive envelopes. He pulled open the little wooden drawers to see a few thumb-tacks, a pencil stub or two, a couple of curled-up, outdated postage stamps, and the usual litter of paperclips, erasers and elastic bands. He felt disappointed, but wasn't sure why.

On the far wall, away from the window, was an old-style hi-fi set-up. It looked like something between a 1950s cocktail cabinet and a Victorian sideboard. Beside it was a rack of LP records. Steve had a quick flip through them. There were no more than a couple of dozen. Eddie Cochran, Elvis, Ricky Nelson . . . they were all there. She had too a collection of audio cassettes. He remembered how she and her friends would swap records and tape them, or try to record her favorites off the radio. He picked out two or three and slipped them in his pocket. Maybe she'd like to have them with her.

Picking up the pad from the bureau, he started on a list. *Check heating fuel. Read electricity meter. Call utilities. Check cisterns topped up.. Flush toilets.* Oh Jesus, he'd better check those now.

He needn't have worried. His sister had remained to the end the neat and tidy housekeeper she had always been. She would never leave home without checking that everything was in good order. He always remembered their father saying she was the kind of girl who would put on fresh underwear for a run to the grocery store in Gordon, just in case she had a wreck and wound up in hospital. So no, no horrors in the bathrooms, either of them.

Even so, he was quickly nauseated with this job, overwhelmed by the atmosphere. He needed to breathe fresh air.

He went outside and walked around the back of the house. There, beyond a bank of overgrown shrubs, was the old place. A tall, sparse hackberry had taken root one side of it and flourished, albeit that it leaned towards the west. Behind it he could make out the mound where the root cellar had been, the remnants of the apple orchard Grandpa had struggled with year after year. Some of the trees had died back, but one or two seemed to be winning the unequal struggle with wind and drought. He recalled their daily attempts to keep them going through endless summers, lugging pails of water across the yard. The roof of the house, he noticed, appeared sound. The shingles were warped but all in place, at least at the front. Apart from one hanging section of guttering, it looked to be in surprisingly good repair. The ground-floor windows had all been boarded up. Walking towards the rusted iron gate that led out of the new house yard towards the old, Steve recalled the pie-plant that grew by the cellar door. He hadn't thought of that since the day he left, but suddenly he could taste his mother's rhubarb cobbler. Distant, sullen, occasionally violent she may have been, but she could cook, and took pleasure in it. He stopped and thought for a moment. Maybe she was simply unhappy. Maybe that was it.

He managed to open the gate, and crossed the yard. He tripped on a bucket, stepped over a tangle of wire, and had to grab the upright that supported the porch to prevent himself from trapping his foot under a board that had come loose and curled up at one end. He looked at the front door, the glass above it cracked, the handle cocked at a strange angle, the last few flecks of paint barely clinging to the bleached, bare wood. Stepping forward, he tugged open the screen door and gave the main door a firm shove. It opened a few inches, then jammed against the litter of dirt and leaves on the wooden floor. It was enough for him to peer inside and see just how dark it was.

He walked back to the truck and returned with a flashlight, noticing once again that his hand was shaking, his heart pounding. He stood on the porch a few moments and reflected. So long since he was here. Forty-five years since he stood, arguing with the old man. Close to half a century since he raised his fist and knocked him down, snatched the car keys from his hand and took off. He shoved the door. It still wouldn't budge. It never did. You had to lift it, then push. Well, he didn't have the patience right now. He leaned back, raised his right leg and kicked it, hard. The pain that shot through his arthritic right knee made him yelp.

He could see his old man standing right there, precisely where he had been that Fourth of July evening. He could see the look of shock on his face after Steve had kicked the door in and swung that punch at him, even though his fist had landed on the doorframe instead. In the background he could hear that damned song 'Strangers in the Night'. Jesus, how he hated it. He could feel the pain in his knuckles, and there it was, his old man's favorite, fueling his rage. He could feel the shape of the words that erupted from his mouth. 'So who the hell are you? Tell me! If you ain't my father, tell me who is.' And then he had his hands on Pete's shirt, gripping tight and shaking him. 'You ain't never gonna tell me what I can and can't do. You ain't got the right.'

Pete was struggling for words. They didn't always come easy to him. He was a man who liked to think before he answered. 'What - what are you saying?' he stuttered. 'Who's been talking to you? Poisoning your mind?'

Steve turned and saw Irena, across the porch, backing away slowly, her eyes on him. He let go of Pete's shirt and pointed at her. 'Ask her!' Steve shouted. 'She knows, the bitch.'

Irena was suddenly on her toes, reaching forward to smack him right across the mouth. 'Don't you use that language to me, you little punk.' She spat the words out. 'You don't know what you're talking about.' She took a step towards her husband. 'Don't you listen to him, Pete!'

Steve's lips were smarting. He snarled at her, his eyes filling: 'Maybe you're not my mom either. Maybe you're just two of a kind, two lying sonsabitches.'

All this time Wanda had been sitting thirty feet away in the car, the window wound down, watching them. It was her radio that was playing the Sinatra song. Now she reached forward and turned it off. The sudden quiet drew Steve's attention.

'You,' he said. 'You started it. Tell 'em what you told me, why don't you? Or are you lying too? Tell 'em about the other guy, whatever his name was. The one she told you about. The one that got killed in Grandpa's car.' He turned to look at Pete. 'You gonna tell me about him or what?'

Pete was looking at the ground. Irena strode towards the car. Her eyes were narrow and her voice low, but everyone could hear her as she hissed at her daughter, 'And I thought I could trust you.'

Steve stepped slowly into the old house. He was shaking his head, as if to rid himself of these memories. Bonny had once told him that the deeper you bury the pain the sharper it is when it rises to the surface. He switched on the flashlight. From the generously proportioned hallway he looked into each of the downstairs rooms in turn. They were crammed with junk. Not the junk of the typical abandoned house, but the kind of things a farmer would stash away in a barn in case they proved handy someday. What was once the the kitchen had clearly been used as a workshop. There was a set of carpenter's tools there, a rusted old electric-powered lathe and bench-saw, a collection of yard tools and, against the walls, several stacks of timber, some of it heavy, much of it in the form of slender boards, some moulded, probably salvaged from another abandoned building. There was a heavy black vise on a work-bench. He remembered how able the old man was, how careful with his tools, how appreciative of a length of seasoned hardwood.

He looked around some more. There was a collection of ornate table- and chair-legs, remnants of some long-ago project. Dry wood shavings had been gathered into corners by generations of rodents. Standing there, he was confused by a brief flicker of warmth towards a father who had taken the time to teach him the rudiments of woodwork, electrical and plumbing repairs, skills that he had put to good use through twenty years as an in-demand handyman in the smarter suburbs of Portland. He remembered being in that room when his mother came in with a birthday cake adorned with thirteen candles. He remembered his sister, later, telling him he was now old enough to know the truth, that they were only half related.

'Where d'you think you got those big brown eyes?' she said.

'Anyone can get brown eyes.'

'Mom don't. Nor me. Nor Dad. Maybe you were one of them – you know, like they found you or something.'

Somehow Steve had smothered that. He needed to. He tried to remember the colours of Grandpa's eyes and realised that, barely a year after the old man's passing, he simply couldn't. So it must have been their grandmother, long gone. She would be the one. Maybe he'd find a photograph of her and prove it. And so the doubts lay buried, until the day he lashed out at Pete and took off.

He went to the foot of the stairs and shone his light up the full flight. At first he trod carefully, holding the stout banister rail with a firm grip. The steps creaked some, but they were still sound enough. He climbed to the landing where he found the wallpaper hanging in strips, and looked up to the ceiling. Maybe there was a leak in the roof, after all. He pushed open the door of what was once his own room. Sunlight flooded in through the window onto a bare wooden floor. He remembered long winter nights, sitting there reading while the wind hammered at the window, and how safe he'd felt, hearing the low murmurings of the adults downstairs – and how terrified, as he grew older, to hear the rows that started to become a regular event. But maybe that was in the new house. Damn, these things were so confused in his memory.

His sister's old room was likewise empty, apart from a tattered rug thrown in one corner. Same with the parents'. When he tried the handle of the fourth, Grandpa's, he found it locked. Now he remembered. After Dad had finished the new house Steve himself had started going back there to sleep from time to time, and slept well. He tried the door again, then looked up, and there it was, hanging on a slender nail tacked into the top of the door-frame, as ever: the little brass key. Now he remembered Wanda telling him that Pete had taken the room over. That way, he didn't have to hear Irena trying to tiptoe in at eleven, twelve, or two in the morning. But that was after he, Steve, had left.

The door opened easily enough, just a little stiff. Inside, Steve stumbled against a portable gas heater. There was a bedstead, but no mattress, a sagging, upholstered swivel chair and a table, hard up against the window, which was set back in a kind of bay that formed the corner of this turret room. On the table were a few sheets of blank, curled-up paper. He saw a *Farmer's Almanac*, dated 1988, a calendar for the same year. Thinking about it, he was sure that was when Dad died. Twenty-three years ago. Was it really that long? He felt a sudden pang at not having returned for the funeral. At the time it didn't make sense. Now, he could see that it might have made a difference. Beside the almanac was a large envelope, covered with dust. He picked it up. It was strengthened with stiff card. He slid his hand inside and pulled out a photograph.

He recognised it immediately. It was the one that had arrested his gaze in his hotel room. The writer, Mari Sandoz. And although he couldn't be sure of the words without his glasses, he could see that something was written in the bottom right-hand corner. He took it to the window, and in the bright sunlight he could read it quite clearly. *For Piotr,* it said, and was signed *Mari XX*.

Steve went to the door. Once again, he felt the need to get outside. At the head of the stairs he paused, took a breath and said the words aloud. 'Easy now.' Stepping carefully, he made the descent without mishap and was out in the daylight. At the car, he fumbled with the door handle. Placing the photograph and its envelope on the passenger seat, he closed the door and retraced his steps, making quite sure the front door and screen door were firmly closed.

There was no way he was going to face Wanda in this state of mind. He drove back to Chadron, his mind racing. Twice he had to check his speed. Why would his old man have a picture of this Mari Sandoz? And what was with the kisses? The discovery mystified and excited him in equal measure. Even twenty-some years after Pete's death, the old bastard was still sowing the seeds of confusion. And Steve felt something else too, an outrage, that this woman he'd only now started reading about, this woman he was finding so intriguing, had affection to bestow on the man who was, but was not, his father.

Later, when he walked into the Olde Main Street Inn, Glenn was at the bar, raising a hand in greeting and looking as though he wanted to talk. It was more than Steve could cope with at that moment. 'Not now!' he said, and hurried upstairs, clutching the photograph to his chest.

10

Lyn felt strangely hesitant about taking the next step in her researches. If her grandmother had been around she would have said it was 'time to poop or get off the pot'. Her project had been so long delayed, so stretched out over the years, that when she finally realized she was free to go at it she almost shrank from the task before her. It felt a little like returning to a leftover meal set aside several days previously. So despite her initial excitement about the sabbatical, there was a certain reluctance about taking the first big step. Was it fear of failure? Maybe.

Over the past few years, all she had been able to do was nibble around the edges of the whole, picking off a little research job here, reading an essay there. Whenever she'd had a free half day - or the precious gift of a weekend - she would attack her chosen task in a kind of frenzy, always conscious of the mountain she had yet to climb, and the constant ticking of an imagined clock. Sometimes when she went back through her previous work, she would be startled to find that she was beginning to forget simple facts that had once been central to her thought processes. Some of the ideas she'd recorded way back at the beginning still seemed fresh and vital, and made her pulse race. Others, viewed years after their conception, now appeared quite banal, unconvincing.

However, with all this time at her disposal, she had drawn up plans and compiled lists, some neatly written in her notebooks, others on computer files, yet more on scraps of paper stashed between the pages of the several books she was trying to get through at any one time. There was always, it seemed, more reading to do. And what had been a youthful delight was in danger of becoming a trial. Yes, it refreshed her knowledge and understanding of some aspects of her subject, but it also cluttered her mind with other people's ideas. She wasn't sure she wanted to hear from all these eager young scholars, plowing new furrows in what had once been a comparatively unexploited field. The idea of being abreast of the latest scholarship seemed beyond her. And what about her ideas? Did they have any value?

Lyn had this simple premise, that there was a common trajectory in the way writers who emerged from the frontier responded to their experiences. As youngsters they couldn't wait to get away and embrace the wider world beyond the cornfield or the corral. Once free from the yoke of unceasing chores, they would write about the worst of pioneer life, its hardships and ordeals. They would lament the narrow world view of their parents, and they would do so with all the vigour of youth, tainted with rancor. At the outset of her project she had delved into the early writings of Laura Ingalls Wilder and found that her *Little House* books were a somewhat adulterated, toned-down version of what she first wrote about her childhood years, which contained some unpalatable truths about the homesteading life. And so she had taken time out to study the life of the author's daughter, the journalist Rose Wilder Lane, who, she discovered, had been instrumental in supervising this re-telling of the past, in essence sanitising it.

All this led Lyn to think more deeply about these transitions. She had seen them in the books of Hamlin Garland, familiar to her from her Wisconsin high-school days. He was another writer who had grown up a pioneer farmer's child. At nine years old he was following the plow, head on to the driving sleet, praying it would turn to snow so that he could return to the shelter of the house. At the start of his career he wrote with anger about conditions for farmers out west, and the way the banks and railroads conspired to keep them in bondage. But when looking back as a middle-aged man on a past that had gone forever, he offered a much more generous, forgiving view, she felt. And she saw the same trajectory, writ large, in Willa Cather - another writer who, in her mature years, wrote with affection about the hard times experienced by her near-neighbors, and chose to celebrate, from the comfort of a home in the east, the way those ordeals fostered their strength of character.

The question was, should she pursue this idea? Was it anything more than a commonplace piece of folk wisdom, that the young don't appreciate what they have until it's gone? That the past always looks rosier when seen from a distance? That growing up involves recognising that all those hardships merely tested your mettle, helped a person develop, strengthen, learn? That they were, in fact, good for you? Could it simply be that Garland, Cather and Wilder developed their writing skills and so produced more lyrical prose as they developed? That that was how they contributed to the mythification of the past?

As she sat in her room, looking at the books she'd brought back from Valentine, she was reminded of her supervising professor's remark, repeated several times over the lifespan of the project. For most students, she liked to say, as it came time to knuckle down and start writing, the temptation was always there: 'I'll just read one more book.' It was a gentle warning against over-preparing, a hint that she should have more faith in her own accumulated knowledge, her mature judgement. Just get on with it! However, here she was with the little clutch of books she'd bought in Valentine. She had long wanted to read Caroline Sandoz' account of her sister's young life, and so she started there, with her little book, *The Making of a Writer*. Within an hour a dozen or more of Lyn's lurid pink Post-it notes were sticking out from between the pages of this slim volume.

As she read, Lyn smiled in recognition of a voice she recalled quite clearly from her single visit with this youngest of the Sandoz brood, back in the early 1990s. In a way, she had met her too soon, before she had fully embraced the scope of her project, before she knew which questions she should be asking. The meeting had come out of the blue. She was in Nebraska, the town of Hastings, to be precise, to attend a week-long conference on Willa Cather, at which she had been asked to present a paper. So she was delighted to find that Mari's biographer, Helen Stauffer, was in attendance, more so to meet her over mid-morning coffee. And it was this gracious woman who encouraged her to drive out to the Sandhills and meet Caroline. 'It's only a few hours,' she had insisted, 'and she loves to receive visitors, especially scholars.' She even promised to phone ahead and prepare the woman for Lyn's arrival. As an afterthought, she gave Lyn the name of a college professor up at the State College who had studied Sandoz for many years and knew a number of the family. And she recommended that she put up at the Olde Main Street Inn.

A glance at the map had suggested this was a good six-hour journey, but clearly worth it. This was primary source material being dangled in her face. So Lyn set out late that afternoon and stayed over at the little town of Hyannis, from where she called her husband to bring him up to speed. He had seemed distracted, but that wasn't unusual. He never fully understood her work, nor the passion with which she applied herself to it.

She completed the journey early that next morning. Less than an hour's drive up a deserted highway she found the turning that pointed to her destination along a dusty two-track. It was alarming enough to be bouncing across open pasture and weaving past clusters of staring cattle, more so when the door of the house was opened by a woman holding a .410 Winchester. But she was quickly put at her ease by her host's insistence that she only kept it there to scare the deer away from the young trees she'd planted around the place.

Lyn would spend the entire day, right through till dusk, in the company of this bright, down-to-earth, eighty-three year old. She had, she now realized, been privileged to see something really special. Even as she lay in her room in Hyannis the previous night, listening to the Burlington freights rumbling past on their way east to Grand Island, she had re-read parts of Mari's early life. It was the young woman's determination to tell her story that had long fascinated her. There was the epic struggle to find a publisher, but before that the more intriguing tale of her several attempts to decide which version of events she would record. It seemed that, long before she accepted her father's deathbed invitation to 'write my life some time', she had written a fictionalised account of life on the Sandoz homestead from the point of view of a troubled child, herself. She had indeed tried several times to get this manuscript published, before abandoning it in favor of her father's own story. Helen Stauffer had asserted that the manuscript, alternately titled *Murky River* or *The Ungirt*

Runner, offered important insights into Mari's personality, her youthful attitudes towards her parents - and her early writing technique.

So when Caroline looked into Lyn's eyes over a cup of coffee and asked, 'What exactly is your interest in my sister?' her answer came, ready formed, as if she'd rehearsed it.

'I'm hoping you can tell me where I can find that unpublished manuscript - her first attempt at a novel.'

'You want to see that old thing?' Caroline got out of her seat. 'Well, you'd better come down to the basement.'

'Really? You have it?'

Downstairs she led Lyn into a room that resembled something between a small-town museum and a thrift store. It housed an apparently random collection of coats and dresses hung on rails, hats on shelves or in cases, framed pictures, papers and books stacked on tables, and several piles of document boxes.

'When my sister died,' Caroline said, 'we took a truck to New York and emptied her apartment. We brought home four tons of – oh, everything, as you can see. Some of it went to Lincoln, of course, but the University only took what they wanted. This is what they left.'

It took Caroline just a few minutes to dig out the ring-binder that held the manuscript. It occurred to Lyn that the University people would surely have wanted this for their own collection, but she wasn't going to ask about that right now. All she could think about was her great good fortune in having the chance to read it.

Back upstairs, the two women sat at the table in the living room and went through it together, Lyn passing the pages across to her host, one at a time as she finished with them. She had no idea how long she had, so she read fast, skimming in places, and making notes. What she read excited her. The jerky prose, awash with superfluous adverbs, revealed a young woman seething with anger and resentment at her violent and abusive father. The young Mari had re-cast herself as Endor, a girl who sought solace in romance, in fantasy, even in imagined friends she could summon up in the night, and through this child's thoughts she gave full expression to her rage, bitterness and scorn for a cantankerous and tyrannical father. She depicted him as a brute, a savage, a roaring terror, her young self as a foundling - absolutely not the natural child of these dreadful people.

Lyn was shocked at some of the words she scribbled in her notebook that day. Could this be the woman who later wrote about Old Jules with such maturity and balance, such generosity, such carefully chosen words? And how had that change come about?

Sitting there in the Olde Main Street Inn, she shook her head. Just what had happened to the notes she'd taken that day? What was in them? She looked out through the window and let out a long, shuddering breath as she remembered the events of that long midsummer day, and how excited she had been with her discovery. How she couldn't wait to get up to Chadron and call home, eager to share her news with her husband. It was, she recalled, getting dark when she finally left Caroline's place, and a stiff breeze was throwing up clouds of dust as she bounced along the two-track and back to the highway. By the time she pulled in beside the Olde Main Street Inn it was going on nine.

She never got to give Marty the good news. Before she could even ask him how things were, she could hear him blurting out the words that would echo around her head for weeks, months, years to come: that he was in love with her best friend and was moving, the very next day, to be with her in Chicago.

The marriage had been in trouble from the get-go. She wasn't blind to that. But loyalty, hope, tenacity, and a vestigial affection for the young man she had met back in their college days together, all those factors had kept her by his side, even through the drinking and the violence that erupted from time to time. And now this. Outright betrayal detonating an explosion that ripped through her life and cost her a comfortable home and, almost, her livelihood. Quite how she managed to hang on to her place at the U she could barely recall. Twice she broke down in front of her class. Once she handed in a resignation, only to be talked out of it by a kind and understanding Dean of Faculty. But in retrospect, all that seemed no more than a brief stay of execution. The following year, renewed budgetary restrictions sentenced her to the fifteen years of serial short-term posts that had only just, finally, come to an end.

As to her project, that went right onto the back burner, and was all but extinguished. As she moved into a friend's basement, and from there to an inner-city apartment, and then another, her research materials went in and out of storage. They became scattered. Books went missing - either loaned out or lost, possibly stolen. And her notes, her precious notes that she'd taken at Caroline's table that long-ago day, twenty-two longhand pages, where the hell were they? The fact was, she had no evidence that she'd even brought them back east with her. Had she, in fact, left them at Caroline's place? Surely not. There had been a sporadic correspondence following the visit, but it had petered out, and now the old lady would be dead. Even so, if that's where she'd left them, Caroline would surely have found them and sent them on. Had she, Merilyn, mislaid them in her hotel room as she threw her clothes into a case and set off on the long drive home that very night? Had she simply overlooked them in the chaos of breaking up the marital home, shoved them into the wrong box as she weeded out unwanted possessions, and hers from his, in the ongoing chaos of successive removals?

Whatever the answer, they were gone, and now her only hope was that manuscript Caroline had shown her. She had either to track it down or reconsider the entire thrust of her project. Finding it, and setting aside the time required, had been a part of her pitch when she applied for this sabbatical. How would it look if she failed in her search? Lyn had long ago forgiven Marty, or so she believed, but once in a while she allowed herself the luxury of unfettered anger. And so, standing in her room and holding a towel over her mouth, she cursed him, volubly, loudly, before setting off for the college.

Outside it seemed that the day was shaping up pretty well. The sun was high in the sky, most of the snow had gone from the streets, and people were walking by in light jackets, baseball caps pulled down over their eyes. Making her way up Main Street, Lyn was reminded of her younger days when she would take regular hiking trips in the country. She still walked regularly, around town and campus, so for her the ten blocks that took her to Chadron State College were no more than a gentle stroll through the tree-lined streets, past neat-looking houses with front lawns, porches, mature shade trees.

It was a modest campus, home to some 5000 students. Its buildings were so much smaller than the tall blocks she was used to, and well scattered across spacious lawns dotted with trees. She soon found the Mari Sandoz High Plains Heritage Center, recognizing it from the pictures she'd seen on the website. It was a single-story brick building with a red tiled roof and a neo-classical portico over the entrance. Out front was a collection of plants and grasses native to the Great Plains. And there amongst them was the life-size statue of Lyn's heroine, in bronze.

The statue depicted Mari as a young woman, a girl really, but one who had all the poise of her older self. She stood, face to the wind, full-bosomed, a broad-brimmed hat perched on her head, her hair flowing behind her and halfway down her back - hair much longer and with more body to it than she'd seen in any picture of the scrawny, wary-looking Mari taken in the days before she made her breakthrough. Behind her, clasped in her hands but out of sight of the passer-by, was an open book. Lyn liked that. It reminded her of the story she'd read, how, as a child, Mari had smuggled works of fiction - gifts from kindly neighbors - up the outside stairs that led to her attic bedroom where she stored them in her mattress. Where had Lyn read that? It could have been in that missing manuscript, possibly somewhere else. It was hard to keep track of every last anecdote or memory. What she knew for a fact was that Mari's father considered fiction as being fit only for hired girls, and anyone who defied his wishes knew what to expect.

Looking down, Lyn saw that the statue stood barefoot. Surrounded as it was by the stalks of last year's prairie grasses, that seemed a nice touch: a woman of scholarly renown, of huge intelligence, an accomplished author, yet one who still loved to stand and face the winds that swept the plains unopposed, who embraced the elemental, who had rarely felt the grip of a pair of shoes until she started school at age nine. So here she was, her toes firmly grasping the coarse, sandy soil that she had known all her young life, her eyes set on a brighter future.

Lyn entered the building. There was a display dedicated to Mari, and to one side a collection of books for sale. She soon found a couple she wanted, and took them to the desk where a young student sat at a computer screen. The person who ran the Center was out of town, he told her. 'So when can I browse in the archives?' Lyn asked. 'Do I need to make an appointment?'

'What exactly are you looking for?' the student asked. He was about twenty-three by the look of him, quiet, and very courteous. Before Lyn could answer he added, 'But she'll be in tomorrow, the director. Do you wanna come back then?'

'Sure, I can do that, but can you tell me exactly what you have here? I'm writing a book about Mari. I need to have some idea. I mean, I don't know whether I'm looking at a couple of days or a couple of weeks, or whether I would be better in the Lincoln archive.'

The student looked doubtful. 'I can print you out the list. But there's a lot of the collection hasn't been catalogued yet.'

'Yeah, I got that. So maybe you can answer me one question. This manuscript Mari wrote and never published - *Murky River*? Do you have that?' The guy looked blank. 'You may know it as *The Ungirt Runner*. It was never published, but it's very important. That's the thing I really need to see.'

'I'm sorry,' the kid said. 'I don't think I've ever heard of that.'

'Forget it,' Lyn told him. 'I'll call back tomorrow. But can you leave your boss a note? Tell her I was in? We have emailed each other, a couple of times. Here's my card.'

Outside, Lyn released a gasp of frustration. In years past, she reminded herself, she might have given that young guy a piece of her mind. But she'd long ago learned that that kind of reaction was best saved for the person who deserved it. She looked around her. This campus was way quieter than any she'd ever been to. Practically deserted. She thought about exploring, but decided instead to go back to town, grab a coffee and re-group.

11

With the light on, and his glasses perched on his nose, Steve sat on his bed and studied the photograph one more time. The inscription was quite clear. *For Piotr. Mari XX*. He turned the envelope over. Had he missed something, a postmark? No, there wasn't even an address on it.

'Jesus.' He got up and started towards the sitting room. Then he checked, came back, picked up the photo again. He went and compared it, side by side, with the one on the wall. They appeared identical. Maybe it was some kind of publicity shot. You could just imagine it on the back of a book. Holding the one up to the other, he reassured himself that they were indeed the same. He then lifted the framed one down and turned it over, hoping there would be a date on the back, or some clue as to who took it, and for what particular purpose. There was nothing that he could see. The one he'd got from the old place seemed a little shabby beside the one in the nice wooden frame. For a moment he thought about swapping them over. Then he had an idea.

He picked up the biography he'd been reading the night before and flipped through that. No, none of the pictures resembled the one she'd signed for the old man. The nearest was on the cover – an artfully composed shot of Mari, half in shadow, her forehead and right eye obscured by a seductively angled hat. This was no Sandhills waif. This was a mature woman who knew herself, knew how to flatter a man, and most likely had the photographer in her pocket as well. The sort of woman who knew what guys were thinking. But the old man? No, surely not.

He slumped into the easy chair, then wriggled to one side and unclipped the fanny-pack. He threw it on the table and sighed. Just what the hell did this photograph signify? What was the connection? He turned the pages of the biography, wondering how old this woman might have been when she and his father . . . Here it was: 1896. That made her the exact same age as Piotr. He looked at his watch. Five thirty. Maybe the woman called Lyn would be around. Maybe she could help. She was researching the damned woman, after all. He put the fanny-pack back on, checked that he had his wallet, and went downstairs.

Jeannie was there at the bar, Glenn at a table by the door. He had a book in his hand and a beer in front of him.

'Hey man, how's it going?' Glenn turned his book over and reached for his wallet. 'Can I get you a beer?'

'Thank you,' Steve said.

'What'll it be?' Jeannie asked.

Steve was looking into the chiller. 'Think I'll try a bottle of that Fat Tire,' he said.

'Glass?'

'Sure.' Then he said, 'And gimme a shot of bourbon, will you?' He glanced at Glenn. 'Don't worry, I'll pay for that.'

Jeannie poured the drinks and passed them across the bar.

'Your very good health,' Steve said, taking a sip of beer and raising the shot glass to sniff at the contents.

'So how's your day been?' Glenn asked 'Speaking as someone who's spent seven hours in a dimly lit room trying to turn a three-chord riff into a rock classic.'

Steve dodged the question. 'What kind of music do you do?' he asked.

'Well,' Glenn said, 'it's been called Dylanesque. It's been called techno folk rock. Been called self-indulgent crap too.' He pointed at the CDs on the shelf behind the bar. 'Songs from my worthless life.'

'Don't listen to him,' Jeannie said. 'He drifted around, like a lot of people. But he learned. This is a wise man you're talking to. And the songs are great. You should listen to them some time.'

'I'm no judge,' Steve said. 'My sister was the musical one.' Then he turned back to Glenn. 'I never met a song-writer before. You make a decent living?'

Glenn laughed. 'Are you kidding? Gigging around small-town Nebraska? I make a few hundred bucks a year. Sometimes a thousand or two.'

'Oh. So d'you have another job?'

'I got a dozen other jobs. Yard work in the summer, cutting grass, trees. Don't charge a lot for that. It's how I feed the wood-burner. And wintertime I got a rancher - big spread. He hires me to help out when he has hunters in from Denver. Deer and turkey, mostly. I get to dress the kill, sometimes cook it. And if they ask me nicely, I play for them around a fire at night. Country standards, mostly. Not my thing. But they do pay.' Glenn looked at Steve and asked, 'So, what have you been up to all day?'

Steve returned his gaze. The guy was like a dog with a bone. Then he glanced at Jeannie. She seemed to trust him, and she was no mug. 'Just digging around old haunts,' he said. 'Out in the hills.' He took a long swallow of beer, then tossed back the bourbon.

'How was your sister?' Jeannie asked. 'You did get to see her, didn't you?'

'Sure I did, yesterday. But she wasn't really with it. She's on some pretty strong pain-killers.'

'That's how my old dad was,' Glenn said. 'One moment he didn't know you, then suddenly he was talking about the old days and you couldn't stop him. We used to take pictures in, old photo albums. That was guaranteed to set him off.'

'It ain't dementia she's got,' Steve said, and passed the empty shot glass to Jeannie with a nod of his head. Then he snapped his fingers. 'Damn.'

'What is it?' Jeannie asked.

'I brought a bunch of cassette tapes from her house. Thought to cheer her up, but . . .' He shrugged.

'Aha!' Glenn said. 'Nothing to play 'em on. Right?'

'You got it.'

'Well,' Glenn said, 'you need to come round my place. I got a few bits and pieces.'

'Just a few,' Jeannie said. 'Boy, he has everything in there. It's like Aladdin's cave.'

'Well, maybe we can do a little business,' Steve said. He was about to suggest a time for a visit when the main door opened and Lyn came in. She walked to the bar and nodded at Steve.

'Hey, Prof,' Glenn said.

'Good evening to you, Glenn. Or is it still afternoon?' She looked around. 'Steve, Jeannie. Kinda quiet, isn't it?'

'It's early yet,' Glenn said.

'Well, early or not, I'm done for the day.' She slipped her bag off her shoulder and let it drop to the floor beside her. 'Just called in at that Sandoz Center. Bought a couple more books. Can't seem to resist.' She gave a long sigh and grabbed a seat at the bar. 'They got quite a stock up there.'

'Yes, they certainly do,' Jeannie said. She turned and

opened the cold cabinet. 'Well, you sound kinda weary. Would a beer help? Non-alcoholic, right?'

'That's the one. In a glass.' Lyn took the drink, then said, 'Thanks, Jeannie. Yeah, I wanted to see the director, but she's out of town.'

'Oh dear, a wasted trip,' Jeannie said.

'Well, it was good to see the place. I loved the statue. And they say the boss is back tomorrow. Not that that's any good to me.'

'Oh,' Steve said. 'You leaving already?'

'No, but I'll be out all day. Going for a little drive.'

'Right.'

'I picked up this flyer about the Old Jules Trail.' She pulled a folded sheet of paper from her shoulder-bag and showed it to Jeannie. 'They say it takes you past all the main sites - you know, like where his buddies dropped him down the well, where his wife lived - the one who went mad. And Mari's grave. So if the weather holds I'm going to pack a lunch and take off.'

Glenn got up from his seat and walked across to the bar. He looked over Lyn's shoulder at the flyer. 'Yeah,' he said, 'but you already had one mishap in that car of yours.'

'Thanks for reminding me.'

'Just saying. That trail,' he said, 'it's kinda rough in parts. Two-tracks, mud hollows. Could be in pretty bad shape after the storm.'

Steve picked up the flyer and looked at it for a moment or two. 'Tell you what,' he said. 'If you can stand a little company, maybe we could take my truck. I know those old roads. Leastways, I used to.'

'Really?' Lyn said. 'Well, listen, that'd be just great. Thanks. So long as you're not in a hurry. I'll be taking pictures, making notes.'

'I ain't short of time,' Steve said. 'Let's call it a date. What'll we do, meet up at breakfast? Eight o'clock - nine?'

'Let's say eight,' Lyn said. She was about to say something else, but Steve was already emptying his beer and leaving his seat.

'Okay,' he said, 'see you tomorrow.' He left the bar but didn't go to his room. Instead, he got into his truck and headed out along the highway. There was a café on the edge of town that served him a halfway decent steak. As he waited for his food he realized he'd glibly promised to spend the day with Lyn when he should have been going back to see his sister, the sister who was going to leave him the ranch. But even as he felt that inner discomfort over the years when he'd barely spoken to her, he reminded himself that the old man had once promised it to him as his natural birthright. So why should he feel bad? Should he back out on the trip with the professor? The fact was, this Sandoz thing was starting to bug him. Ah hell, he would honor his promise. From what he'd seen of the map Lyn had showed him they ought to get done early enough for him to visit Wanda in the afternoon.

He lingered over his food, and sank a couple of beers. When he got back to the hotel he took the out-of-hours staircase to his suite. The last thing he wanted right now was company, and questions. How was he doing? Where had he been to eat? The folk down in the bar were okay, but he wished they had more going on in their lives.

Sitting in the easy chair, with the copy of *Old Jules* in his hand, he was reminded of what Jeannie had said, that he should brace himself. She was a wise old bird, he had to admit. And dead right when she talked of the impact all this shit was going to have on him. He was already finding himself overwhelmed with fatigue at odd moments. There was no doubt about it, the past was crowding in. He'd half expected that, that he might find himself going over the crap between himself and the old man. What surprised him was the way Grandpa had started to appear, both in his dreams and in waking moments, how conversations he'd had fifty years ago were starting to come back to him. It was almost as if the old fellow was trying to tell him something, that he should have been listening more carefully, those quiet afternoons when they sat together, talking.

'I didn't vant to go. I built that house to stand - a hundred years. More. You and your sons and they sons. I was plan to die there. God damn, I vill die there. You must promise.'

It was clear to Steve that they were in the new place when the words were spoken.

Grandpa wasn't in his comfortable old chair by the window that looked out across the grass he'd come to love over the years, the seat from which he could greet the rising sun. He was propped up in bed in the back room of the new place. His window looked out to the north, over an empty corn-crib and a straggly apple tree. Beside him was an oxygen tank, a table with one of his Polish novels and his magnifying glass on it. They'd tried to tell him he should get his eyes tested but in the end they gave up. It worked for him. When young Steve sat down he accidentally kicked the old china piss-pot. Luckily, it had been emptied.

'Your mother want new place, always new place.'

Steve knew what this was about. Even as a twelve year old he'd been used to hearing his mother complain about the old house, how it was spooky, draughty, old-fashioned. She talked about her friends, whose husbands were putting up modern places, open plan, single-story, with big windows. 'Light,' she'd say. 'It's too gloomy and depressing in here. I need more light.' Never occurred to her how damned hot it would get in the summer, and sure enough, no sooner had they moved in than she was nagging Pete for Venetian blinds and air conditioning. It was around that time that he first heard his father mutter under his breath about 'the witch of Endor' and wondered what the hell that meant.

'She want, she get. Every time,' the old man said. He leaned towards Steve, a wicked sort of grin on his wrinkled face. 'But she didn't get the bootlegger. Your Pa and me, we fix him good.' His bony fingers were around the boy's slim forearm, and he was laughing. 'He never come round no more. Ha ha ha.'

At the time he had no idea what Grandpa was talking about. Didn't even know what the word bootlegger meant. What he most wanted right then was for Grandpa to let go his arm.

Strange how all these things were coming back to him now. Who the hell was this bootlegger? Whatever Grandpa had been talking about, it could have no significance after all this time. Surely. But the memory wouldn't go away, and that night he dreamed it all over again. The fingers on his arm, the pleading look on the old man's face. And then the words, *'Your Pa and me, we fix him good. Think he know how to drive? Ha.'*

The dreams came in fits and starts. Steve kept waking up. That was nothing new: he was regularly up once, sometimes twice, for the toilet. This night though, it was memories. Of Grandpa, of his old man, of Wanda and his mother on the front porch – and there beside them on the top step the big glass jar with a tea bag in it. All through the summer they would be brewing one lot of sun tea while they sat and sipped yesterday's, iced. And then his father came storming out, accusing them of plotting against him. And his sister whispering about Grandpa's car. When Steve revisited those days he felt confused, but above all isolated and alone.

12

By the time Steve dragged himself out of bed he didn't feel much like a ride in the Sandhills with the woman Lyn. He told himself he'd made the offer out of a sense of guilt for the way he was talking about her when she was there, sitting in the bar, that night after he'd pulled her out of the ditch. But an arrangement was an arrangement. He showered and dressed. As he shaved he took another good long look at the photo of Mari. Of the woman who had been sweet on his old man. It was taking a bit of getting used to. He tried to remember the previous night's dreams, but they were melting away.

When he went downstairs to the bar Lyn was already there with her coffee, a book in her hand. She wished him good morning and then suggested they should go and get themselves a big breakfast. 'My treat,' she said. 'I mean, you're driving. It'll set you up for the day.'

'You don't have to,' he tried.

'Hey, rule number one of the road. Keep the driver happy. And it could be a long day.'

'I guess it could at that.' Again he realized that he ought to tell her he needed to visit his sister, but was aware that a part of him was looking for an excuse.

They went to a new coffee-house, just a couple of blocks away. As they sat waiting for their food to arrive Steve asked, 'So you're seriously clued up on this Sandoz woman?'

'Oh yes. I've been studying a number of authors for this book I'm writing, but she's the one.'

'The one who what?'

'I mean she's my favorite. The more I've gotten to know her, the higher I rate her. Not just for her work, which is great, but for her journey, I guess. The gap between where she started and where she ended up. That's how you measure a person's stature, wouldn't you say? The distance they've had to travel.'

Steve thought for a moment. 'Never saw it that way myself, but yeah, it makes sense.'

Looking at him, Lyn saw the ghost of a smile cross his face. 'You thinking of someone in particular?'

Steve was surprised by the question. 'Matter of fact I was thinking of my old grandad. Came all the way from Poland to settle out here. But go on – about this Sandoz woman.'

'Oh, okay. Well, I just rate her amongst the finest writers from the Great Plains. Don't get me wrong, I mean there's Willa Cather – you know her?'

'Heard the name.'

'Great, great writer. Laura Ingalls Wilder, likewise. They lived the life of the pioneer homesteader: how to butcher a pig, build a log cabin, hang a door, hone an axe, fight a grass fire - it's all there in the Little House books. But Mari Sandoz, you've got the books and then, wow, take a look at the life.'

'I've only just got started on that,' Steve said. He paused as the waitress placed the food in front of them. Then he said, 'So go on – tell me about her.'

'Okay. Number one, this is a woman who didn't speak English till she turned nine. Think about that. Nine years old before her old man allowed her to go to school. God, he was a tyrannical whatever. And violent, of course. Number two, she never even went to high school, never mind getting a college degree. Number three . . .' She cut herself a triangle of toast, picked it up, thought for a moment, then put it back down.

'Let's talk about dedication. She half-starved herself while she was learning to write. Had her work rejected over and over. And every damned time she just sat down, rewrote it and sent it out again. Over and over. D'you know, there was a period when she lived in Lincoln, every time she earned fifty dollars she quit work so she could concentrate on her writing. I'd call that heroism, wouldn't you?'

'Not sure about that. Crazy, more like it. But hey, don't forget to eat.'

Lyn laughed, broke her other egg on the hash browns and mashed it with the back of her fork. She took a mouthful, then carried on. 'Just imagine her, a barefoot kid in a pioneer shack. She was on the highway to nowhere. An early marriage, a brood of kids and a life of drudgery. That's what was facing her, what her old man assumed she would do. But she ends up one of our most important Great Plains historians. And not just white man's history. Oh no. She wrote the Indians' too. I mean, she was around them as a kid. Used to sneak out of bed at night to listen to them trading stories with her old man.'

'Whoa there. You need to slow down. How come there were Indians in the house?'

'Old Jules traded with the Lakota. Furs, tobacco, rifles.

They'd bring him broken ones. You see, he could fix guns just the same as he could doctor people. He delivered babies, for heaven's sake. He was a clever man, educated - but boy, was he lazy.' She broke a slice of bacon in two and put a piece in her mouth. 'You just have to read the books. It's all there.' She smiled at him. 'You see what happens when you get me started?'

'Yeah, you spill egg yolk down your blouse.'

'Oh, shoot.' She grabbed a napkin and cleaned it up. 'This subject gets to me, every time I start talking about it.'

'That's okay,' Steve said. 'Always figured it must be something to be fired up by the work you do.' He waited a few seconds, then asked, 'She ever get married? Any boyfriends?'

'Well, there's a question.'

Steve waited, took a sip of coffee. 'So you gonna answer it?'

'I can hazard a guess. The thing with Mari is, she played her cards close to her chest. Especially where men were concerned. You know about her marriage?'

Steve shook his head. 'I told you, I only read a few pages. Busy enough with *Old Jules*.'

'Right, well, she did get married, which was what her father wanted. Demanded, more like. She was eighteen years old.'

'And?'

'Hah! She canned the guy five years later. Or was it four? I forget right now. Divorced him and took off for Lincoln. Started a new life and never spoke about it. Nobody there ever knew. But that's not to say she didn't have boyfriends.'

'Yeah?'

'She liked male company. Liked dancing and skating. Knew how to enjoy herself. Someplace there's an album she made of all her beaux - photographs. I'm hoping to find it. Think it's in the university archive in Lincoln.'

'Listen,' Steve said. He pulled a paper napkin from the dispenser, wiped his mouth and leaned forward across the table. 'I'm gonna tell you something.'

'Go on.'

'I was back in our home place yesterday.'

'Where your sister lives, right?'

'Sort of. There's her place, the house my dad built in the nineteen sixties, and right behind it there's the original house my grandfather built.' Steve paused as the waitress refilled their coffees. 'Now, he was a guy. Grandpa and I, we kinda hit it off. But then he died. Ninety-some years old.' He paused for a moment and looked out the window. 'I guess I was lucky to have the time I had with him.' He went on: 'You see it everywhere on the plains - the two places side by side, the old and the new, and the old one slowly falling apart. It was a typical frame house.' He thought for a moment, then said, 'No, that's not true. It was more than that. My grandfather put a few nice details on it. He took a lot of pride in it. After my parents and my sister and I moved into the new place my dad still used the ground floor in the old place as a workshop. And he kept a room of his own upstairs. Like an office, except sometimes he slept there. Grandpa hung out there full-time at first, until he got really weak towards the end.'

'And when was that, exactly?'

'I guess we moved across about sixty-two, three. Come to think of it, we watched the Kennedy assassination - I mean we saw it on the news. Lee Harvey Oswald and all that. We watched it on our television in there, so it would be sixty-three at the latest.'

'Yeah, I remember that, just about, and I was only four.'

'November, wasn't it, so I guess I'd just turned seventeen. I left when I was nineteen.'

'And you've not been back since? Till now?'

'Correct. Been as far as North Platte one time, and thought about it. But I talked myself out of it.'

'Wow.' She tapped her brow with a forefinger. 'You must be churning up some dust in that head of yours.'

'I guess so. Anyway, this office in the old house. There wasn't much to get excited about up there. Mouse-shit and cobwebs, mostly. All except for one thing.' Steve paused. It wasn't for dramatic effect. That had never been his style. He simply found this stuff tiring. The words didn't come easy. Lyn seemed to understand that. She didn't nudge him, just finished off her toast and waited.

'Okay, what I found was a photograph of Mari Sandoz.'

Another pause, Lyn waiting, head cocked to one side.

'It was for my dad. Signed by her, with two kisses.' He folded up the paper napkin, placed it on his plate and shoved it to one side.

They sat silently for twenty seconds, maybe thirty. Then Lyn said, 'So what do you make of that?'

He didn't answer immediately. His head was still teeming with possibilities, most of them disturbing. 'What I make of it is - hell, there must have been something between them. Y'know, he and my mother weren't happy. Fact, they were miserable as sin, especially later on. And there's a whole other bunch of stuff I wouldn't trouble you with. Fact is, he was fifty when they married. She was more than twenty years younger, and pregnant.'

'Wow, that's an age gap. And a half. And that was you she was carrying?'

'Yes. My sister was born a couple years later.'

'Sorry, when was he born? Your dad?'

'The year1896.'

'Same year as our heroine.'

Steve nodded. 'I spotted that too.'

'Of course,' Lyn said, apparently choosing her words carefully, 'there are other possible interpretations.'

'Like what?'

'How about he found this photograph in a junk store, and just kind of took a fancy to it? Like, he'd read her books and wanted a picture.'

Steve disagreed. 'No,' he said. 'When I told you it was signed, that ain't the whole story. What it said was, *For Piotr*, spelled the Polish way, PIOTR. That was my old man's name, but nobody knew it. Only us. He always went by Pete, American-style, all his life.'

'Oh. Your family were Poles?'

'Still are. Family name's Kaminski.'

'Well, that is interesting. You know, Mari wrote a number of stories about Poles. When they moved out to the hills they had Polish neighbors. She had quite a soft spot for them.'

'Hm.' Steve was silent for a moment, thinking. Then he said, 'But like I said, she put Piotr. And then, those two kisses.'

'Wow.' Another pause, before Lyn said, 'Well, who knows? Maybe there's something there. If I were in your shoes . . .' She tailed off.

'What?'

'I guess I'd dig a little deeper.'

'Yeah. Maybe.' Steve pushed away his empty plate and clasped his hands together. 'Let's leave it there,' he said. 'I'm due to call on my sister around three, so what do you say we get going?'

They drove east about twenty miles, mostly in silence. The road was quiet, and the land around seemed only half awake after its long winter rest. Lyn sat and studied the flyer she'd brought with her. Just past Hay Springs she told Steve to turn south down the county road that took them to Walgren Lake. They parked and got out. There was a gentle breeze blowing, and the sunlight sparkled on the waves. One or two waterfowl were bobbing about in the reeds around the fringes. It was an unexceptional feature, and meant nothing to Steve.

'We used to get around some, me and the old man,' he said, 'but I don't recall ever coming here. That other lake - Smith, is it? - I used to go there, time to time. But not here.'

Lyn didn't seem too interested in the place either. She took a couple of photos, but never strayed far from the vehicle. 'I guess they had to start the trail somewhere,' she said. 'There was an old folk tale about a monster that lived in the lake. Mari wrote a short story about it, but that's the only connection, as far as I know. Happy to move on?'

'Sure.' He turned the truck around and headed back to the road.

'So the next stop . . .let's see.' Lyn was checking her guide. 'Here we are, Mirage Flats, where Old Jules had his first homestead. About ten miles, it says here. Don't get too excited though.'

Lyn was right. There was little to see there either. The landscape was, as the name suggested, more or less featureless, and still drab in its late-winter colors. Steve stayed in the cab while Lyn got out with her camera. 'Saves making notes,' she said.

Back in the truck she studied the map. 'Now, if you wanna take it steady, just a mile or two and we should come to the Sacred Heart Church.' She was leaning forward, peering through the windshield. 'And wow, look at that: it's still there.'

Soon as Steve stopped, Lyn was out, striding across a patch of mown grass to a modest, neat little building, immaculately maintained. Steve followed her, almost losing his cap as the wind picked up. By the time he caught up with her she was already telling him the history of the plot. 'This land belonged to Old Jules,' she said. 'He gave it to the church.' She was trying the door.

It opened, and he followed her into a clean, freshly painted interior, plain enough but with old-style wooden pews and life-sized figures in plaster either side of the altar. Steve was struck by the Christ, draped in a dark red robe and appearing to step out from His alcove, arms held as if to embrace the visitor.

'Jules wasn't a churchgoer,' Lyn continued, keeping her voice low. 'He was against all forms of religion, but this priest liked a game of chess and Jules didn't want to let him go. He needed to have bright people around him, educated people he could talk with, because he was always reading, picking up new ideas. Plus the fact that he was dedicated to the idea of building a community.'

'So he gifted him the land?'

'That's about it, as far as I recall.'

They stood there for a few moments before Steve said, 'Yeah, I used to go to church when I was a kid. In town. Grandpa liked to go. I just went along for the ride, and then he'd take me for brunch. But after he died, that was it. I never went again. '

Back at the truck Lyn studied the map. 'Okay, so now we need to keep our eyes open. We're looking for a stone marker.'

'You mean like a grave?'

'Hah. Could've been, but wasn't. Jules had a couple of buddies, Swiss guys he'd dragged out from Ohio, I think it was. One was called Tissot and - no, I forget the other guy's name. Anyway, they'd come to look over the area, see if it was everything he'd built it up to be. They'd picked out some land and needed to register their claims. In return for locating them he got them to help dig a well, and because he was such a royal pain in the ass they decided to have a little fun with him. He was down the hole, seeing whether they'd shored it properly, and when it was time for them to haul him to the surface they started to jiggle the rope around.'

'That doesn't sound like a great idea.'

'It wasn't. The rope snapped and he fell to the bottom. Broke his ankle, badly. Multiple fractures.'

'They played rough in those days.'

'Jules had a way of nettling people. Not that I'm saying he had it coming, but . . . Anyway, somehow they managed to get him to the surface. They were planning to take him to a doctor, but he insisted they didn't have time. Said they needed to take the wagon to town and file the claims on their land before it was too late. That was going to take them a week.'

All the time she was speaking, Lyn was looking along the roadside for the marker. 'So he just sent them on their way. Told them he could self-medicate till they returned. Except they didn't.'

'So what happened?'

'Luckily for him, a party of soldiers came by. By this time he was delirious, and the leg had turned gangrenous. They took him to Fort Robinson and handed him over to the post surgeon, who was none other than Walter Reed. The guy who found the cure for Yellow Fever?'

'That right?' Steve thought for a moment, then said, 'The Walter Reed Hospital, is that named after him?'

'It is. You ever been to Fort Rob?'

'You know, I never did. There was a school trip one time, but me and my buddies decided we had better things to do.'

'It's on my list. There was a POW camp there, for Germans. Those places always intrigue me. Anyway, Reed is all set to amputate when Jules pulls a gun on him. Tells him to put his saw away or he'll shoot him. "Shoot you so dead you stink before you hit the ground" were his exact words, according to Mari.'

Steve gave a short laugh. 'You could grow to admire a guy like that.'

'Well, Mari sure did. Anyway, he survived, but he was semi-crippled for the rest of his life. Perfect excuse for being a lazy s.o.b. Hey, here we are, on the right there.'

It was no more than a couple of feet high, a creamy-colored stone slab set in the long grass with a likeness of Old Jules carved on it. They both got out to look at it and read the inscription.

'No sign of the well,' Steve said.

'No. I guess it just got abandoned.' Lyn handed him the camera and stood beside the monument. 'Can you take a couple of shots of me?'

They were back in the truck and making for the next stop when Lyn asked, 'You okay? I mean, it's not exactly a thrill a minute.'

'I'm fine. Kinda interesting seeing an author at work.'

'This is the fun part,' Lyn said. 'Trying to find something clever to say about it, that's where the hard work begins. Okay . . . any minute now and we should be crossing the Niobrara.'

'The Niobrara,' Steve repeated. 'Jesus, I swam in there a few times. Used to meet a couple of girls.' He let out another quiet laugh, more a sort of murmur. 'They call it skinny dipping now, don't they? We had some good times.' He fell silent, watching the road. They were on dirt now. It took them to a bridge made of wooden boards, and below it was the river, no more than a ribbon meandering across a meadow.

'This it?' he said.

'According to the map, yes. The mighty Niobrara.'

'Hell, you could jump clean across that,' Steve said. 'Where we swam it was thirty-forty feet wide. Mind, you had to hunt around to find the swimming holes, but we knew where they were.'

They both leaned on the sturdy fence, watching the water flow. Steve was conscious of the sun warming his back, the sound of the breeze shushing through the scrub that overhung the river. He flicked a couple of little rocks with his boot and watched them splash into the stream.

'They tell me the creeks out here are dried up most of the year, with all the irrigation and center pivots. Water-table's dropped since I was a kid. But this one, she just keeps on flowing. Guess that's how she got her name,' he said. 'The Running Water.'

'Spring-fed, was what they told me.' Lyn was busy with the map again. 'So we're closing in on what they call the river place, where Old Jules settled with his fourth wife. That's the one who couldn't escape. You read about her yet?'

'She the one who arrived by train to meet some other guy?' Steve asked. 'I just got to that part.'

'That's her, and the guy didn't show, so Jules took her to his place. Next thing you know she's pregnant and that was her young life over.'

'I guess it would've been. What they call the good old days.'

They returned to the truck and set off along what was now a graveled road.

'Okay, we're looking for a track to the left. Should be an old barn or two.'

Steve wound his window down and hung his left arm out. 'This ain't a bad way to spend a spring morning,' he said, and glanced across at Lyn.

'Well,' she said, 'thank you for chauffeuring me around. Hey, look out there, on the left! That's our turn.'

He swung the vehicle over an auto-gate, and they entered a narrow dirt track that led down to a corral and a couple of barns.

'Looks like someone still uses this place.' Steve was out of the car, looking at the ground, which was littered with dried-up cow pies.

'One of the Sandoz clan, is my guess,' Lyn said. 'Funny to think of it. There's Jules fighting the ranchers all his life on behalf of the homesteader – and all his kids go into cattle.'

'Except Mari, right?'

'Yes, except her. But she did write a damned fine history of the cattle industry. I mean, Old Jules proved his point - that you could grow fruit out here and support a family - but only in a few favored spots. This land was made for cattle, wasn't it?'

Steve looked around. The hills still wore their winter coat of dried grasses, with here and there a soapweed breaking the horizon. 'You mean bison,' he said.

Lyn laughed. 'Ha. Round two to the gentleman, to quote our friend Tina.'

The land here was more undulating. Trees grew along the side of the infant river. A couple hundred yards away to the east was a small eminence, in the form of a promontory.

'That'll be what Mari called Indian Hill,' Lyn said. 'Said she found the remains of their signal fires up the top, arrow heads and suchlike. She used to climb up there when she got a break from looking after the babies. To think her thoughts. Dream of a better future.'

'Babies?' Steve looked puzzled. 'Thought she never had any kids.'

'No, but her mother did – three boys and two more girls, and soon as they got to two weeks old Mari had to look after them. Papa was busy cleaning his guns and trading stories with his Lakota buddies so Mom had to get back to work.'

'What do you mean work?'

'The house, the garden, the milk cow. Cleaning up the mess when he was through gutting the animals he trapped.'

Steve nodded, and looked at the hill. Towards the top it wore a threadbare look where the wind had scoured out hollows in the sand. 'You wanna climb up?' he asked.

'That was my intention.' She looked at him and said, 'You realize this is a big deal for me?'

'I guess so. Like a pilgrimage?'

'Exactly that. I've been waiting years for this.'

'Well,' he said, 'this'll do me good. These old knees of mine are inclined to seize up if I don't keep flexing them. I do a lot of walking. Or used to, till I left Portland.'

'You lived there? What made you leave?'

'Let's say someone got tired of being married to me.'

They crossed the dusty corral. At the far end they had to bend a length of barbed wire to get over the fence. Then it was a short climb, maybe a hundred feet, through the loose sand and threadbare grasses. Lyn had the map out again, trying to hold it flat as it caught the wind. She was looking to the north, over the river.

'So on that far bank,' she said, pointing, 'that must be where Henriette lived.'

'Henriette? Remind me who she is.'

'Wife number two. When he married her they settled over there. Just a dug-out at first. And when Jules moved over to this side Henriette stayed put. At least, I think that's how it went. I need to check all that. Anyway, the point is, she went crazy. And then . . . then he dug in here. Planted fruit trees, a garden. And along came his third wife, mail order. He'd written to the Old Country, bigging himself up. Took her two weeks to realize what she'd gotten into and get the hell out. Just waited until he went on a hunting trip and - *boom*. Gone. And then along came poor little Mary Fehr. She was

German Swiss, but she'd been living in . . . where was it, Arkansas? I need to check. It's frightening how much you forget. Anyway, she arrived at the railroad depot to meet some other guy she'd corresponded with, but he didn't show. God knows what Jules was doing there, but he brought her back to his place.'

Lyn turned to look at Steve. 'Frontier rules were pretty informal, I guess you'd say.' She shielded her eyes with her hand and scanned the scene. 'So this is where Mari was born, and all her siblings. No sign of the old house though.'

'So let me get this right. He had a place all set up here, and then he left it to go and live in the hills. Why would he do a thing like that?'

Lyn walked to the very edge of the little promontory and squatted down on a slab of crumbly limestone. Steve watched her, taking in the slim cut of her jeans, the relaxed look on her face as she leaned into the breeze, closed her eyes and breathed it in, deep and slow.

When she spoke she said, 'Jules felt hemmed in, I guess. Too many neighbors, and he fought with most of them. He used to go off on his own, hunting and trapping. So he knew these hills. Knew them intimately. What grew and where. Knew where there was water. Could read a soil. And he found this valley, east of here. Decided he could grow fruit there, and he was damned well going to prove it. You didn't argue with Jules Ami Sandoz.'

'We going to go there? What's it say on that map of yours?'

'Sure. Take a look for yourself.' She passed it to him, and he studied it for a few moments.

'It's pretty much as I figured it,' he said. 'I mean, our place isn't far away from these orchards, just a little to the north. Not far at all. So my old man when he was growing up, he would've been her neighbor.' He handed her the map.

'This is all new to me, you know that? Takes some digesting.'

'Maybe you're starting out on a research project of your own.'

'Wasn't what I planned,' he said. 'Wasn't what I planned at all.'

Lyn was quiet for a few moments. Then she said, 'You're reading *Old Jules*, right?'

'Yeah. And I been flipping through the biography by the woman Stauffer.'

'She's a good woman,' Lyn said. 'I met her once, corresponded with her for a while. So helpful. Generous with her time.' She stood up and brushed the sand off the seat of her jeans. 'I was going to suggest you dig out a short story of Mari's.'

'Why's that?'

'Remember what I said, that she wrote about a Polish family?'

'Yeah, I meant to ask you about that.'

'The one I have in mind, it's a while since I read it. But I have a copy back at the hotel. Her sister reckoned it was based on some actual neighbors they had. She told me all those stories were. She wrote a lot of short pieces before her career took off. Remind me, and I'll dig it out for you.'

They climbed down from Indian Hill, back over the fence and across the corral.

'So what's the next stop?' Steve asked as he settled in the driver's seat.

'Smith Lake, according to this. You said you knew it, right?'

'Used to. Used to fish there. Sometimes we camped, me and my parents and my little sister. That was before she discovered boys and before our parents started to fight -

seriously fight, I mean. They were always sniping, but that seemed normal. Later it got far worse.'

'Can I ask what about?' Lyn spoke cautiously.

Steve didn't answer. He seemed to be concentrating hard, even though he was now driving on tarmac, heading south on 250. He didn't speak again until they reached the entrance to the lakeside parking lot. Then all he could say was, 'We'll get there. I mean the crap about my folks. Just bear with me.' He parked the truck under a giant cottonwood.

'Well,' Lyn said, 'I doubt this place has much to do with Mari's story. I think they put it in here as a good spot to picnic.' She got out and he walked after her, to the water's edge.

'I got beer in the cooler,' Steve said.

'I don't drink, remember? But thanks anyway.'

Steve didn't answer. He was standing perfectly still, facing out over the water. She followed his gaze and saw a gaggle of pelicans that were browsing out in the middle.

'Jeez, I never expected to see them,' Lyn said.

'You'll find them all over the Sandhills. Wait till you're driving around in the dusk some night and you stumble across a flock of them on a lake. Grey sky, fading light - and then a great splash of white. Boy, it's a sight. I must've seen that dozens of times, but every time – man, it makes you jump. Especially in moonlight.'

They stayed there for several minutes, soaking up the sunshine. Steve was remembering the time he came down here with his buddies and they hunted up a bunch of snapping turtles - and how his neighbor Luke almost lost a thumb when he made the mistake of grabbing one by the tail. He was lost in thought, once again taken aback at the way his memories seemed to be debating the past, evaluating it. It was a crock; no, it was okay. There were good times, yeah, but what about . . .? He didn't at first notice that Lyn was by his side. When she spoke it startled him.

'Reckon we should move on now?' she asked.

'Sure. The gravesite, right?'

The gravel road that Lyn had got stuck on just a couple of days previously held no terrors this time. The snow was gone and it had dried out in the sun and wind. Just a few hundred yards took them to a large timber sign, *Mari Sandoz Memorial Drive*, and a left turn.

'Looks like we're almost there,' she said, as Steve steered the truck onto a narrow dirt trail that led across rough pasture, and along the northern side of a broad, shallow valley.

'That it over there?' Steve was pointing to a wire-fenced enclosure, partway up the hill.

'Must be. I could almost have walked it, instead of sitting in the car, freezing.'

He parked the truck a couple hundred yards short of their objective. It was an old habit. He'd always been aware of how stiffly old cowboys walked, guys who'd spent their lives on horseback or at the wheel of a truck, and he'd tried to keep limber. Wild horses wouldn't get him into a gym, but he'd never objected to walking, even as a youngster. One time he and his buddies had driven out to the Black Hills and he'd made them all hike up Harney Peak. Momentarily he remembered how much he'd also loved riding his horse in these hills. Easy to imagine right now, with the weather almost balmy, the breeze gently caressing them as they strolled towards the grave. A rickety gate led into the plot, and on the post was a metal box. Lyn lifted the lid.

'Look, they have a register you can sign,' she said, and started flipping through the pages. 'Wow, it goes back ten, fifteen years. People from all over. Florida, Ohio. One here from England.'

Steve was already at the grave. It was marked by a plain granite slab, dark pink, just a foot or two in height. It bore a simple inscription: *Mari Sandoz 1896-1966.*

'So this was what she wanted, was it?' Steve said. 'To be buried here.'

'She felt a spiritual tie to this place.' Lyn turned and looked out over the valley. 'See the old house?' She was shading her eyes against the sun. At the far end, perhaps half a mile distant, Steve could now see a couple of buildings among a cluster of bare trees.

'Yeah, that the place Old Jules built?'

'That's it.'

Steve stood, trying to take it all in. Aside from the tiny farmstead there was nothing but grass and rolling hills from one horizon to the other. There were only two colors: the pale tan of the land, the pale blue of the sky. It had a certain beauty, but he was remembering what it looked like in bad weather, or in snow, when land and sky merged in a terrifying bleakness. Slowly, he realized that a very specific memory of this place was coming into focus. Without saying anything to Lyn he left the little enclosure and walked towards the truck, turning every so often to look back at the gravesite and the great sweep of land that surrounded it.

He stood there and half closed his eyes. Then it came to him. Damn, he'd driven the old man out here. Sure he had. Pete had got hurt by a cow. He was trying to get her to adopt an orphan calf and she kicked him. Nearly busted his hip. For several weeks he couldn't drive farther than the mailbox. Wanda was pregnant by this time - or maybe she'd had the baby, Steve couldn't be sure. He was certain that Irena was working in town, so although the two of them were barely speaking Steve took his old man out to the gravesite. It was a bitterly cold day, snow on the ground, the sky slate-grey, and he had stayed in the car, engine running, while Pete joined a bunch of people on the bleak hillside. It seemed a crazy damned place to have a funeral, but then adults were always doing things that perplexed him.

As soon as he was on his own it was radio on, feet up on the dash, light a cigarette and let the old bastard do whatever it was he needed to do. Steve remembered opening his eyes long enough to catch a sight of the pall-bearers trudging over the snow with the casket, and pausing, once, twice, before stumbling on. There had been some kind of discussion, with people gesturing. Then they'd just got on with the job.

Shit, so Dad had come out to see his old sweetheart buried. He'd forgotten all about the incident until now. But then, why would he remember? As far as he was concerned it was just another old-timer who'd died and his father was there out of good manners. Pete was always attending burials. Many a time he'd be reading the paper and announce that some old guy had gone, someone he'd been to high school with, or their mother or father, or that they'd come from Poland, and he'd take an afternoon off to go pay his respects. It was what you did in the Sandhills, where everyone knew their neighbors for miles around. Some folk would show up to a funeral just for the social side and the spread that was served afterwards, the glasses of schnapps. It was another chance to catch up.

Within the family such an outing generally passed without comment, but not this one. And now he remembered the row that had erupted, back at the house the previous night when Pete had told him he'd have to drive him out there. He remembered his mother screaming at the old man: 'You shoulda married the damned bitch!' And his father's reply, 'Don't think I don't tell myself that every goddam day I live here with you.'

By that time, Steve was in the habit of shrugging off such an outburst. He had been on the point of leaving home, and barely gave a thought to what might lie behind the savage animosity that flickered back and forth like lightning between his parents. But now, the thought that his old man had been that close to the Sandoz woman, that he'd harbored thoughts of marrying her . . . Shit.

He started back towards the gravesite. Jesus, the crap that was getting stirred up - just like Jeannie had said it would. As he approached the gate Lyn was coming out. He was about to tell her what he had just remembered, but stopped himself. He wasn't sure yet what it meant to him and decided it was best left unsaid.

Lyn was looking to the east, towards the trees and the half-hidden buildings. 'Okay if we head down there now?' she asked.

'Sure.' They returned to the truck. On the way down the hill he asked, 'So this is where he dragged his family, from the river place?'

'Yeah. He reckoned he could grow his fruit here, and he succeeded.'

Across the valley Steve now saw a few rows of gaunt trees. 'Is that it? His fruit farm?'

Lyn shook her head. 'I don't think so. The old pictures I've seen show the whole of the valley floor planted up, in rows. But all that's long gone. Combination of disease and old age, according to Helen Stauffer. The ones you see, they must be what's left of Flora's planting.'

'Flora?'

'Daughter number two. Mari's little sister.'

'So here's a question for you. If Mari was so miserable here - I mean, living under the old bastard's fist - how come she chose to be buried here?'

'Keep reading the book and you'll get it. First thing Old Jules did when he bought the place was to send her out here to watch over it. Her and her brother. She was fourteen.'

'You mean just the two of them?'

'Sure.'

'What about the boy? How old was he?'

'I guess Jim would be ten, maybe eleven.'

'Ha, they'd have you in court today, wouldn't they?'

'I guess they would. But Mari always said it was the best days of her childhood.'

Steve thought about that for a moment. Then he said, 'You mean because she was free?'

'Right. Think about it. Suddenly she had no babies, no chores, no grizzly old man on her case. I mean, he provisioned them well enough. Sack of flour, sack of beans. Not sure what they did for water. And a gun, of course, so they shot prairie chickens, rabbits. Picked sand-cherries - it was that time of year. They did fine. And according to Stauffer that's when the Sandhills cast their spell over her. By being alone here, she discovering their magic for herself. They had a few weeks, she and Jim, maybe a couple of months, just the two of them. Then the family moved over.'

'Guess I can see why she might have enjoyed that. Yeah.' They drove down to the valley floor, pausing to look at the fruit trees. They weren't in the best shape, but they seemed to be alive. 'Apples, most of them,' was all Steve said.

They reached the old house, got out and walked around. There were a couple of other buildings. One of them seemed to be used as a hunting lodge. A notice on the door had a phone number for enquiries. Steve hardly said a word. Lyn went about her business, taking photos, making a note here and there. Then they were in the truck again.

'How you doing?' Steve asked.

'I'm fine.'

'Whaddaya say to a little trip out to my sister's place?'

'How far is it?'

He pointed to the northern horizon. 'As the crow flies

five or six miles beyond that hill, maybe less. But it'll be a twenty-thirty-mile drive to get there. Gotta head west, north, east and then back south. Nobody ever thought to cut any diagonal roads when they settled this land.'

'You planning on visiting your sister, or just the house?'

'Most likely call by on the way back to Chadron. See how I'm feeling. Fact is, I keep looking for excuses to put it off.'

They drove out of the valley and onto the highway. It was close to forty minutes later when they arrived. Steve parked the truck outside the old place.

'This is the house my grandpa built in 1909,' he said, as they walked towards the door. 'The one I was telling you about. It's where I was born, where I lived. Until I was in my teens.'

'Was that the date when he settled here?' Lyn asked.

'No, there was a sod house at first. In fact, there was a dug-out before that, I'm not sure where exactly. He was on his own that first winter, maybe two. That would be 1894, or '95. Then he built the soddy. My old man grew up in it - used to say he liked it. Story was, by the time Grandpa started cutting sod his wife was expecting.'

Lyn was down on one knee, camera in hand, looking at the abandoned house. 'Oh,' she said, 'do you mind? Is it okay for me to take pictures?'

'So long as they don't get plastered across the damned internet,' Steve said.

'No, of course not. I just like to keep a record.' She clicked, and clicked again, then stood up, taking a long, appreciative look at the house. 'Besides, this is beautiful.'

Steve was surprised by the remark. 'You think so?'

'I know so. And it was your home.'

'That it was.' He thought for a moment, standing there on the rough grass as a meadowlark trilled somewhere close by, a liquid song that sent a shiver down his spine. 'And the weird thing is, every memory I ever have of my childhood, when they come back to me it always seems they took place there. Although that thing' - he pointed to the new house - 'hell, I lived there three-four years before I took off. But not Grandpa. He flat out refused to move. Until he was too weak to argue with them.' Steve was at the door, lifting and shoving. 'Come on in. I'll show you where I found the photograph.'

He led her upstairs, and they entered Grandpa's old room. He was looking at the floor, and the footprints he'd made in the dust the previous day. Neither had spoken, and when Lyn asked, 'When did you say he died?' her voice made him jump. It occurred to him that the last words these walls had heard were probably Pete's.

He looked up. Lyn was at the table, with the calendar in her hand. 'I'd have been twelve,' he said, 'so nineteen fifty-eight? I need to check with Wanda. He was ninety-three, I believe, maybe ninety-four. After that my father took his room over. Turned it into what you see - a kind of office, although to tell you the truth, it was more of a refuge. Him and Mom, they were at each other's throats most of the time. According to my sister he still used it after she'd gone. Even slept here, from time to time, right up to when he died. And this is where I found the photo, lying right here.' He tapped the table with a forefinger.

'Amazing, for it to be just sitting there all those years. And your father died . . . sorry, when did you say?'

'In 1992 or – hell, somewhere around then. My sister dragged all his things out and then just left the place as she found it. Or so she says. Never came back in. I find that hard to swallow – and how could she miss the photograph?' He leaned forward, his hands on the table-top, and looked out through the window. Beyond the trees he could see the dun line of hills against a blue sky. He gave out a deep sigh and said, 'I guess he had his own issues, as they say.'

'Who, your father?'

'Yeah. Grandpa was a hard man, leastwise with his own. To me he was just this gentle old guy. But back in the day, I guess he couldn't see why his kids should have it easier than he did. And he believed in this place - when it was a ranch. Just that it needed manpower, so I guess he was disappointed not to have more sons.' Steve was silent for a while. He was still looking at the hills. 'There were two others, but soon as war broke out in Europe they were gone.'

'This is the first war, right?'

'Yeah.'

'What happened to them?'

'One was killed. 1918. Just a week before the ceasefire. Less than that. Four days, I think the story was. His brother, Uncle Waldemar - Waldo they called him - he survived okay, but only came back just long enough to tell them he was going to California. Grandpa again, I'd guess. I think he kinda drove him away. My father was the youngest. He never went to war. I guess Grandpa needed him to help around the place.' Steve turned away from the window. 'Well, no good standing here all day, reminiscing.'

While he was talking Lyn had been studying the table, leaning across it with her hands flat on the surface. Now she peered over the edge by the window. 'You know there's a drawer under here?' she said.

Steve looked, and for the first time he noticed the depth of the thing. 'Reckon you're right,' he said. 'Here.' As he started to drag it away from the window, it immediately became evident that one of the legs was loose. 'Looks like it broke off and Dad wedged it up against the wall here. Unlike him. He was always such a perfectionist.'

'But there is a drawer,' Lyn said.

Steve got the thing turned about, tapped the leg back into place then pulled at a little brass handle. It came out a few inches and then stuck. He reached inside and pulled out a sheet of paper, folded in four. He opened it out. 'It's a list. Number one is Irena - that's my mom. Number two, someone called Clouser - I've no idea who that is. Three, Nadia, that's one of the sisters, my aunt. Then Pete.' He took hold of the drawer and worked it side to side till it opened to the fullest extent. Inside was a faded cream-colored envelope, bulging.

'Will you look at that?' He gave out a brief whistle. 'Got a three cent stamp on it. How old does that make it?'

Lyn was at his side, looking over his shoulder. He could feel her breath in his ear. *'Return to Sender,'* she said.

Steve picked it up, feeling the weight of it in his hand, then turned it over. 'Still sealed,' he said quietly.

Lyn reached out and pointed at the name on the envelope. 'Macumber,' she said. 'That was Mari Sandoz' married name.' Then she read the address. '1226 J Street, Lincoln. J Street was where she lived. Right up until she moved to New York City. No, Denver. She went to Denver first.' Lyn peered closer at the faded postmark. 'Looks like . . .1946? Wow. You gonna open it?'

Steve already had his finger inside the flap. He slid out the contents: a dozen or more sheets of lined paper. He unfolded them. 'That's my old man's writing okay. Christ.' He started reading. It was written in a scrawled hand. It looked hurried, the letters large. There were as few as two to three words per line in places. He flipped to the second page, then folded the lot and slid them back in the envelope. 'Let's get out of here,' he muttered.

All the way back to the highway Steve was silent. Lyn was bursting to ask him about the letter, but she held her tongue. In Gordon, at the junction, she saw that he was hesitating.

'Listen,' she began, 'just you do whatever you need to do.'

'Yeah,' he said. 'My sister's gonna have to wait.' He swung the wheel and headed back towards Chadron. 'I got some thinking to do.'

13

At the hotel they parted with no more than a glance and a nod. Lyn went to her room, Steve to his. He locked his door, opened a window and sat in the armchair under the standard lamp. He unfolded the letter, then put it down. He went to the little kitchen and collected a bottle of bourbon he had there. Poured himself a generous shot in a glass tumbler and sat back down, the bottle beside him. Then he began to read.

Dearest, it began. Even that one word made him pause. His eyes hovered over it for some time. It didn't sound like any word the old man could or ever did utter. He tried to imagine his father's lips parting and saying it out loud, but couldn't. He then tried to remember what Pete called Irena. Sometimes it was 'Mom'. It was never 'Dearest'. Steve checked the date at the top of the page: 15 March 1946. Just after his mother and Pete got married. And he was still addressing Mari as 'Dearest'.

Steve went on reading.

Dearest, I know you told me not to write again, but I never was much good at taking orders. Right, but you could dish them out okay, Steve thought, couldn't you?

Things are working out, and I think I'm ready to accept your decision. It's been a long road we've been down, you and me. Specially you, with your success. I want to be happy for you, but it isn't easy. Every time I pick up the Omaha paper I'm reading something by you or about you, and all I can think about is who you used to be. The young girl who walked along the banks of the Niobrara with me, the barefoot girl with a garland in her hair that I made out of wildflowers. I can smell them yet. You're the girl who swam in the river with me and raced her little pony against mine that summer when you and your little brother were alone in the hills. Bareback. And there was the time you came tearing down the hill past our place in the buggy with your eyes wide and your dad about to fall off any second. You didn't even see me standing by the corral, gaping like an idiot. That was the time he got bitten. A rattler, wasn't it? I'd forgotten all about it till I read it in the book. Just think how strange that was for me.

And then he found out about us. What did he have against me, Mari? What did he think we were up to, at that age? Guess he figured you were worth more than a goddam Polander. And then before I knew it you were married to that creep Macumber. You know that's why I took off, don't you? Never even said goodbye to anyone. Just - went. I was barely turned fourteen. And it didn't take me long to fall in with bad company, and go wild. And you know what? I didn't give a damn. Jim looked out for me. Treated me like a brother. Jeez, Marie, is it any wonder I ended up in trouble? It could've been different, but I didn't give a damn for anyone. Specially not me.

'Well, that soon changed.' Steve breathed the words aloud, and they hung in the room. He wondered whether this woman knew quite what his father was capable of. He also wondered briefly who Jim was.

I remember one time working a freight out of Omaha, picked up the paper and read one of those stories about you. I got to North Platte and went into the engineers' hall and I wanted to show the guys and tell them that I once danced with you, held you in my arms. I told you we would get married, didn't I? And you squashed me flat. Said you were never going to have children or keep house. Said you'd had your fill of it. Seen what marriage does to a woman.

And then you went and hitched yourself to that jerk Macumber. Why? I never understood that. It never made sense to me. Unless you had to. Was that it? Have you any idea what it did to me when I heard? You really think I would've got mixed up with guys like Jim, with Clouser and his outfit if I hadn't given up all hope, all caring – for myself or anybody? Oh sure, bootlegging seemed like fun at first . . .

Bootlegging? Steve stopped reading. Grandpa talked about a bootlegger. He laid the letter on his knee for a moment and closed his eyes. Was this really his old man? Writing from the heart, exposing his deepest feelings? Why did we never see any of that? Why were we left to be raised by a man who never seemed to feel any damned thing except anger? 'Who knows,' he said aloud, 'if you'd opened up a bit, you fucker, we might have got somewhere. And bootlegging? Shit.'

He read on.

Easy money, fast cars. You should've seen me, Marie. In my double-breasted suit. A proper gangster. I once bought myself a violin case, just for the hell of it. Sure frightened a few people. And boy, that little grey roadster of mine, she could move. It was like being in a movie, looking back and seeing the cops eat my dust. They were never going to keep up with me and Jim. You wouldn't understand this, but being the bad guy gave me a good feeling. Real good. We weren't doing anything so terrible. Jim, maybe, but not me. What was so bad about bringing people a bottle of good cheer? Dumb stupid law. Then you look around and see the people you're dealing with. They really did carry guns, they'd shoot anyone who stood in the way, guys who called themselves friends and then ratted on you to the cops soon as they'd got what they needed. Sure, I had my thrills. Car chases, fast women. One time I threw a suitcase full of dough on a hotel bed and opened a bottle of champagne with some little hotsie totsie throwing handfuls of dollar bills in the air. But don't forget, we sent money home. Remember how bad things were for farmers in the twenties? My old man disapproved of the life I was living but he never turned down the money.

But of course it was only ever going to end one way. Not that they were that hard on us. Ninety days wasn't so bad, and it cured me of bucking the law.

Steve was struggling to take it all in. So Pete had done time? Had been in a gang?

You're a strange one, Marie. Keeping me at arm's length the way you did, and then writing those letters when I was in the joint. They sure gave me comfort. And hope. Wish now I'd kept them, but in a prison cell you don't do that. I read them all two, three, four times. Memorised the best parts. Then burned them, every page.

Maybe you should've cut me off there and then. Did you think I was going to drop you just because you told me to? Marie, had you forgotten who we were? Had you forgotten the time we held the bottle of strychnine in our hands and tried to work up the courage to do ourselves in? Had you forgotten the ring you gave me? You found it on the road and we pretended it was gold. Remember how I wore it, and how we laughed when it turned green? Do you remember your old man threatening to shoot me? 'So dead you'll stink in an hour,' he said. I never forgot that.

Maybe you choose not to remember. That's okay - go ahead. Forget it all, if that's the way you want it. It's over. You can stop worrying. I've got me a good enough woman and we're settling back in the home place. She's too young, but I got something she wants. I'm coming up to fifty now, and I figure a guy should be settled at that age. My old man struggles on with the ranch, but he won't last forever. So after all these years I'm back where I started, living the life I never wanted, except I'm ready for it now. Ready to take over the ranch and hand it on to the next generation. Irena says it'll make her happy, and I believe her. She's hatching out some goose eggs, plans to grow a garden. Maybe that'll make her smile. That's what I most wanted since I got to know her: to put a smile on her face.

Her life was no bed of roses. First her old man got at her. Her mother called her a whore and kicked her out. Then she ended up doing Jim's dirty work for him. Fact is, she had to play his tune or be turned out on the street. And then I had to face up to him, take a long hard look at what he had become.

Getting rid of him was a problem, but I got lucky. I didn't have to dirty my own hands. I can live with what happened.

I've accepted the way things turned out. I don't know whether I can be happy with this woman and the child that's due in a few months - I mean truly happy, the way you and me could've been. But it's what I got to try to do.

Never forget me, dearest. Never forget that we could have had something. I will never forget you, but I will stop bugging you now.

Goodbye, Pete.

Steve sat with the letter in his hand, then started again at the beginning. Christ. So much to take in.

Somehow, by the time he'd got to the end a second time, the idea that his old man and the Sandoz woman were childhood sweethearts - that at least had taken root. Okay, he told himself, that was plausible. Make that reasonable. Surprising, yes, disorientating for sure, but perfectly reasonable, if he could only forget that these were his parents and not some characters in a book.

He closed his eyes and thought it through. They were neighbors, and they were the same age, so of course they would be friends. That was nothing unusual. If this had been someone else's story, and not his old man's, it would have been no big deal. It might even sound romantic, or was it tragic? His old man had a childhood sweetheart, and he carried a torch for her. What was unusual about that? That's what first love is.

He himself still felt a fondness for his first girl, back in junior high. Had even traced her on the internet, like everyone else does, and as hard as he'd looked into her sixty-year-old eyes he could see nothing that was the tiniest bit familiar, just the name and the place of birth. It could have broken his heart, but it didn't break the spell. Far from it. Whatever it was the two of them had at twelve, thirteen, fourteen, it kind of set the standard for any feelings he had towards any woman for the rest of his life. That, that first eruption of feeling, the thrill of it, was the standard against which every subsequent affair was measured. So why would it be any different for his old man? Or anybody's old man? It's just that kids aren't meant to find out that stuff, he now told himself. Not about your own parents. It can't be healthy.

But what about all the other business? The bootlegging? The time Pete had spent in the slammer? That, Steve would never have guessed at. And strychnine - what the hell was *that* all about? Was it even true? Could it be? Or was it just a memory of two kids playing at being grown-up? He could understand why that had never been mentioned. But what about the time when Steve had his little run-in with the cops, when he was nabbed for buying liquor underage, when they showed up with him on the front porch? How come that nearly caused World War Three? His dad had been a bootlegger, for chrissake. Did it never occur to him that a son might like to hear that kind of story about his father? To know that he was someone besides a sorry old bastard in shit-streaked jeans, trapped in a crappy marriage in a place he'd sworn never to return to? And who was this guy Jim? Whatever happened to *him*? A thought skittered across his mind, a memory of what Wanda had told him, about the guy who got killed in Grandpa's car. Skittered across his mind and hid itself away.

He went through the letter a third time, and thought about his mother. He had learned, slowly and painfully, over the many years of drifting, through a tempestuous marriage to Bonny and the trials of living with her kids, year by year he had learned that you cannot simply judge a person by what you see, that you need to know where they've come from. Yes, he'd learned that, but it had never really occurred to him to apply the same principle to his own parents. Whenever Grandpa had talked about his young days, everyone had rolled their eyes. They thought they'd heard it all before. It was just an old man reliving his past. Steve excepted himself from that, of course. He had been an avid listener to those tales. But when he'd asked Irena about her young days - where she'd grown up and suchlike - she'd brushed him off.

'Look ahead,' she'd said. 'The past has gone. You aren't going to change it, so forget it.' And now this, the dark hint that she had a turbulent back-story of her own, maybe one she was genuinely ashamed of. Did he have the right, now, to learn it? And what did his sister know? Hadn't the two been thick as thieves those last few years before Mom died, when Dad had started sleeping in the old house?

When the smoke had cleared from his head Steve placed the letter on the table beside him. His mind was seething. He was back to wondering why none of this had ever come to the surface. All those rows and accusations flying to and fro between his mother and the old man, and none of it had ever been hinted at. Or had it? Pete had been fifty when Steve was born. From where Steve stood now he could see he'd been little more than a child when it all started to go crazy. Sure, Wanda seemed more aware, young as she was, but she was around their mom more than him. Maybe Irena confided in her. But if things had leaked out in the arguments, they passed right over his head. Boy, how different life might have been if only one of them had opened up to him. But that was the family way. Sit on your feelings, hang onto your secrets.

He guessed he must have been fifteen, sixteen when he first started to realize his sister was right, that he really was different. It was the time he got pulled in by the cops, him and Luke, drinking beer in the park in Gordon. Or was it Hay Springs? One of those towns. They brought him back to the house to confront his old man. Wanda was there. And this young cop, he remembered, looked at his sister and asked, 'You related?' Wanda told him she was Steve's sister, and it was just the look of mild surprise on the guy's face, nothing more, that he remembered.

Steve stood up. On an impulse he decided he'd take the letter to Lyn. Maybe it would help to share it with someone, and he was growing to trust her. She was probably sitting there right now wondering what the hell was in it. He went out into the corridor and walked down to her room.

At first she didn't answer. He knocked again. He heard a sort of thump from inside, then a muttered expletive. When she came to the door she had a dressing-gown wrapped around herself. Her hair was all over the place.

'Sorry,' she said, 'I was just napping. That was pretty intense, our little drive in the country.'

'Look,' Steve said, 'if this is a bad time . . .'

'No.' She was making a physical effort to gather herself. 'Just need to get myself awake.' She frowned and said, 'D'you think the bar's open? I could do with a coffee.'

'Yeah, sure. Lemme go down, see if Jeannie's around. I could do with something myself.'

By the time he'd returned, Lyn was dressed and tidied up.

She ushered him into her room and gave him a seat. He placed the two coffees on her desk.

'Thanks. Should help to calm me down,' Lyn said.

'Why, what happened?'

Lyn gave a short laugh, then stared at him. 'You kidding? Only that I watched you pull out a letter your dad wrote to Mari Sandoz about sixty freaking years ago. How often does that happen in a historian's life? And it turns out they were lovers or something. Jeez, do you realize how flat out tumultuous that is?'

Her tone grated on him. 'It's pretty tumultuous for me too,' he said. For a moment he thought about telling her to forget it. Instead he said, 'But from your point of view, yeah, I guess I see that.' He pulled out the letter and handed it to her. 'So maybe you'd better read it. See what you make of it.'

As she unfolded it he picked up his coffee and went to stand by the window. But he didn't feel comfortable, trying to imagine how she might react, line by line. 'Tell you what,' he said, 'I'll be downstairs. Leave you in peace.'

GLENN WAS IN THE BAR. 'Hey, feller,' he said, 'when you coming to root around in my garage?'

Steve stared at him blankly. What the hell was he talking about? 'You said you needed a cassette player,' Glenn reminded him. 'Or did you find one already?'

'Oh, that. Yeah, sure. Maybe tomorrow? I'm planning to call on my sister, so yeah – that would be great, thanks.'

'Any time after nine. You got the address?'

'No. I guess it would help, right?'

Already Steve was wishing he'd stayed upstairs. Glenn was okay, but he sure liked to talk. As he was writing down the address, Tina entered. She was another one, but she did kind of intrigue him. He generally liked sparky women, but right now the last thing he needed was a bout of verbal sparring.

'So how's our visitor?' she said. 'How you coping with the pace of life in the Panhandle?'

'You're forgetting I grew up here,' he said.

'Is that right?' she said. 'I don't think you told me that. Whereabouts?'

'South of Gordon, about twenty miles.'

'That a fact? My folks were from down that way too. A bit further on, towards Ellsworth.'

'What were they into, cattle?'

'What else is there?'

'Organized crime?'

'Oh, very good. Hey, I like it.'

Steve's problem, and he knew it, was that he could do this sort of jousting all day long. He was well practised at it, all those years of shooting the breeze with truckers and sales guys in family-run diners across the Great Plains. Then his years as a self-employed fix-it guy. You had to know how to oil the wheels.

Tina didn't seem to like silences. 'I'm hearing you took the trail,' she said. Steve didn't answer immediately, so she prompted him. 'Old Jules?'

'I did, yeah.'

'Enjoy it?'

'It was more of a research exercise. Lyn wanted some company.'

'Oh yeah, Lyn. The professor. She get what she wanted?'

Steve looked up and saw Lyn entering the bar from the far end. 'You'd better ask her that,' he said, nodding in her direction.

Lyn glanced at Tina. 'Hi,' she said. Then she looked at Steve. 'You wanna come and talk it over?'

'I think we should, don't you?' Lyn was watching Tina, who was taking it all in. Without a trace of a smile she said, 'My room or yours?'

'Whatever.'

'Sleep well,' Tina said as he walked past her.

'Jesus. Grow up,' he heard himself say.

'WELL . . .' Steve began, as he sat down beside her desk. And then he dried up.

'Well indeed,' Lyn answered. 'I mean, jeez, what can I say? There's a lot of stuff in there. Are you okay for me to talk? Or do you want to kick things off?'

'I wanna hear what you got to say,' Steve said. 'Right now I'd trust your thoughts more than I'd trust my own.'

'Okay then, in no particular order.' She sat there, the letter on her knee, sifting through the pages. Then she picked up a notepad, looked at him and forced a sort of grin. 'I made a list. If you don't mind.'

'Go ahead.'

'Okay. Number one, I guess you're learning things about your dad you never knew, is that right?'

'For sure.'

'So I'll try not to tread on your toes.'

'That's okay. They're tough old toes.'

'The fact is, Steve, this is the kind of document any historian would give their eye teeth for. What can I say? It's genuine historical evidence.' She paused, and seemed to be straining to find a way to say what was on her mind. 'One of the things I'm trying to do in this book I'm writing is to connect up the young Mari, before she hit the big time you might say, and the mature self-confident woman she would become. How did she change and why, sort of thing. Does that make sense to you?'

'Sure. We all go through a lot of crap. I guess it makes us who we are, unless we fight it. But you gotta understand, every notion I ever had about my father is . . . I mean . . .' He threw his hands in the air and gave her a questioning look. 'My old man - a frigging bootlegger?'

'Yep. Looks like you've got some working out to do,' Lyn said. Another pause. More shuffling of the pages. 'So listen, let's see whether we can piece the jigsaw together. Or maybe what I mean is, if we can set you off on the trail.' She turned the pages once more until she found the place she was looking for. 'This guy Clouser, right? Wasn't his name on the list we found in the drawer - back there at the house?'

'You're right. It was.'

'Well, that's one lead, isn't it? We can maybe check his name in the archives. That's part of my immediate plan, going through the archives in Valentine, then in Lincoln. A guy like that, he'll surely have had run-ins with the law. So he will have made the newspapers. There are other leads you can follow.' She was still going through the letter, sifting the pages between her fingers. 'Shall I go on?'

'Sure.'

'Mari wrote a lot about her Polish neighbors. I told you that, didn't I?' Steve nodded. 'And I think I said there were a number of incidents from her childhood that pop up more than once. I mean, incidents we can assume may have taken place, that she incorporates in her fiction. Like the garland of flowers your father mentions.' She looked at Steve. 'Yes? Still with me?'

'I'm listening, don't worry.'

'I can point you to at least one story where that crops up. And the gold ring that turns out to be copper. Pretty sure I can find that too.'

'Seriously? She wrote about those things?'

Lyn nodded. 'Absolutely. She wrote a lot of what we call fiction, but most of it was based on real events. Just about all of it. I mean, that's what makes this letter so . . .' She hesitated, then went on. 'Look, it's personal to you and your family, but it's also a piece of historical evidence, I guess.'

'So you're saying that all these things in the letter, they're likely to pop up in her work. But the strychnine? What about that, for chrissake?'

Lyn nodded and looked him in the eye. 'I just know I've seen a reference to it. Or maybe Caroline wrote me about it. If only I had those notes. I'm pretty sure I read it in that missing manuscript.'

'Missing manuscript?' Steve asked. 'What are you talking about ?'

'Didn't I tell you? Mari wrote a whole novel based on her young life. Called it *Murky River*. Well, that was one title. Sometimes she called it *The Ungirt Runner*.'

'Say what?'

'*The Ungirt Runner*. It comes from a poem, a Scottish soldier who was killed in the First World War. Just a kid. Nineteen or twenty years old.'

'But why would she call it that?'

'Good question. I did read the poem one time. It seemed to be about the joys of running through the landscape, freedom, that kind of thing. I guess it would have appealed to her as a young writer.'

'And ungirt? What the hell does that mean?'

'Boy, your teachers must have loved you when you were in grade school. It means something like when you've loosened your belt to free up your movements. Like you're going into battle, I guess. I dunno. Anyway, my point is it's really raw stuff and she never published it. I got to read it, years ago, at her sister's place. I mean it was very adolescent -

a great long tirade against "my awful parents" and "what a raw deal I had", all based on her family and all dressed up as the history of a pioneering family. Part of why I'm here is to track it down, read it through again. But so far, no luck.'

'Okay, so what next? On your list?'

Lyn checked her notepad. 'Next is the sister who drowned. Did you say you had an aunt?'

'Yeah. But they didn't talk about that. We kids weren't supposed to know. The way they avoided it I'm guessing she might have taken her own life.'

'Is that right? Well, Mari has a similar story. Very lurid. Two sisters, one gets pregnant and kills herself. I can point you at all this stuff if you wanted to read it.'

'Jesus.' Steve looked at Lyn. This was all new territory for him. 'Do all writers do this? I mean, just steal things from other people's lives? Damn, it's almost like they're . . . I dunno, grave-robbers.'

Lyn couldn't suppress a smile. 'Well, I've never heard it put that way,' she said, 'but in essence, yes. People say they invent things, but look around you. Is there any need to make up a story about human frailty? Poke around in any family. I teach literature for my living, and when I was younger I imagined I'd be a novelist, but a part of me wonders why anyone would bother to write fiction. Real life is way more dramatic.'

'I hear you,' Steve agreed. 'So what about Jim? I got a bad feeling about that. 'Cos there was some guy Wanda mentioned, when I had the big bust-up with Pete. And I swear she was trying to tell me Pete killed him. Or maybe my Grandpa. Maybe that was him.'

Steve was struggling with the reins here. The story was like a rogue stallion, pulling him in too many directions at once. 'Yeah, a real bad feeling. Same as I have about the child,' he said. 'He tells her Wanda is pregnant, but he doesn't say "our baby", does he? Just "this woman and the child that's due". I mean, would he say that if it was his? Christ. Maybe that's the truth of it. Like Wanda said. Like I always suspected.'

Lyn didn't respond. Just looked at him, then at the letter. Steve shook his head. 'All my life,' he said, 'I've done the Kaminski thing, throwing up a barricade, hiding behind a shield. And here I am, sixty-five years old. I been to war, I been through all kinds of shit that's supposed to toughen you up - and damn me if I don't suddenly feel . . . I dunno.' He sat there, head down towards the floor. Lyn managed to keep quiet, to let him breathe. When he sat up, his eyes were wet. 'It's like a part of me never really grew up,' he said shakily. 'Guess I suddenly feel kinda young.'

She got up from her chair, walked over to where he sat and stood there, facing him. 'Here,' she said, and held out her arms. 'Feeling young is okay.'

He stood up. They embraced in silence for a full minute. It was a warm, tight embrace and for the first time he smelled her, close up. It was a sweet, uncomplicated womanly smell, and he realized it was something he'd been missing. He drew back quite abruptly. 'Sorry,' he said. 'Sorry.'

'Come on,' she said, 'sorry for what? Since when did a person have to apologize for being in need of comfort?'

'Okay,' he sighed, 'just that every time I get involved with someone it goes wrong.'

Lyn looked at him and frowned. 'We're not getting involved,' she said. 'Just being kind to each other. There's nothing wrong with that.'

14

When Steve went down for coffee next morning, the place was empty. Lyn had told him she would take off early. She was going to see what the library in Valentine had to offer, and while she was there she could call in at the Land Registry. Her next job would be to have a dig through the Chadron archive, once she was sure that the curator was back. As to Lincoln, that might be quite a long job. It would wait. She wondered whether Steve might go with her, when it happened. He wasn't sure, but he said he might. He hadn't been there since his high-school senior year, when the whole class visited the Capitol. He'd think about it. Today, he decided, he was going to take it slow. Give himself time to get over yesterday, prepare himself to visit his sister in the afternoon.

He sat with his coffee. Jeannie seemed to get the message that he didn't want to talk. She was an astute woman, he figured. So many of them felt the need to probe. But not her. Lyn had left him a little book, not much fatter than a magazine. Edited by Mari's sister Caroline, it was entitled

Victorie and Other Stories. There was a Post-it note on the cover. *The title piece ought to interest you. Lyn.* He decided he might do worse than spend an hour or so looking through it.

Back in his room, he struggled with the story. It seemed lurid, almost melodramatic, and the sense wasn't always clear. He was no literary expert, but the writing seemed jerky, not at all like *Old Jules*. Even so, what he read soon had his heart thudding. Sandoz was writing about a Polish family.

He tried not to get swept along on a tide of speculation; after all, Grandpa wasn't the only Pole around Nebraska in settler times. And for sure, there were plenty of guys called Pete, as the young lad in this tale was. But the more he read, the more convinced he became that it might just be his old man. He reminded himself that Grandpa had been located by Mari's father. Those early settlements, everybody would know everyone else. If young Mari had been looking around for inspiration, why would she bother to look any further than her own childhood friends and acquaintances?

Then he thought about the signed photograph. How long had they known each other? Did their friendship really go all the way back, back to when they were kids? The letter made it plain that it did.

He read on, trying to make sense of a tangled tale clumsily told. There were other echoes of the little bits he could remember about his family back then. This character she called Pete had two older sisters, just as his father did. There was one who died, but it was plain that she had killed herself. In his own family nobody could ever figure out how his aunt Mata had managed to die in a gently flowing river like the Niobrara, and a shallow one at that. Sandoz had the answer: a deep fishing hole created by the guy who farmed the land adjacent to it.

In Mari's story, the big sister had left the home place and gone to live in town, a thinly disguised Rushville. Meanwhile, the younger one fell under the spell of an older guy. He had accumulated a lot of property in the neighborhood. She was only fifteen, but pretty soon she was pregnant. A 'hurry-up' wedding was arranged. Had to be. That was the way they did things. And then along comes the big sister. She meets this man that little sis is about to marry and decides she wants him for herself. He could be her ticket to a better life, and she doesn't see why her kid sister should get him. Little sis is only young - there will be other men for her. So big sis sets about seducing the guy. Next thing, she's telling him she's pregnant and they're going to get married. Later it turns out she lied. But by then the guy had already walked into the trap. When the younger girl, Victorie, kills herself, his revenge on her sister, now his wife, is sustained, cruel and pitiless.

There was more to the story, but Steve was already weary of it. He skimmed through the final pages. It was almost as if the author was relishing her foray into a world of Gothic awfulness, and the tale seemed to spin out of control.

He rose from his seat and went to the window. He'd told Glenn he would call by, and it was another beautiful spring day out there. He picked up his jacket and checked his stash of money. Well over three grand left, but of course he was running up bills here. That couldn't go on.

Downstairs he found Jeannie sitting at a side table, flipping through the newspaper. 'They say it could reach seventy today,' she said.

'Is that right?' Steve paused, then said, 'Listen, I gotta feeling I'm gonna need to stick around here for some time yet. Think I'll check out the State Park. Give it another night or two and then make a move.'

'You'll like it down there,' Jeannie said. 'And you'll most likely have the place to yourself.' She looked at him and added, 'I guess that might suit you.'

Steve nodded and gave a tired smile. 'Yeah, you got my number.'

It was only a short walk up Main to the small neat house where Glenn lived. It was set back from the sidewalk and surrounded on three sides by small trees and shrubs. Steve knocked at the door, and waited. Then knocked again. Just as he was about to give up and return to the hotel, Glenn appeared from around the side.

'Well,' he said, 'if it ain't the man from Oregon. And how can I help you this beautiful morning?'

'You said you might have a cassette player.'

'That I did, and you chose a good day to come by. You're about to find out what musicians do when the right notes won't come.' He ushered Steve towards the garage entrance. 'They call it displacement activity. You might call it rearranging all the crap I've accumulated over twenty years since my mom passed.'

The place was piled high with old furniture, boxes, garden tools, a stack of tires, and in one corner an assortment of TVs, radios and beat-up hi-fis.

'People hire me to throw out their junk and I always find - I dunno, interesting things. Photos, ornaments, things they maybe shouldn't be dumping. Sometimes I just see something in a box of trash and figure it might be worth holding onto. Books, letters. You'd be surprised what people throw out. Personal stuff sometimes. So I just file it away,' he laughed, 'then I forget about it.'

When he saw that Steve was barely listening to him, he said: 'Okay, cassette player, huh?' And started shifting things around. 'I know I got one someplace. More than one. Just let me . . . here, grab this, will you?' He handed Steve a tall speaker in a wooden cabinet. 'Just dump it behind you there.' He hauled out its pair. 'I bought these for the cases. Good hardwood ain't gonna get any cheaper. Okay, let's see . . .'

Glenn was leaning over a stack of cartons and a set of dining chairs that were piled up above them. 'There ya go,' he said, and emerged with an old-style portable cassette deck with integral radio.

'It work?' asked Steve, taking it in his hand.

'Should do. Wanna come in the house and try her out?'

'I'd appreciate that.'

Glenn gave the garage a parting glance. 'Jeez, I'm gonna have to sort this place out some time soon. Have a great big yard sale. Or a fire. Open up a bit of space in there.'

The house wasn't a great deal different from the garage, except that in here it seemed to be all books and records - on shelves, in piles on the floor, spilling out of cardboard boxes. In the middle of the room they had entered was a large table. On it was a pc, a laptop, a couple of portable amplifiers, the body of a guitar, an Indian flute, a pile of notebooks, an old glass pie-dish full of coins and dollar bills, a china plate with a half-eaten slice of toast on it, three or four mugs, and a teetering piles of CDs.

'The nerve center of my world,' Glenn said, and pulled out a seat for his guest. Then he picked up an electric razor, saying, 'Full life-support system for the busy songwriter.' He reached into a cup full of pens and pulled out a toothbrush. 'See, I can spend fifteen hours here and not want for a damned thing,' he said. 'Except a little company sometimes. Can I get you a beer?' He looked at his watch. 'Kinda early, but this bar's open seven days a week.'

Steve looked at his watch. 'What the hell. If you got something light.'

'Okay, just let's check this machine.' Glenn crouched down under the desk and plugged it in. 'Works on batteries too,' he said. 'Triple As.' He crawled back out and held out a hand. 'Got a tape I can try?'

Steve had them in his jacket pocket: he was planning to play them to Wanda. He shook his head. 'Not that I wanna hear right now. You got any kicking around?

'Somewhere. Here, lemme get you the beer.' Glenn disappeared out back, returned a few moments later with a couple of cans of Miller Lite and handed one to Steve.

'Y'know what,' he said, 'I believe I have what we need right here.' He went to a tall metal filing cabinet and opened the top drawer. 'Aha! *Road trips: ambient sounds.* Nineteen eighty-seven.' He had a tape in his hand and was looking at it. 'Yeah, I used to record a lot when I was on the road. Things that came into my head that - hell, we're talking a younger version of me. When you're a crazy twenty year old turned loose for the first time, everything seems so damned, you know, profound.' He waited for Steve to respond, but there was nothing. 'I was always getting ideas and putting them on tape. Except sometimes I just recorded what I heard. Atmospheric stuff: traffic on the highway, a loco horn, the wind in a cottonwood tree. I got a whole stack of recordings of the Niobrara River. Figured I was gonna write a guitar symphony around it.' He stopped short. 'Okay, let's try her, shall we?'

There was some hissing, then Glenn's voice over the sound of a car engine. 'Gravel road, Sheridan county, April 26. Windmill.' The engine cut out and almost immediately came the sound that Steve himself had stopped and listened to just a day or two earlier - the clanking of rods, the trickle of water into a tank, cattle exhaling. Then the liquid trill of a meadowlark, followed by a few high chords on a guitar.

Glenn hit the STOP button. 'That was me trying out my

new art form.' He laughed. 'That's what I told myself, anyway.' He removed the tape and handed Steve the machine. 'Good as new,' he said. 'Man, I should go through this old stuff of mine. Get it to CD. Probably got some good material hidden away. *Sounds of the Sandhills.* How's that grab you? Could be an internet sensation.' He unplugged the machine and handed it to Steve. 'You gonna take it?'

'Sure,' Steve said. 'How much do you want?'

Glenn shook his head. 'Have it. I got more in there someplace. Just need to dig around. All a matter of stirring my lazy ass, I guess.'

They sat in silence for a few moments. Steve wiped the dust off the player with his sleeve, and sipped at his beer. Then he asked, 'Ever had any of your songs recorded? Ever make any money?'

'Yeah,' Glenn said. 'Good question.' He thought for a moment. 'I had a buddy once, in Omaha. He was trying to get into record producing. I laid down a few tracks with him. I think he put a couple out, but I never got a dime. He's in Philadelphia now, doing okay. I gig here and there. Coffee shops, bars. County fairs in the summertime. But I enjoy myself, that's the thing. What about you? Ever felt like dropping out? You're about that age, aren't you? Summer of love and all that?'

'No, I was more the beatnik age.'

'Right. Jack Kerouac. You read his books?'

Steve gave a short laugh. '*On the Road*. Sure I did. Read it when I was hitch-hiking west. Yeah. Nineteen sixty-six. Buddy of mine loaned it to me. He never saw it again. Or me, come to think of it.'

'Wow, a child of your time. And was that what made you go - reading the book?'

'No. I was fighting with my old man.'

'It's an old story.'

'Yeah.' Steve sighed, and shifted in his seat. 'Took off one day and never came back.'

'Till now?'

'Till now.'

'And that's what, forty years?'

'And more.'

'Jeez, so this is a huge big deal for you.'

'I wouldn't be here but for my sister being ill, and . . .' He stopped. He'd already said more than he wished to. Then he looked at his watch. 'Shit. I need to hit the road. Listen, Glenn, thanks for the machine, and the beer. Catch you later.' He picked up the can, tipped back his head and finished it.

IT WAS one o'clock when he drove into Gordon. He was hungry now. He stopped at a little café and ordered the lunch special. The place was busy and he shared a table with a veterinarian, a specialist in horses. He introduced himself as Vince, and asked Steve where he was from. To his own surprise Steve told him he was a Nebraska boy, that he'd moved away as a young man and was only now revisiting old haunts.

'So where do you live?' Vince asked.

'I was out on the west coast twenty years or so, but this last year or two I been kinda footloose.'

'Are you thinking of retiring here?'

'No,' Steve said. 'No, I can't see that happening.' He looked at the other man. He looked about fifty. He was lean, well-groomed, and wore expensive-looking clothes. 'What about you?' he asked. 'Where you from?'

Vince waved a fork towards the highway. 'Some way east. Little place called Johnstown. Towards Ainsworth.'

Steve felt as if he'd heard of it, but couldn't be certain.

The waitress came and handed Vince his bill. He stood up and held out his hand. Steve shook it. 'Well,' Vince said, 'nice talking to you but I gotta go see a sick horse.'

After he left, Steve remembered that he had been to Johnstown. It was one of the many places he'd called on with the old man. He felt he could recall a tiny place set back from the highway. There was a cozy little bar there where he'd tasted his first beer.

The crowd was starting to thin out, and Steve lingered over his dessert and coffee. He had a couple of refills and waited until a little before two o'clock before making his way to Sunny Acres. He was pleased to find Lejla on duty, and smiling at him.

'Ah, Mister Kaminski. Good to see you. And your sister, she just woke from a little nap. She's bright today. Very bright.'

'That right?' He enjoyed being around this young woman, the way she greeted him like he was an old friend. She exuded warmth, and she seemed happy. He wondered whether she'd been born that way, what her parents might have been like. Or had she adopted this cheerfulness, this effortless conversational ability, by act of will?

'Sure, she been out in the garden, enjoying the sunshine. Is a beautiful day, isn't it? You'll find her back in her room now. I just took her a drink. You need me to walk you down, or you going to surprise her?'

'I'll manage, thanks.'

Lejla noticed that Steve was carrying the cassette player. 'Ah, you brought her some tapes?' she asked. 'She will like that. She will be happy. But be careful with her.'

'Careful?'

'The painkillers. They make her sometimes a bit confused. Irritable.'

Steve appreciated the warning. His sister was scowling at him before he'd even opened his mouth.

'Why didn't you come yesterday?' she said. 'I sat waiting for you. Hours I sat. Waiting for you to come and take me home.'

'Have they given you the all-clear?' Steve asked. 'I mean, are you fit to go home?'

'I am if you'll get off your high horse and come stay with me.' Wanda looked at him, her head held sideways. 'Or are you too busy? Listen, I can still get myself to the can, if that's what's worrying you. I just need someone to cook and clean up, make sure I get my meds.'

'Look,' he said, 'far as I was concerned I came out here to . . .' He had his face half turned away from her, but forced himself to meet her eyes with his. Christ, why was it so hard? The truth was, he'd assumed she was dying. That she'd be gone any time soon, that she might be gone by the time he showed up, that he'd arrive just in time to collect the inheritance he'd hoped for twenty years ago.

'What did you think?' Wanda asked. 'That I'd conveniently die? Huh?' She was giving him the hard stare now, unblinking, daring him to look away. 'All I'm asking you, brother of mine, is to fix it so that I can die in my own home. If I get really bad, you call in a nurse.' She stopped then, and asked, 'So you been out to the ranch, you say?'

'Yeah,' he said. 'I went out to the old place. Checked things over. It took longer than I thought. Here, let me sit down.' He held out the tape player. 'Look what I brought you.'

'What do I want with that?'

'Thought you'd like to put some of your music on. Y'know, the old songs. I brought some of your tapes from the house.'

'You been to the house?'

'I just told you. Checking it over.'

She looked at the tapes in his hand. 'So what have you got for me?'

'Elvis, Everly Brothers . . .'

'Oh, the Everlys,' she said. 'That's nice.' Her face widened into a beautiful smile, the way it might have done thirty, forty years previously. 'Go on,' she said, shifting her chair into the reclined position. 'Put it on.'

He slotted the *Greatest Hits* tape into the machine, and pressed PLAY.

They sat there in silence through three or four tracks. Steve watched her expression as she nodded to the beat of each tune in turn, transfigured by the joy she found in those familiar old songs. 'Till I Kissed You', 'Bird Dog'. Steve found himself smiling with her, briefly. The songs brought him memories of the last of their happy days, before things really kicked off between Mom and Dad.

She was laughing now, trying to sing along. Then she said, 'How's Bonny?'

'Don't do that, Wanda. You know damned well she threw me out.'

'I forgot. What was it? Another woman?'

'No. Try again.'

'She didn't like you drinking.'

'Correct.'

'So why didn't you quit?'

'Chrissake, Wanda. I've always drunk. I got a lot to forget about. And I never touched her, if that's what you're thinking. Or her daughters. Just . . . '

'Just what?'

'Just that I was starting to let my work go.' He was tempted to tell her about the big job he screwed up, the best job he'd had in years, and the legal case that followed. But what was the point? Soon as he inherited he could sell up and it would be history. 'Look,' he said, 'I didn't drive twelve hundred miles to pick over the bones of a dead relationship.'

'Seem to remember there's been a few.'

Steve let the remark pass. She had always had an acid edge to her tongue, and he guessed the drugs were eating away at her inhibitions. He looked at his sister. She seemed distracted. Suddenly she was scrabbling in an old leather shoulder-bag. She pulled out an audio cassette. There seemed to be others in there with it.

'Here, put this in your machine,' she said. 'Little treat for you.'

'Sure,' he said, turning it over to see whether it had a label of any kind. But it didn't 'What is it?'

'Just play.'

There was a lot of hissing and a few odd noises, like someone banging against a microphone. Then he heard his sister's voice the way he remembered it. Clear, expressive, musical. She always had good diction. That was something their mother had encouraged. 'Gives you a touch of class,' she used to say. It didn't work for Wanda. People thought she was acting superior and as a teenager she strove to lose it. Only later did she realize its value.

'Okay, Mama, so today we're going to talk about how you met Dad. It was in North Platte, wasn't it?'

Steve shot forward out of his chair and whacked the PAUSE button. 'When the hell did you record this?' he said.

Wanda looked at him, held the stare for several seconds. 'Just play it,' she said.

He shook his head. Whether she was being deliberately provocative or not, what did it matter? He was already scrabbling through his memory trying to recall when he'd last heard his mother's voice. Most likely on the phone, one of those stilted, awkward conversations after he'd got together with Bonny and Irena decided she had a right to see the children, even if they were Bonny's and not his. And then before she had the chance to come, she took ill.

'Come on, tell me. When did you do this?'

'I went to visit her in Colorado.'

'And Pete was still alive?'

'Of course. But I knew she hadn't got long. So did she. I just figured, let's give it a try. Get the story straight.'

'And she agreed?'

Wanda pointed at the tape player. 'You're looking at the evidence. Or hearing it. Shall we continue?'

Steve nodded, and Wanda pressed PLAY, and there she was again.

'I was young. You need to understand that. And I was alone.' She sounded defensive, as though she was about to excuse herself for something she was ashamed of.

'How old?' Wanda again. 'How old were you, Mom, when you met Dad?'

'I met Jim first.'

'Jim?' Steve cut in. Wanda paid no notice. Her eyes were closed.

'Your dad was kinda tagging along. Like he was Jim's little brother. Except he was the same age, just not so savvy. He was cute enough, although not in Jim's league. No damned way. Jim could charm the birds off the trees, whereas your dad . . .'

'Not a charmer, that what you're saying?' Steve heard his mother's faint chuckle. 'And how old were you, Mom?'

'How old was I? What is this, the Spanish Inquisition?'

'Just trying to get the picture in my head.'

'I'd say I was seventeen. But I didn't get to know them right then. Not really. I was working in the saloon, and they were just a couple guys outa the yard who came by after their shift finished. There was a whole gang of railroad men. Most of them were younger guys. But there was a few older ones used to hang around. You learned to watch out for them. Hustlers and pimps, a lot of them.'

Steve shut the tape off. His sister opened her eyes. 'How long have you had this?' he asked. 'When did you record it? Why didn't you ever let me hear it?'

'One question at a time, if you don't mind. Take it easy.' That was the old Wanda speaking, the little sister imitating her mother, trying to sound grown-up.

'How the hell d'you expect me to take it easy when you're setting off firecrackers like this?' Steve had his hands on his head and was rubbing his hair forward and back. 'Okay, okay,' he said, 'let's frigging well get it over with.' Then he glared at her. 'And who's this Jim guy? His name came up in a - no, forget it,' he said. 'If you had this you shoulda let me know.'

'Oh sure, and you on the west coast, never picking up the damned phone.'

Steve wasn't listening. 'You any idea what I been through?'

'Just play the damned thing.'

He reached forward and placed his forefinger on the PLAY button.

It was Wanda talking again. 'So let me get this straight, Mom. You were working in the saloon at seventeen?'

Steve heard his mother's familiar short laugh as she dismissed the objection. 'Why not, for heaven's sake? They didn't have so many dumb rules in those days. ID cards and such. If you were good enough you were old enough. Hell, there were kids of fifteen taking beer to the tables. Not boys, but girls for sure. Runaways, most of us. They liked to hire us. We didn't argue about the pay. And we weren't going to get ourselves fired if we could help it.'

'Us, you say? So you were a runaway too?'

There was a moment's silence, the sound of a cigarette

being lit. Steve could plainly hear his mother take a deep breath and exhale, real slow. Man, she sure enjoyed her smokes. In the background was the faint noise of a door opening and closing. Then another of her deep breaths out, followed by a muffled cough. He thought of the times he'd asked her to quit. Even as a kid he could see it was bad for her.

'Three times I ran away. First from my beloved father, after Mom died. Then from his sister's husband. She was okay, Alice, but he was such a damned creep.'

'You said three times, Mom. You ran away three times.'

'Why so impatient?' She drew on her cigarette again. 'Third time was from the poor farm. You get to a certain age and men . . .Come on, Wanda, I don't need to tell you about that. Can't keep their damned hands to themselves. And I was a good-looking kid. It's a mixed blessing, as you found out for yourself.'

'Christ.' Steve paused the tape to give himself time to absorb what he was hearing. He glanced at his sister. She had been sitting upright, concentrating hard.

She turned to him now and scowled. 'What you stopping it for? Keep going.'

'There's a lot to take in, is all. I never heard about any damned poor farm.' But he was in no mood to argue with her. He pressed PLAY.

'Okay, Mom, the railroad guys - what year was this, by the way?'

'Year? Let me think. It would be . . . when was the Republican Valley flood? The one that wiped out all those farms?'

'Hell, that,' Steve said. 'Grandpa was always talking about it, d'you remember?' Wanda held her finger up to shush him.

'No, don't tell me,' Irena continued. 'It would have been nineteen thirty-five. I was coming up to eighteen. The line was washed away down south and they diverted all the traffic through North Platte, so all these Burlington men were working double shifts. And Saturday night, they'd come in with their fat wage packets, and Jim and his buddy - your dad - they were in there too. I liked them from the start. They had more about them than the average railroad guy. They'd been around. Seen a few things.'

Wanda cut in. 'But he must've been forty. And you, I mean you were just a girl. Eighteen.'

'I didn't say I went with them, did I? Just that I liked them. Later, well - I mean a lot later, after the war . . .' A long pause, then Steve could almost hear her smile as she added, 'Course, they liked me. They made that plain enough. Like I said, I was a looker. And I knew it.'

Steve paused the tape again. He needed to know where the hell this was leading, but he wasn't sure he wanted to go there. He had a story in his head that made sense to him, and which legitimised the anger and resentment he'd had in his heart these past forty years. Did he need to hear a new one? He glanced at Wanda and saw her eyes were closed and her head was slumped forward. She started to snore, lightly.

Lejla was back in the room, looking at her. 'She'll maybe sleep for a while now,' she said. 'When she wakes up she'll need more medication.'

'So is that it for today?'

'I think yes. You must keep these visits short. Maybe around six she'll be ready to talk again. Or tomorrow?'

'Tell me,' Steve said, looking deep into her eyes. As he spoke he was aware of Wanda stirring, her breathing coming in a series of little gasps. 'Look, I need to ask you . . .'

Lejla put a finger over her mouth and beckoned him to step outside. In the corridor, sitting on a bench with her, Steve said, 'C'mon, I need to know. Realistically, how long does she have?'

'I can't say,' Lejla told him. 'Nobody can. Our job is to make her as comfortable as we can, to ease the pain.'

'I see. 'Cos I got questions I need to ask her.'

'You can do that. You just got to be patient. Patient and gentle. It's not good for her to be upset.'

'Okay. But listen, you know she's asking me to take her home?'

'Well, of course she would. Anyone would.'

'So, is it a possibility?'

'Sure, if you can arrange stand-by nursing care for when she gets really weak.' Lejla paused. 'You willing to do that for her?'

'I dunno,' he said. 'I never looked after anyone before. I mean, not a terminal case. What do you think?'

The young woman looked at him, and smiled. 'What would you want, if you were dying?'

He didn't answer, just got up from his seat. 'I hear what you're saying. I'm going back to Chadron now. I'll come again, soon as I can. Most likely tomorrow.'

'She will like that. Believe me.'

Steve returned to the room. He was aware of Lejla standing in the doorway. He looked into Wanda's shoulder-bag, which had fallen to one side, its contents now visible. More tapes. He reached in and took them out. He hesitated, thinking it through. Would she notice? He glanced at Lejla, still watching.

'She wants me to copy these,' he said. 'Then bring 'em back.' He rose to his feet. 'Yeah,' he said, 'that's what she wanted. She was clear about that.' He fastened his jacket, picked up the player and made for the corridor. 'Okay,' he said, 'I'll come again in a day or two. Maybe see you then.'

Once he was out of town he drove fast. He wanted to hear the rest of this stuff. Maybe he would find some answers at last, things he should have known years ago.

When he got to Chadron he went directly to the hotel, then hesitated on the doorstep. He'd said he was going to move out, didn't he? Or meant to. Did he or didn't he? Damned if he could remember now. Too bad. It would have to wait. He hurried upstairs.

He sat in the rocking chair and wound the tape back to the beginning. He had the bottle of bourbon on the table beside him and a glass in his hand. As the tape played, he paused every so often. As well as trying to take it all in he was trying to work out why his sister had made these recordings, and when. It might help if he could remember exactly when their mother had died. He knew that he hadn't gone to her funeral, any more than he had for his father's. It had taken place in Colorado, where she'd settled - Fort Collins. That was all he knew. He realized that most people would have a clear recollection of the date their mother died. But he wasn't most people. Besides, he had dramas of his own going on at that time. He and Bonny had been arguing – about her kids mostly – and she was telling him it was no wonder he was estranged from his family. She said he was 'emotionally illiterate'. It was the first time he'd heard the phrase.

The tape rolled on, past the point where they'd left off. 'So let's get this right,' Wanda was saying. 'When you ran away from the poor farm you were what - sixteen, seventeen?'

'About that. You got to a certain age, they couldn't hold you. But I wasn't going to wait that long. I mean, they would try to hold people, but they had no legal right. Not that that always counted for much.'

'What do you mean?'

'Some of those places, before the war, they had people enslaved, as good as. They ran all kind of rackets, and when the authorities came sniffing around they paid them off. Got away with murder, some of them.'

'You mean like that woman Cook?'

Steve knew about her okay. Some years ago he'd read a book about her. Christ, she was into everything - prostitution, bootlegging, gambling. And still at large when she died of old age. They couldn't lay a finger on her. She had them all in her pocket.

'I never came across anyone as flat out evil as Annie Cook. Around North Platte you only had to mention her name and people clammed up. They were frightened to death of her. Partly because she was a real scary woman, but there was also the power she had. Anyone in public office, you could bet she had some dirt on them. She knew everyone's secrets. But that was all news to me when I arrived in town.'

'You came from Omaha, right?'

'Near there. You got to understand none of those places were a bed of roses. You were there because you were a loser, either you personally or your family, and they treated you that way. You had to be tough; if you showed any weakness you'd go under. They just destroyed people. Anyway, I had a friend who'd gotten away. She had an uncle in North Platte and he fixed her up in a hotel in town. She wanted me to come join her, so I just skedaddled.' Steve could hear Irena suck on her cigarette. 'Night-time. Took my first ever ride on a train. I spent the whole trip glued to the window, even when it got dark. Just looking at the lights out on the farms and trying to imagine the people and what they were doing.'

'How'd you manage to afford a ticket?'

'I had ways,' Irena said. 'Anyway, my friend fixed me up with a job, same place as her. Sort of a hotel, night club, some would say brothel.'

'So did you live there?'

'We shared a room, tried to save money. We made plans. One time we talked of buying a place together; we were going to grow fruit and raise chickens.'

'I never knew that.'

'Why would you? As it panned out, I pretty much got what I wanted anyway.'

'You did?'

'Well, look where I ended up. If there was one thing I wanted it was to get away from people and towns. Being a rancher's wife sort of appealed to me.'

'Really? So Dad was like your ticket to the good life?'

'I didn't see it that way. When I got to know him he told me stories about growing up in the hills. And it kinda spoke to me.'

Steve was sitting upright now, listening intently. All he remembered was the old man saying that he had never wanted to come back to the ranch. Wanda seemed equally perplexed, but for a different reason.

'But you and Dad were always fighting,' she said. 'Like you never even wanted to be with him in the first place.'

'Well, I didn't. That's the whole damned point. I wanted his best buddy.'

'Jim?'

'Sure. Dear old Jim.'

Steve could hear his mother sigh. It was a sound he recognized, having heard it many times. Sort of wistful, and sad.

'After the flood the two of them became Saturday-night regulars.' Irena laughed, a gentle sort of laugh, born of some long-forgotten affection. 'They sure stood out from the crowd, those two,' she told Wanda. 'Like I said, it was mostly young, single guys coming in to sink a few beers, play a little pool, maybe join the card school in the back room and hope the evening ended with a girl, of course. But for that they had to dance. Dance?' She laughed. 'More like wrestling. You had to fight them off sometimes. Boy, they were all hands. And then there were these two, Jim and his buddy Pete. Couple of more mature guys.'

Wanda gave one or her dismissive little laughs. 'Yeah right, you could say mature. You could say old enough to be your father.'

'Listen, little lady, I'm not denying that. But you need to remember where I came from. Finding a guy who offered protection, who treated you with respect, that was always on my mind.'

'But there must have been younger guys, surely?'

He heard Irena sigh again, listened as she lit another cigarette. 'You may find it hard to understand this, Wanda, but those two - to us they were like gentlemen. And we sure appreciated it.'

'You mean compared with the other railroad guys?'

'Compared with any guy I'd ever met. I'm not saying they were like knights in armour or something. Just that they tried to treat us as if we were worth something. All those young studs, they came in with their roll of dollar bills and before you knew it, it was "Hey sweetheart, let's go upstairs." Jim, and your dad, they weren't like that. They'd put money in your hand at the end of an evening, sure they would. But it was like they were tipping you, for doing your job. Thanks for a nice evening kind of thing.'

'So what was your job?'

'It was what you made it. We knew what was required. Look pretty, sell drinks, laugh when the guys cracked a joke. Dance if they wanted. I guess today you'd call us hostesses.' Irena paused, then said, 'We dispensed hospitality.'

When Wanda repeated the word, 'Hospitality,' and added a snide sort of 'I get it,' Steve could just see his sister's smirk. She could be such a superior bitch at times.

There was another silence, and the sound of Irena drawing on her cigarette. Then she said, 'Okay, Wanda, yes. Your mother sometimes took a guy up the stairs. And more often than not, money changed hands, or a gift. But tell me this, Snow White, were you a blushing virgin on your wedding night? Huh? Were you?'

'Okay, Mom. Let's move on. I got more things I wanna ask you.'

Steve's mind was racing. Why was his sister doing this? And why was his mother playing along? And what difference would it have made if he'd known all this years ago, while Irena was still alive? How come Wanda had never even hinted that their mother came from such a place? He wanted to drive back to Gordon right this minute and shout at her: 'Things could've been different!'

Even as the thoughts tumbled around in his head, he heard Irena asking, 'What's this all about anyway? Why the sudden interest in my young life? Looking for someone to blame for your own misfortunes, are you?'

Steve pressed PAUSE. He picked up the third tape. No sign of what it contained. What the hell had he got here? He shrugged, took another slug from the bottle and snapped the tape out of the machine then inserted a replacement. It was labelled 2. He pressed PLAY.

'Okay, Dad, so let's talk about you and Jim, and how you . . .' His sister's words were quickly strangled by a squeaking noise. Then there was a sharp snap! as the thing turned itself off. When he opened the machine up to remove the cassette, several feet of twisted tape came with it, and there was more in the machine.

He got up from his chair, unsteady on his feet. Damn. He picked up the player and tried to pull the tape free. It was never going to shift. He wondered whether he could fix it with a pencil, like he used to. Or a ballpoint. Damned things were always getting screwed up. He went to the table, then the kitchen, and couldn't find a thing. Looking at the machine once more, he could see it was never going to work. The tape was tangled tight around the heads.

The place suddenly felt stifling hot. He went to the window and opened it. The sun was shining and the air was still. He slumped back into the rocker, drained his glass of bourbon and started thinking over what he'd just heard. He'd never had a good feeling about coming back. He'd let his mother and father die without the benefit of his company. He should've done the same with his sister. But then what if she changed her mind about the ranch? Was that the only reason he'd come out here?

He got up and went to the bathroom, filled a glass with water, drank it and filled it up again. He stared at himself in the mirror. Christ, did he look this bad to other people, his face lined, his hair sticking out in short gray tufts, his brown eyes so doleful? What had happened to that upright posture he used to have? He'd always made a thing of standing upright as a young man, ever conscious of his lack of inches. He held his own gaze, and it didn't feel comfortable. There was something he needed to ask the man in the mirror. He didn't say the words out loud, but he did run them slowly and deliberately through his mind. *Tell me. Look me in the eye and tell me that you aren't here just to nail the inheritance? C'mon, say it.*

He backed away, and retreated to the sitting room. Took another slug from the bottle. Rocking gently in the chair, he wondered. What would he feel when his sister died? Relief? Would it be at her funeral the way he figured it would've been at Pete's, and Mom's? In each case he'd thought it through several times before deciding not to come. He could only imagine people standing by an open grave and shedding tears, and him dry-eyed, itching to get it over with because really, deep down, he was glad to see the end of them. That was one thing he might get from being here. Closure. Except of course there could be no such thing till he'd worked this all out.

He was startled by a tapping at the door. Screw it, he wasn't home to anyone right now.

But there it was again. What the hell? Whoever it was would go away in the end.

15

Lyn had put in a good morning's work at the library in Valentine. She'd known what to expect, having worked on microfilmed newspapers before, and she'd learned the hard way that an hour at a time, with a coffee break between, was as much as she could manage. She'd learned too that there was no point in trying to take in the full content of every page, corner to corner and top to bottom. There was just too much. You had to skim. You had to get into a groove and trust your eyes. Let them act independently of your mind, sorting the ads from the headlines without your conscious self taking too much notice. In the end, your eyes learned to cover the shifting landscape and find key words with surprising ease.

The odd thing was that here, today, most of the few stories that caught her attention related to Steve in some way. There were number of articles about bootleggers; amongst others the name Clouser had cropped up. He'd been convicted of running a still and sent away for a spell in jail. All it said about him was he was a resident of Sheridan

County. Later, she decided, she would go to the Land Registry and see whether she could find his place, which she suspected would be out in the hills, close by the Sandoz orchards. So she photo-copied the articles, and went for lunch, satisfied that she had something, at least, to show to Steve, but feeling a little weary of the essentially drudgery of her task.

It was during the afternoon, just when she was starting to think she was wasting her time here, that Lyn stumbled upon a second story citing the man Clouser. It referred to his earlier conviction, when he'd paid a modest fine and had a few cases of moonshine destroyed. Now, it appeared, he had gotten mixed up with a bigger outfit, one of whose members, the prosecution claimed, was called Peter Kaminski, described as a native of Sheridan County now resident in North Platte. It gave few details, but there could be little doubt that this was Steve's father. Why else would the story have been deemed newsworthy in the Rushville paper? He was charged on a number of counts, among them transporting liquor with intent to sell. With him in court was an accomplice, one Diego Jimenez, described as a Mexican. The pair had been apprehended after a high-speed chase over dirt roads in Lincoln County. Liquor had been found in their car, and the pair were to stand trial.

Suddenly Lyn was focused on her work. In a later edition of the same paper she found the trial of Kaminski and Jimenez written up in some detail. The pair had smashed through a barrier erected by the police, and driven at reckless speed. Had they not blown a tire on a railroad crossing, they might have been free yet. When they were finally stopped, they were found to be carrying two cases of whisky. The prosecution claimed that they had thrown several other cases, along with firearms, into a roadside ditch along the way, charges which both denied. They were found guilty of transporting liquor and sentenced to ninety days in jail; their vehicle was impounded. Jimenez, the report stated, would be deported upon completion of his term. His claim that he was an American citizen was dismissed. He had no evidence to offer in the matter.

When Lyn went to collect her photocopies the curator surprised her by asking, 'Oh, you have a special interest in the Kaminski case?'

'Well, not really,' she said, 'just gathering information for a family member.'

'Oh,' the woman said, 'because there's more. Quite a bit.'

'Really?' She glanced at the clock. The place would be closing before long.

'Shortly after the war,' the woman said. 'I only remember because I had a student researching the period a few weeks ago. I think it was early 1946. Would you like me to find the reels? You should just have time to go through them.'

It took Lyn less than an hour to go through the relevant pages. What she discovered, and what she had copied for her, was going to blow Steve's mind. She couldn't wait to get back to Chadron and show him.

SHE ENTERED the Olde Main to find a few of the locals already at the bar. Jeannie was busy at the far end signing in some new arrivals. Glenn was sitting with Seb and Tina. There were another couple of people with them that she hadn't seen before.

'Any idea where Steve might be?' she asked.

Glenn shook his head. 'He went to see his sister, didn't he? Maybe he's still there.'

'No, he's back,' Seb said, nodding towards the side door. 'I seen his truck, right out front.'

Lyn had parked around the side 'Oh,' she said.

'Mebbe he's in his room,' Seb suggested.

'Oh, okay.' Lyn hesitated. She wondered whether she should wait for him to come down.

'Nothing to stop you calling on him,' Tina said, lifting a bottle of beer to her mouth. 'You know, just go knock on his door.' She turned and grinned at Lyn, placed her bottle on the bar and made a rapping gesture with her right hand. 'He could be sitting there right now, waiting to hear that little tap tap tap.'

Lyn returned her stare. 'Listen,' she said, 'do you have anything better to do than trying to provoke people?'

'Guys,' Glenn said. 'C'mon now.'

Tina put down her beer and held her hands up. 'Hey, lighten up, for chrissake. I'm just making a suggestion.'

'Well,' Lyn said, 'maybe it isn't such a bad one after all.' She gathered up her bag and coat and went round the back of the bar. As she walked up the stairs she heard laughter. She shrugged it off. Small towns, she told herself.

Outside Steve's door she stopped and looked at her watch. Five thirty. What if he was napping? Oh hell, this couldn't wait. She gave the door a couple of sharp knocks. At first there was no answer. She tried again. Nothing. She tried a third time, and was about to give it up when she heard a muffled, 'Okay okay, who is it for chrissakes?'

'It's me, Lyn.'

He half opened the door. He seemed drowsy. 'Yeah?' he said. 'Whaddaya want?'

'You okay?' she asked. 'Something happen?' His hair was tousled, and there was a wet stain down the front of his shirt. His eyes were half closed and he seemed unsteady on his feet.

'Nothing's up,' he said. 'I'm doing fine.'

She smiled, tentatively 'I've just come back from Valentine - the library. I made a couple of really interesting discoveries.'

'Well, bully for you.'

She could smell the booze on him now. 'Look,' she tried, 'it involves your family - in the old days.'

Steve put out a hand to support himself against the door-frame. As he spoke his head was nodding, slowly. 'My family, huh?'

'Yes, I was in the newspaper archives and - '

'Listen,' he interrupted, and now his eyes were wide and looking right into her eyes, and she could see they were bloodshot. 'My family's nothing but a buncha fucked-up losers and most of them's dead in any case, so why the hell . . .?' He broke off, wiped his mouth with the back of his hand and leaned towards her. 'Look, do yourself a favor, will ya, and back off. Just – go back to your damned research. I mean, good luck with whatever it is you're doing, but leave me and my family out of it, okay?'

She took a step back, half fearing that he could stumble and fall against her. 'I'm only trying to help you. '

'Help me what?' He lurched towards her, a look of genuine menace in his eyes. She glanced along the landing, at the same time reaching in her bag for the key to her room.

'I thought you wanted to find out about . . .' She tailed off. 'Okay, okay.' She stepped back onto the landing. She needed to end this.

'Whatever I want, I don't need no help from a fucking airhead professor. Ya got that?'

'Yeah,' she said, 'I got it.'

He looked at her, a steady, unblinking gaze, then backed away into his room, swinging the door firmly in her face. She stood there a moment or two, trembling. She wanted to shout something back, but she wasn't sure what. Instead, she threw herself forward and kicked the door, twice.

Safe in her room she fought back tears of hurt, anger and rage. She'd gone to see Steve in a mood of unguarded joy and been casually slapped down, as if she were a fly on the back of his hand. While she was mad at him, she was also angry with herself. She prided herself on being able to spot a boozer, but she'd managed to kid herself with this one. She'd told herself Steve was just a guy who liked a drink, and what was so bad about that? She used to be like that herself. Sociable. And so she'd dropped her guard. Idiot.

Why did she waste so much energy persuading herself to be reasonable, not to pre-judge people? Over the years she'd tried to learn never to lay herself open to that kind of assault, yet here she was, still willing to lower her guard – and why? Because she'd taken the trouble to listen to someone else's story, and gotten interested. Because this guy, sober, seemed okay. And look at the result. There was a rage too, that this man she was trying to help was no different from her ex - a slave to alcohol and the moods it brewed up. Which meant he was weak. But as soon as that word - weak - entered her head she was asking herself the question, So what does that make me? She knew she really ought to have passed the point of being stung by the words of a mere drunk. She knew, from her marriage, that nothing said under the influence of booze meant a damned thing; and yet at the same time it meant everything.

She glanced around, at her papers, neatly arranged on the table, and her books, lined up on the shelf above her bed, the working tools of the committed scholar. What was the point? What was it all for? All this trying to make sense of the lives of people long dead and she couldn't even spot the danger standing right in front of her. A boozer. At least she'd had the good sense to stop drinking once and for all after the divorce. Because sure as hell, if this had happened fifteen years ago she would've been on her way to the liquor store right now to buy herself a good night's sleep. Instead, she kicked off her shoes, lay back on the bed and wrapped the cover around her shaking frame.

16

It didn't take Steve long to get his things together. The sooner he got the hell out of this place the better he was going to feel. Just a couple of trips down the side stairs, and he had everything stowed in the back of the truck. Before he left his room for the last time he pulled out a bunch of twenty-dollar bills and stuffed them in his pocket before securing the fanny pack about his waist. The weight of it in his hand reassured him. Then he went down to the bar, where Jeannie was mixing drinks for a young couple. He stood waiting.

'She find you okay?'

Steve turned around. It was the woman Tina. 'Who?' he asked. 'Who you talking about?'

'Your friend Lyn. She was looking for you.'

'Yeah,' he said, and turned away. No point in encouraging her.

'Ah. That's okay then.'

He spotted Glenn, who held up a hand in greeting and said, 'How's your new toy?'

Steve couldn't think what he meant, and didn't answer.

'The cassette player,' Glenn said.

'Oh, that.' Steve shrugged. What did he expect with a machine rescued from a dumpster or someplace? 'Chewed the damned things up,' he said. 'Twisted all to hell.'

Glenn exhaled, puffing his cheeks. 'Hey, sorry to hear it. Guess that's why we all loved CDs when they came along.' Steve hardly heard the remark. He was watching Jeannie. All he wanted right now was to pay up and check out. But Glenn carried right on. 'You want me to see if I can fix it for you?'

Steve took a good long look at him before he answered. Was the man trying to be helpful, or just plain nosy? 'Okay,' he said at last. 'But I'm busy right now. Maybe call by tomorrow.'

'Any time, buddy. I ain't going anywhere.'

Steve turned and saw that Jeannie was now looking at him, her eyebrows raised.

'Yeah,' he said. 'Listen, I'm taking off.'

'Home? No, you mean the State Park, right?'

'Yeah. I need a change of scene.'

'And when you planning to go?'

'Right now. Before it gets dark. Meant to check out this morning, but . . . Listen, just tell me what I owe.' He reached into his jeans pocket and pulled out the cash.

'You sure you're okay to drive?' Jeannie asked. She was looking him right in the eye and he didn't like it.

'Yeah, I'm fine,' he said.

Jeannie stood there, still looking at him. 'You're quite certain?'

'Okay, maybe I could do with a coffee.'

'Just don't want you getting pulled over, is all.' She was already at the hot-plate, filling a mug for him. 'If you want to hang around till you feel better…'

'Yeah,' he said. 'Yeah, sure.'

While he drank the coffee Jeannie wrote him out a bill.

He didn't bother to check the details, just handed over the cash. He wanted to be on his way. It was a familiar feeling, this urgent need to move on, right this minute, to go someplace where nobody was around to offer advice, apply pressure, ask awkward questions. But he knew Jeannie was right. He wasn't fit to drive just yet. He accepted a refill, which he took to the far end of the bar, away from the regulars.

It was about an hour later that he left. He drove the short distance to Safeway, where he bought a few groceries, ice, beer, some firewood, coffee. He remembered at last to buy a replacement charger for his phone. He'd given his number to Lejla and then clean forgotten about it. Before he left town he filled up with gas. Turning out onto Highway 20 he was almost blinded by the sun, now sinking toward the western horizon.

At the junction he swung onto 285, heading south. He put his foot down, and opened the windows. Within a mile or so the scenery started to change. Rolling hills, occasional bare rocks, pines that scented the cool evening air. He eased back on the gas, remembering what Jeannie had said.

He remembered riding a horse in these hills, way back when he was in high school. He had a friend lived south of the town. One summer he invited Steve over for a few days. They camped in the hills. Ricky fetched along a couple of mounts from his parents' place, and a third to carry their gear. Steve had never camped out before. Short of an occasional picnic beside the Niobrara and the swimming parties at Smith Lake he had rarely explored the country beyond his immediate surroundings. It was, he guessed, the lack of shelter, the inescapable nakedness of the rolling grassland that drove him always to town. This was a more welcoming, friendly kind of country, so different from the Sandhills with its warm yellow rocks jutting out from the hillsides, the shade afforded by its trees, its occasional bluffs. He'd seen his first mountain lion up there, and the memory had stayed with him. He'd gone out alone one early morning, leaving his buddy to sleep. He'd climbed to a rocky outcrop and paused to take in the view when he spotted it prowling along an adjacent ridge, barely a hundred yards from him. As he took out his binoculars to get a better look, it slipped quietly over the edge and vanished.

Steve closed the window on the past and concentrated on the road ahead. As far as he was concerned, he'd dealt with all that years ago. He knew the precise shape, the color, even the taste of those times. Knew damned well what they meant to him. Didn't need memories like that to challenge his view of the past.

The State Park was almost deserted. He'd expected as much this early in the year, especially midweek. As he cruised around the perimeter of the campground he counted just three motor-homes. The only sign of life was a TV flickering through a louvred window, the dying embers in a barbecue pit sending up a thin curl of smoke.

He found a spot in a far corner and backed in. Behind him and to either side was a grassy ridge with a few trees scattered across it. In front was a circle of unoccupied sites, well shaded by tall pines. He pulled out a folding chair from the back of the truck, gathered a few dry sticks and lit a fire in the pit. As the flames climbed, yellow and eager, he arranged a few logs around it. Later, when it was good and hot, he would slap a steak on. Meanwhile, he could sit, and think. The dying sun was peeking through the low branches. One or two insects were darting around, but the temperature was dropping rapidly; they would soon be gone. He went to the truck, pulled out a thick jacket and a woollen hat then took out the bag of groceries, grabbed a beer and squatted down beside the fire.

Maybe he should have come out here sooner, he thought. Then he wouldn't have got tangled up with the woman Lyn. Would never have set foot in Chadron in any case, but for that snowstorm. Here he could think more clearly. That was how it usually worked for him. Around people he so easily got confused. And yet he knew he needed company once in a while.

The fire crackled and drew his gaze. A distant peal of laughter coming from one of the motor-homes started him thinking. It was a woman's voice, musical, and he found himself wondering who she was and who she was with, what she looked like. He knew from his experiments with telephone dating that you could never judge a woman by her voice, but that didn't stop him trying to picture her, and to wonder. Was he, despite the ease he felt in his own company, actually lonesome? He always told himself that when he retreated into himself he was going to a safe place, into sanity and clear-headedness. But was he? Or was he, as Bonny had said, simply running away, wary of engagement, frightened that the truth might leap out and ambush him?

Well, in the end it was she who left. Then wrote and gave him notice to quit. The house, after all, was in her name. So what gave her the right to preach at him?

Steve went and picked up a long stick from under the pines. He poked and stirred the fire. The logs were starting to catch. With his boot he shoved them closer together. He liked tending a fire, always had. He stood up stiffly and stretched his arms above his head before strolling around the neighboring sites where he picked up a few old, charred sections of log. Plenty now to keep him going for a night or two. From the back of the truck he pulled a light metal grille, tapped it against the trunk of a pine tree to shake off a few bits of dirt, then put it to one side, ready. He opened another beer and sat, waiting. Through the trees he could see a fat moon rising, pale red. Away in the hills a coyote yipped once, twice, and then was quiet.

The woman Lyn. Christ, how had that happened? He knew she was only trying to help. And the truth was he was on the point of liking her. Then this. Goddam it, she just chose the wrong time to come banging on his door. Bad enough to hear his mother's voice like that, but all those revelations about her past: who wants to hear that his own mother was some kind of hooker? And then Lyn comes bounding up, grinning and eager like a frigging pup and wanting to tell him about his family, about his own goddam past.

The flames had died down. He had the grille set over the glowing coals. He laid the steak on it, then opened a tub of potato salad.

Well, he'd most likely seen the last of her. Couldn't blame her if she just took off. She said she had plans to visit Lincoln, didn't she? Women come and women go.

He turned the steak. In places it had stuck to the grille and he had to use a knife to free it. The fact was, she'd told him things that had him questioning what he knew about his family. All that business about the Poles. And the stories she'd shown him, written by a woman his old man had pursued for years. Part of him wanted to shove everything back in the box, to forget all these complications. What purpose did they serve? But part of him resisted, wanted to chase these new leads, hunt down an alternative truth. That damned woman had unsettled him - that was the fact of the matter. And now he'd got sucked in by these tapes. What else was he going to unearth?

The steak was done. As he ate Steve thought over his options for the next day. He had to get back to Wanda. See if he could get any sense out of her. Yeah, that was it. Get the tapes fixed and go see what she made of them.

He had one more beer before setting off to find the shower block and set up his phone with the new charger. Then he sat a little longer. He took out his harmonica and tried to get a tune out of it. But he never had managed, and doubted that he ever would. It was just an idea he'd had, years ago, that it would be a neat thing to be able to do.

He let the fire die and turned in for the night.

17

Lyn stayed in her room that evening. She didn't even go out for supper. She felt no hunger, just a dull, bruised sensation in her heart. That, and a quiet rage. Only slowly, as fatigue set in and her anger abated a little did she have any inclination to start making plans. She needed to be out of here. That was clear to her. The last thing she wanted was to run into that sonofabitch Steve - and God alone knew when he would pack up and go. So how about Lincoln? Why not give herself the pleasure of an excursion? Sure, it seemed a little extravagant, crazy even, to be going all that way only a few short days after her long drive across the state. But the capital had always been on her list.

Circumstances change, she reminded herself, and you have to adapt. And if there was one thing she needed to hang onto right now it was the pleasures and satisfactions that had been presented to her by this gift of time. Whatever else happened, she needed to nurture the joyous feeling in which this whole project was cocooned. So she would go to Lincoln, spend a few days there, dig around in the Sandoz archive, check in with her contact at the State Historical

Society. The Center up at the College, that could wait. She'd come back to it refreshed, ready to try again. Besides, who could say what new material she might have unearthed by then?

She didn't sleep well. Never did when she was troubled, or excited. And the fact that she planned to be up at six, she just knew she would wake up every hour or two to check that she really had set the alarm clock.

She was on the road a little after seven and driving south. Her immediate destination was Alliance, where she would pick up Highway 2. She had always had fond memories from that earlier trip, back in '93, when she followed its gentle undulations more than two hundred miles from Grand Island to Hyannis. It was a relaxed, easy ride through seemingly endless crop and grasslands. Next to no traffic, just the occasional company of the mile-long freight trains carrying coal along the tracks that paralleled the highway for long stretches. 'If ever you want to understand how huge and empty Nebraska is,' she'd tell friends back home, 'take a trip along Highway 2.'

By the time she made Thedford it was midday. She stopped to buy a sandwich and ate it at the wheel. She had seen on the map that there were picnic areas in the forest outside Halsey, and that was where she broke for a brief nap, parking in a patch of shade, tilting her seat back and placing a silk scarf over her face. Twenty minutes later she was back on the road, only stopping to stretch her legs in the square at Broken Bow before setting her sights on Grand Island. From there it was a straight ninety minutes along the interstate to the capital.

She'd got a good deal at a chain hotel in the downtown area, a rare treat for her. Generally if she had to go away she'd stay in cheap motels, or sometimes a friend's sofa, but at this time she knew she needed to treat herself kindly. By three in the afternoon she'd found the place, checked in, and was on foot in the city, feeling light of step and mentally unburdened. She carried nothing more than a camera and a notebook in a hessian bag draped over one shoulder. In the warm sunshine it felt like being on vacation, and maybe she was.

Her first stop was the Capitol, just three blocks away. She'd seen its majestic limestone tower from way out on the interstate, twenty miles before she reached the city. Approaching the enormous building, she looked up at its gold-tiled dome, some four hundred feet high and topped by a huge bronze statue. Entering, she immediately felt awed. In every direction were huge enclosed spaces, cathedral sized, with monumental stonework and ornate tiling, a kaleidoscope of images and symbols harmoniously integrated.

On an impulse she joined a party setting out on the final conducted tour of the day. She followed her guide in a daze of wonder as he led a straggling line of ten or twelve through the foyer to regroup under the towering rotunda. They took an elevator to the fourteenth floor, went out onto the stone parapet to take in the views that stretched over the city and the flat croplands that surrounded it, reaching out to far horizons. Lyn was close to being overwhelmed – by the size and scale of the building, the variety of its architecture and decoration, the opulence of its very materials. She felt the power of the messages implied in the artwork or explicitly set out in the words carved in stone, from the sober reminder that *The Salvation of the State is Watchfulness in the Citizen* to the calming reassurance of the Navajo song:

In Beauty I Walk
With Beauty Before Me I Walk
With Beauty Behind Me I Walk

Even as she followed the guide and tried to take in a steady stream of information, she knew it would take more than one visit for this magnificent building to reveal its more subtle meanings. But two images of that first visit had already taken root in her mind. One was a pair of tall mahogany doors. She hadn't expected to see here, in a Midwestern state, such a bold and unequivocal recognition of the area's Native past. Guarding the entrance to the eastern legislative chamber were the carved forms of a man and a woman in full tribal regalia, standing under a cruciform tree of corn-stalks, both of them looking up at what she could only assume was a thunderbird. The image reminded her of Mari's work with, for and about the Native Peoples, her advocacy for their cause, her lobbying of government offices in defence of their rights.

The other image that would stay with her was the bust of her heroine in the Nebraska Hall of Fame. Seeing Mari's familiar face there, cheek by jowl with authors of the stature of Willa Cather and John G Neihardt, with Lakota chief Red Cloud and the brash showman she held in such contempt, William F Cody, Lyn considered the possibility of grabbing a stool, of climbing on and reaching up to whisper a congratulatory word in Mari's bronze ear. Then she walked on, smiling at her own whimsy.

Outside in the late-afternoon sunshine, she decided to circle the entire Capitol complex, to view the building from each side in turn, to get a true appreciation of its size and scale. She soon found herself looking along across 14th towards J Street, where Mari once lived, and crossed the road to take a closer look. 1226, the house that had been Mari's home for twelve years, was no longer there. In its place stood an office building. But that didn't really matter to

Lyn right now. What she got from simply standing there was an understanding of just how close Mari had lived to the heart of the expanding city in the 1920s and '30s, how she had been able to watch, over a full decade, as the ambitious vision of the Capitol's architect was realized, step by step, culminating on the day they brought in a crane and hoisted the stylized figure that is *The Sower*, thirty-two feet tall and cast in bronze, and placed it on top of the tower.

From the Capitol area she walked the several blocks to the Haymarket, once a warehouse district fed by the railroad, now a place of bistros and coffee shops and arty retail outlets. She visited a photographic gallery and spent half an hour looking through a collection of gorgeous Plains landscapes, but although she was tempted she didn't buy. Maybe, she thought, she'd find time to capture her own images of places that mattered to her.

Being in no particular hurry, she called in at the depot and fantasized briefly about taking a train to the west coast, or back to Chicago some time. She was feeling better as afternoon gave way to evening and the streets started to fill with workers heading for home or for one of the many bars and cafés around the area. After the previous day's troubles she was getting back to that state of mind when all manner of things seemed possible. Not far from the depot she found a place where she could linger over a coffee, then called in at a used bookstore, but her initial excitement at the prospect of browsing amongst their western Americana gave way to a sudden weariness. Hungry now, she went in search of food and chose a Mexican restaurant. After she'd eaten, she hiked back to the hotel, feeling blissfully tired, fit only to immerse her weary bones in a bath. When she got into bed she slept, as she had hoped she would, for nine hours straight.

18

Steve awoke with a sore head. He had expected it, and he knew it was his own damned stupid fault. It was a cold morning and his breath came in clouds. He crawled out from under his blankets in the back of the truck and threw on every warm thing he possessed, then his boots. His arthritic foot was already making its ritual morning protests, sending out spasmodic darts of pain that found an echo in his right knee as he swung himself around and slid to the ground a little too abruptly. He found himself thinking about his father, some fifty years ago, constantly reminding Steve that he was 'not as young as I used to be.' He shook off the thought, even as another of the old man's sayings picked up the theme. 'Damn me if I don't sound like your Grandpa already.'

He climbed a few yards up the grassy bank and took a leak. Back at the fire-pit he reached out and stirred the ashes with his boot, raising a tell-tale wisp of smoke. He threw on a handful of dead pine needles. They caught readily, and he gathered a few sticks to build it up. Twenty minutes later he had a pan of water coming to the boil. He shook a good dose of coffee into a tin mug, poured water over it, extinguished the fire with what remained in the pan, then walked up the low hill, high enough to catch the rays of the sun that would be appearing above the horizon any minute now.

He sat on a flat rock, and shivered as the chill cut through his jeans. A darting movement caught his eye and he turned in time to see a chipmunk skitter away behind a rotting stump. He hunched forward, his gloved hands wrapped around the mug, and breathed deep the fragrance of the coffee. His mind turned to thoughts of the day ahead.

Like it or not, he had to get back to Wanda. He'd come a hell of a long way to see her. After all, she was the point of the whole damned trip. She'd paid for it, and he was allowing himself to get distracted. But he wasn't making the drive to Gordon until he'd got that damned tape unscrambled. Maybe listened to it too. He needed to find out what was on there.

The sun was almost up now, its first rays touching the tree-tops above him. He sat for another fifteen minutes, watching the golden light work its way down towards the ground. He savoured every last drop of his brew, then threw the grounds in a wide arc across the earth. After checking that the fire was truly dead, he straightened out his bed and got into the cab of the truck.

IN CHADRON he headed for the little diner he'd adopted, out along the highway west of town. It was still barely eight o'clock, so he took his time over ordering. He had his copy of *Old Jules* with him and sat reading for a while. He was around halfway through the book now. He'd read of the Swiss pioneer's battles with the Sandhills weather, with the land itself, with the cattlemen; of his court battles with the owners of the Spade ranch, his neighbors, and the unfortunate women who married him. And here at last the author was making her first appearance. Old Jules' fourth wife, the long-suffering Mary, had given birth to two boys, and now came a girl-child, christened Marie. As he read, he frowned, puzzled that the author would change the order of the children, make the boys older. And why the different spelling of her name? Well, she must have had her reasons. He read on.

Two pages and barely three months later the baby girl was crying in the night and her father, livid at having his sleep disturbed, was whipping her 'until she lay blue and trembling'. Steve was finding it hard to credit that the same child would one day write this balanced, sober, generous account of her father's life. Why, he asked himself. What would motivate a person to do that?

He laid the book face down on the table and looked out of the window, his face reflecting the puzzlement he felt inside. How the hell did this all happen? How did a woman who had suffered at the hands of this monster come to write about him without rancor, without anger, without passing judgement? Where was the rage? The hatred? The desire for revenge? Steve had never had children of his own. Sure, he'd had a hand in raising Bonny's three, but he would never claim to know all the trials of parenthood, certainly not the hard years of babyhood and infancy. Even so, he knew, as sure as he knew his own name, that if he'd come across a man treating a kid like that - a babe in arms, for chrissake - he would have beaten the crap out of him. The guy should have been locked away. No wonder, he thought as he turned the pages, that the young Marie of the story 'retreated into fancy'. Had she ever fully emerged, he wondered?

He wasn't sure he wanted or needed to read any more about this detestable man, although it went against the grain with him to leave a book unfinished. He knew, however, that he would persevere with Mari's biography. He wanted to know more about his father's one-time sweetheart. The thought occurred to him that during this period that he'd been reading about – this month and year, May 1896 – his own father had been born, just a few miles away, and that this brute of a man who had thrashed his own baby had once shaken hands on a deal with his beloved grandfather. The thought both drew him in and repelled him. On the one hand he wanted to walk away from this journey of discovery and spare himself whatever horrors lay in wait. On the other he knew he must proceed, albeit warily, with eyes shielded. There was a connection there that he could not loosen.

It was just after nine when he showed up at Glenn's place. He turned down the offer of a beer and Glenn seemed to get the message that he was in a hurry. They went to a little workshop in the rear of the garage. There were all kinds of electronic bits and pieces in there, and a workbench, complete with a vise.

He watched as Glenn teased out the first few inches of twisted tape, slowly, patiently. 'Okay,' he said, 'I'm gonna have to cut it free now. Once it's wound around the heads it's the only way. But don't worry. I got a little splicing gizmo somewhere.' He laughed and added, 'But you can use scotch tape. It works. All you hear is a little hiccup.' A minute or so later he was holding up a skein of twisted brown tape, looped over his outstretched arms. 'Course, it'll be a little jumpy through this section, but if I rewind it good and tight . . .'

'That's okay,' Steve said. 'Just do your best. I appreciate your help.'

Glenn had found the splicer and was already at work. 'So what's on here?' he asked. 'Favorite albums from long ago?'

'No,' Steve said. 'It's an interview with my father. Years ago, before he died.'

'Oh shit. I didn't mean to . . .'

'No reason why you should know,' Steve said. 'My sister recorded it. Did one with our mother too.'

'Wow. How old?'

'How old what?'

'The tapes. When did she record them?'

'Good question. When were people using cassettes? Some time ago now, isn't it?'

'They stopped making them around the millennium,' Glenn said. He studied the cassette in his hand. 'But looking at this, I'd put it at early eighties? Late seventies?'

'That would make sense,' Steve said, taking the tape that Glenn handed him. 'So is that it? You fixed it?'

'Done my best. Just a matter of trying her out. And keeping your fingers crossed.'

'Okay. Well, thanks for your help.' Steve was already moving towards the door.

'You gonna be back in town any time soon?' Glenn asked.

'Maybe. But I checked out of the hotel.'

'Yeah, Jeannie said.' Glenn watched as Steve got into the cab. 'Well, maybe we'll get to crack a beer or two sometime.'

'Maybe we will,' Steve said, then drove off.

19

Lyn was up early and hurrying through the doors of the State Historical Society just minutes after it opened. She had decided to start her work here by going through old copies of the Lincoln newspapers, starting in the fall of 1919 when Mari, newly divorced and looking to make a fresh start, left her Sandhills home and came to the capital with her Cousin Rosalie. Lyn hoped that scrolling through these back numbers would give her a flavor of the place and the times, a background against which to view and assess this young woman, fresh from the frontier, who would further her education, learn to be a writer and indeed, find literary success, during her two decades in the city.

Lyn didn't consider herself any kind of historian. She'd avoided the subject as much as she could through high school and university. It wasn't that she had no interest in the past. She did, but in her experience most history courses dwelt on politics and international relations, on leaders and power-mongers, almost exclusively male. History only really grabbed her when it was about what she thought of as real people living real lives. That was why she'd been so enthralled by the Little House books as a youngster. They seemed to tell her what life was actually like in those days - at home, in the woods and fields, or on the streets of a small frontier settlement, for mothers and children, rather than dwelling on events in the corridors of power, or the battlefield, on the lives of men. So she always had some idea of her country's most treasured story about itself, and thanks to her parents, and the various books they'd had around the house, the kinds of serious TV they watched and the stories they told her, she had a broad appreciation of how the twentieth century was shaped.

She understood something of the significance to the older generation of the monolithic events that overshadowed their young lives: the two world wars, the Great Depression and the explosion of prosperity that was ushered in by the nuclear age. Like Steve, she'd been born to a father of mature years. Her grandfather had fought in Europe in 1917-18, had found himself unemployed within a year or two of his return and readily embraced the opportunities afforded by the New Deal, working on Federal projects, often far away from home. That was an experience that had deeply affected his political stance.

Her father, born in 1924, was of an age to serve in the final stages of the next war, fighting his way through France and Germany in the aftermath of the D-Day invasion. He stood against any form of political extremism but, unlike so many people of his generation, he was a strong opponent of the Vietnam war. As for Lyn's mother, she had grown up a country girl in southern Illinois, a town called Carbondale where her father had run a hardware store. She had gone north to college and later joined the Peace Corps, teaching primary skills to the children of farmers on the slopes of the Chilean Andes. That was where she met Lyn's father. By the time the couple returned to the States, they were married and expecting their first and only child.

Despite this inheritance, despite the story about bootleggers that she'd discovered in Valentine, Lyn was taken aback, when she started browsing through the Lincoln papers of eighty and ninety years previously, by the number of column inches dedicated to stories about Prohibition. This was not a topic that had been discussed by her parents. She knew little about it. She vaguely associated it with tough-guy gangsters and their molls, as portrayed in the old black and white films she'd watched on late-night TV as a teenager.

Now, she found herself reading almost daily accounts of the crimes and characters generated by that bizarre experiment. In Lincoln, it seemed, speakeasies were being raided by the police with monotonous regularity, and the people involved were appearing in court to receive what seemed very lenient sentences. Thirty days in jail; a fine of $25. There were stories of high-speed car chases, pictures of axe-wielding agents destroying barrels of beer, rumours of corruption, and the naming of people who were well known to be involved in bootlegging but appeared to be beyond the reach of the law.

Lyn found all this intriguing, the reported exploits of the law-breakers entertaining. Some of these people engaged in illicit activity had become celebrities for a public who frequented underworld bars and night clubs for the sheer thrill of it, it seemed. They reminded Lyn of the self-conscious delight the pot-smokers of her own generation took in being, as they saw it, subversive. She read about the range of establishments that were being raided, from industrial-sized affairs in the city to makeshift stills in rural outbuildings, and as she did so, she thought again about the Sandoz' neighbor who, by Caroline's account, ran a still just over the hill from Old Jules' orchard place. Was that the guy Clouser, or someone else? Maybe everyone was at it, even Jules himself. Jules would presumably have been in the market for a little moonshine. He certainly considered it necessary to have liquor around the house, and would surely have resented the Volstead Act as yet another infringement of his liberties.

In order to make sure she wasn't imagining all this, Lyn checked her copy of *Old Jules* and, to her satisfaction, found several passages on the subject that she'd highlighted years ago, on first reading the book. She was reminded of the time the 'State booze hounds' were on the prowl, destroying a neighbor's still, of Jules' distaste for the bootleggers' product, yeasty and muddy. 'Damn the women and the Methodist preachers,' he said, and to ease the pain of his old age, went for 'the colorless bottle he kept in his safe'. She wondered where that came from, but the book offered no clue.

The work in the archive was tedious at times, and physically tiring. She took breaks, walking around the plaza, drinking coffee on a bench beside the fountains. One time she took an hour to browse in the Sheldon Museum of Art and found a single picture by Georgia O'Keeffe, an artist she'd known and loved since a long-ago visit to the Art Institute in Chicago. She was reminded that O'Keeffe, like the writers she'd studied for her project, was born on a farm, this one in Wisconsin, then had gone to the big city - New York - and only later become immersed in landscapes. But they were in New Mexico. Would that trajectory, she wondered, be worth noting as grist to her mill? Might it fit her thesis? Even as she started to consider the possibility she realized how easily she could get side-tracked if she wasn't careful.

She discovered too a solitary work by George Catlin, whose writings on the Northern Plains Indians she had devoured as an undergraduate. It was a simple, but such a delicate sketch of three Natives, two men and a woman, standing together. She had forgotten just how detailed were his observations of their dress and adornments; and she marveled now, as she had done thirty years previously, that he had produced such a record during what was in effect a camping trip, made on horseback in the 1830s. Reluctantly, she tore herself away. It was it was time to get back to the job in hand.

20

It was around eleven-thirty when Steve showed up at the care home. His sister seemed much more lively than the previous day. There was no sign of that brain-fog. It had dispersed, along with the apparent vexation with which she'd greeted him.

'And how's my brother, this fine morning?' She was sitting on a sofa. Beside her was a TV guide, her glasses and a book. Some sort of romance as far as he could make out.

'I ain't doing so bad,' he said. 'How about you? Got that pain on the run yet?'

'The pain comes and goes,' Wanda said. 'It's the damned fatigue that gets to you as much as anything. Boy, I hope you never have to go through this. That chemo kicks like a mule.'

'But you're done with that, right?'

'For now, yes. There's no reason why I shouldn't go home – if I could persuade my ever-loving brother to come spend a little time with me before I fade away.'

Steve was looking at the drip that fed pain-killers into her arm, the oxygen tank. 'But how the hell would I deal with all this crap?' he said.

'You don't have to,' she snapped. 'God, I've seen people wheeled out of here with a zillion tubes and wires stuck into them. It's modern medicine, Steve. Most of this I can deal with myself. I already said I'll pay for nursing help. When I get to needing it.' She slumped back in her seat and said, wearily now, 'Tell me, if you were dying, would you want to be in here, or somewhere that you loved to be?'

Steve didn't answer for a moment. Her question almost made him flinch, and he wasn't sure why. Finally he said, 'Maybe that's my problem with all this. I can't think of a place I want to be.'

There was a silence. Neither of them knew where to take it. After a while Wanda raised a finger towards her purse, which sat on the coffee table. 'Anyway, you gonna put my tapes back where you found them? Assuming you've quite finished with them, of course. What did you think - that I wouldn't notice?'

'Oh jeez, them.' Steve removed his coat and hung it on the back of a chair. He took the tapes from the pocket, and handed them to her. 'Wanda, you threw me a curve ball with those damned things, you know that?'

'Yes, and maybe I meant to. But that doesn't excuse you taking them away without asking.'

'You'd fallen asleep. We were halfway through the one with Mom on it. And then I saw the others in your purse. I figured on taking them back to Chadron and going through them in my own time.' He pulled his chair closer to her and sat down. 'Anyway, turns out I was doing you a favor.'

'Oh yeah? How's that?'

He held out the tape Glenn had mended. 'This,' he said.

She picked it out and looked at it. 'What about it?'

'It wouldn't play. It had gotten all screwed up.'

'Oh.'

'So I got someone to untangle it.'

'That's good. And you played it?'

'I changed my mind, Wanda. Maybe I got cold feet. Whatever, I decided I'd rather go through it with you.'

Wanda shrugged her shoulders. 'We can do that.' She turned over the cassettes one by one. 'It's been a long time since I made these.'

Steve looked at her. Sitting there with the sun on her face, she really looked like her old self this morning. She looked like their mother had done when she was young, and he felt closer to her than he had done in years. Quietly, he asked, 'What made you do it?'

'What, get them on record?'

'Yeah. I mean, what were you thinking?'

'Time ticking by. Dad getting frail. He'd stayed pretty fit into his eighties, and then he started to slip. You could see it. That moment when you suddenly realize people aren't going to be around forever, and I needed to get a few things straight.'

'And did you?'

'You'll see. If you can sit still long enough.'

'You ever played them back?' he asked.

'No. I made the records for posterity, not to comfort me in my old age. Maybe I still hoped you'd make a family of your own and they would hear it. Anyway, don't expect too much sweetness and light.'

'What about your kid? The one you had adopted. You ever get in touch with him?'

'Her, Steve. She was a girl.'

'Excuse me, her. You ever think about her?'

'Sure I do. Thought about trying to trace her more than once, but never followed it up. I reckoned it could have done more harm than good.'

'Ever wish you'd – I dunno, met someone and raised a family?'

'From time to time, yes. But no more than I've wished I'd taken a trip to Europe, or learned to play the piano. I guess I burned a lot of that energy training to be a teacher. That took me long enough.'

'How so?'

'You know me. I kept finding things to argue about. Two courses I quit, and then third time I managed to stick it out.' She sighed. 'Maybe we have that in common, that we always fall out with people.'

'I guess so. I could never work for a boss. Maybe it's a thing that afflicts farmers and ranchers. And their children. They teach you to be self-reliant and it turns you into someone who just can't stand to be told what to do.'

For a moment they both sat there, the past weighing on their shoulders. Then Wanda picked up the tape and passed it across to him. 'But I guess you're just busting to hear this. Aren't you?'

Steve slotted the cassette into the machine. 'That's not the word I'd use, but sure. If there's something to know I'm ready to hear it. I got as far as you saying you wanted to talk about this guy Jim. I wanna know where he fitted in.'

Wanda stifled one of her dismissive little laughs, which gave way to a rasping cough. She smothered it with a Kleenex, then dabbed at her forehead, which was moist with perspiration. 'Well,' she said, 'hold onto your hat.' Then she pressed PLAY and sat back on the sofa, her eyes closed.

'Okay, Dad, so let's talk about you and Jim, and how you got together.' This was the young Wanda, in her best schoolmarm voice, trying to make it sound like they were writing a Christmas card to a beloved aunt.

For the first time in half a lifetime Steve heard the old man's familiar voice, fainter than it used to be, and sounding weary, but unmistakable in its deep throatiness. 'Do we have to?'

'Dad, I told you. If you're really serious about getting Steve to come see you, this could be the way to . . .'

'Whoa there!' Steve's hand came down on the machine, feeling for the STOP button. Wanda opened her eyes, and gave him a questioning look. 'Are you telling me this was all cooked up to persuade me – what were you thinking? That you'd send me a goddam tape, the confessions of a bitter old man, and it would change everything? Just like that? Jesus, Wanda!'

'Take a deep breath, Steve. Just calm down. Always were on a short fuse, weren't you?' Then she gave him a hard, cold look. 'That why Bonny left, eh? The best woman you ever had?'

'Let's leave Bonny out of this, shall we?'

'You left home in a rage, Steve. You slugged your old man, remember? All but busted his jaw.'

'Busted my damned knuckle is what I did,' Steve said.

'I believe it. You were blazing. And I don't think you've ever put the fire out, have you? Maybe you never wanted to. You thought you'd figured it all out about Dad, and that justified your behavior.'

'He's your father, not mine,' Steve cut in.

'Yes, so we can forgive you for leaving when you did. Even the way you did. Twenty year olds behave like that.' She sighed. 'Especially when they feel hurt. Then they're supposed to grow up.' She held up a hand to stop him interrupting. 'Steve, you only knew half the truth. Not even that.'

'Is that a fact? And what about you? If you knew it all, why didn't you let me know?'

'Steve, we're talking about 1960 something. I was in the dark, same as you. Just had a couple of half-truths to chew on.'

'Right. Except there was Mom feeding you her lies.'

'Not lies, Steve. Just her version of things. She was trying to help me see it from her side. Look, when I started to hear Dad's story I figured you ought to hear it too. I thought maybe you'd understand. And forgive. Simple as that.' She waved a resigned hand at him. 'Okay, I have nothing more to say. Just do yourself a favor and listen to him. He was dying, Steve, and he knew it. He had no reason to hide the truth. Hear what he has to say, and then tell me you still hate him.' She reached across him, and started the tape again.

Her voice again: 'Just tell the story, Dad. Take your time. Tell it the way it happened.'

'Where do I to start? How far back you want me to go?'

'Well, how about you and Grandpa? Tell me about him. I mean, when you were a boy. How was it between you?'

There was a long pause, then the sound of Pete lighting a cigarette. 'What you gotta remember is, I was the youngest. The others always told me I got off light. I believe it's the same in every family. Because he was hard on them, no doubt about that. Things were okay at the beginning - that's what the boys said, anyways. I don't know what Nadia thought. After Mata drowned she moved out. Went to live in Valentine and got married. Had three sons. Only one of them stayed around. Became a sheriff's deputy, years later. Your grandpa liked that, having a lawman in the family. Then Mom died. It was around the time we moved out of the soddy. I was coming up to thirteen. She got a cold and it turned to pneumonia. I don't know that she ever got to live in the new place. I don't recall, but maybe she did. The old man was real proud of that house. He put everything he had into it. Everything.'

There was a long pause. They could hear Wanda helping him get comfortable, fixing him a drink.

'You want to rest up?' she said.

'No, I'm okay. What was I saying?'

'About how things were okay at the start with your dad.'

'Oh sure. And then Mom died. So on top of running the ranch we had to find for ourselves at home. We tried to tell your grandpa to hire a housekeeper but he said we couldn't afford it, which was a damned lie. And then of course, come 1917 my brothers had to go to war.'

'What do you mean, had to? They weren't drafted, were they?'

'Couldn't resist it, is what I meant to say. It was all going to be one big adventure. They were all fired up about it. Kept joking about the French girls they was going to meet. I was all set on going with them. Damned if I wanted to miss out - but Dad put his foot down. Said he needed one of us to stick around.'

'I thought it was because you'd lost an eye.'

'No, that was way later.'

'Ri-ight. Remind me how that happened.'

'We'll get to it. Thing about your grandpa is, he drove himself hard, and he expected other people to do the same. My brothers started to question the way things were. "This was his place, it was his choice - his dream, you might say, but it doesn't have to be ours." I know I heard Waldo say that more than once. It's why he went to California. He wanted to work regular hours, earn a wage and spend it on himself, not wait around to inherit the place when he was forty or fifty. I believe Pavel would've gone too, if he hadn't got blown to pieces.'

'So they went off to war, leaving you at home.'

'No, that's not the way it was. It was the other way around.'

'I don't follow.'

'I'd left home already, see.'

'Really?'

'Sure. I was down on the Gulf Coast, working for my living. Didn't I ever tell you about that?'

'No. When was this?'

'It would be 1914. Not long after Mom died. I'd just turned eighteen.'

'That's kinda young.'

'Those days, Wanda, you were expected to grow up quick. I wasn't that unusual.'

'But even so . . . And why the Gulf Coast?'

'You wanna hear the story? Or you wanna keep butting in?'

'Hey, excuse me.'

'I had this girl.' There was a long pause. Then, 'Not just any girl, as it turned out.'

'Ma-ri San-doz.' Steve said the words slowly and deliberately.

Wanda had had her eyes closed. They were wide open now and staring at him. 'You knew about her?'

Steve shook his head briefly and held a forefinger to his lips. Pete was talking again.

'Marie. Daughter of Old Jules Sandoz. You know, they lived just south of us. And of course she grew up to be the big-shot writer.' He fell silent again. Wanda was looking at Steve. 'Well? Did you?'

'No, I didn't know, not until a coupla days ago. Tell you about it later.'

On the tape, Wanda's younger voice resumed: 'You were sweet on her?'

'Oh yes.'

'How'd you get to know her?'

'Well, we all knew the Sandoz family, especially Old Jules. Every time his name came up your grandpa used to tell us how Jules had located him, helped him get a start. People had mixed opinions about him. To some folk he was just an ornery, dirty old sonofabitch. He was certainly dirty, I can vouch for that. Plain smelly, as I recall. Never saw him without his pipe. God alone knows what he put in it. But other people, and your grandpa was one of them, admired him, the way he'd stood up to the cattlemen. You know his own brother was shot dead by a hired gun? Right there on his front porch. He's buried out there in the Swiss graveyard.' A few seconds' silence. Then: 'Okay, where'd I get to?'

'You were going to tell me how you got to know his daughter.'

'Oh, right. Well, I had this colt I'd broken. I was out exercising him and I just ran into her. She was sitting on the grass, high up, overlooking her old man's place. Not much of a place at that time, just a shack or two. She had a book in her hand. I stopped and asked her where she was from and what she was reading. I was a pretty shy kid at that time, but she seemed glad of the company. Admired my little colt too. So we talked for a while before she had to run and do her chores.'

'So then what? You arrange a date or what?'

'You didn't date people in those days. Where the hell were you going to go? No, it was weeks before we met again, and after that, sure, we started to set a time to rendezvous, so yeah, I guess it was like dating if you wanna call it that. It always had to be out of sight of her place, of course. And things kinda developed.'

'So this was like a teen romance?'

'It felt like more than that. We were real close. Seemed to have the same fears, the same hopes. But yeah, we did all the things I guess young kids do. Sending each other - oh hell, I guess you'd call 'em love tokens. And letters. Carving our names on things, fence-posts mostly. Years later I read a story she wrote about a boy and a girl. Polish boy at that. He makes a garland of sweet peas . . . and I reckon that was little old love-sick me. Picked the flowers along the river and rode all the way out just to hang them around her pretty little neck. Not sure they were sweet peas, but . . . could've been.'

'So how long did this go on? The thing with Mari.'

'Till she started teaching school. It wasn't like she dropped me, just that she started taking longer to reply when I wrote her. And I was getting busier around the place.'

'I'd no idea about all this,' Wanda said.

'Why would you have? It's not a subject to talk about when you're married.'

'No, but I remember Mom flying into a rage, the time of Mari's funeral. When was that, exactly?'

'March 1966. In the snow.'

'Right. But why would Mom get so excited about a teenage crush? I mean, all that was way before you two got together. Why the big drama?'

'Because for me it never did end, and Irena knew it. I thought it had, but when Marie upped and married that Macumber guy, it all but destroyed me. I wrote and pleaded with her, but I never heard back. So I took off.'

'And that was when you went south?'

'Yeah. I was just heartbroken. Wasn't ever going to come back. Really didn't care what happened to me. Had no idea where I was going, although south seemed a sensible direction. I think I had a notion that Texas was the place to be. I tramped as far as the Burlington tracks, hopped a freight to North Platte. This was spring time, month of May. All I had was the clothes I stood up in, a hunk of bacon, a loaf of bread. One time I got so thirsty I drank from a puddle and made myself sick. Met a lot of hoboes, and boy they put the fear of God in me. Wild, crazy guys. Dangerous. Finally I fell in with one who acted friendly. He was heading Texas way. Said there was work to be had on the coast, and I figured I might as well head that way with him. Took us three days and I don't know how many different trains, but he got me there.'

'Wow. Sounds like some adventure.'

'Now it does. At the time I was mostly cold at night, thirsty in the daytime, and hungry the whole damned time. Frightened too. I mean, I watched guys fall asleep and drop off the train. Saw one go under the wheels and – just cut in half. Those trains just kept rolling. Then you'd end up in some yard and if you didn't make yourself scarce the yard bulls would beat the crap outa you. It was like war. There were a lot of desperate men. I just kept my head down and did what my buddy told me, and he got me as far as Houston. That's where I got lucky. Met Jim.'

'Was he hoboing too?'

'Nuh-uh. He was living with his uncle. Came up from Brownsville, down on the Rio Grande there. That was his hometown. He'd seen me skulking around, back of a railroad workers' cabin. I was hungry. Real hungry - the kind that hurts. He took me to his uncle's place and I got fed. Stayed there a few nights, then Jim said he was going to work on the fishing boats with one of his uncles, and why didn't I come with him.'

'So how long were you away altogether?'

'Close to four – no, three years.'

'And what about Grandpa?'

'I wrote home, time to time, let 'em know where I was. And one day I got a letter from Waldo. Pavel and him were going to sign up for the Army. I wrote back and told 'em to wait for me, and hopped a train northbound. Arrived home just before Christmas 1917. That's when your grandpa told me I had to stay. I said I'd see him in hell first, but my brothers backed him up. Most like they saved my life, thinking about it.'

'And you stayed through to the end of the war?'

'Yeah. I was always gonna wait until the boys returned. But of course only Waldo did.'

'Then what?'

'Well, Dad hadn't improved – in his attitude to us, I mean. Still thought he could work us like dogs and never pay us a nickel. Course, I ran a few head of my own, but you know what cattle prices are. Sometime you'll make a few bucks; other times nothing. And the work just never stops. Anyway, my brother didn't hang around long, and that left me alone with your Grandpa.'

'Why didn't you just head west, with Uncle Waldo?'

'Well, that was one idea I had. Once he got settled out there I was going to join him. Then I heard Marie had gotten divorced. Read about it in the newspaper and a few days later I ran into one of her brothers in town. He told me she'd gone to Lincoln, so I decided to go look her up. I still had most of the money I'd saved down south, so what the hell. I'd treat it like a vacation, buy myself a train ticket. Your grandpa raised hell, of course, but he soon found himself a hired man to take up the slack.'

'And did you find her, Mari?'

'Sure. Took a while, but I tracked her down. She was living with her cousin, Rosalie. They were taking classes. Shorthand typing, kind of thing.'

'So how did she react when you showed up?'

'Surprised, I'd say. She was seeing this guy, some kind of mechanic, and he was hanging onto her like a goddam leech. Not that she didn't seem pleased to see me, but the writing on the wall was plain as day: nothing doing.'

'Did you stay in Lincoln?'

'For a while. I went looking for a job, but I didn't see anything that appealed to me. You gotta understand, working on the boats doesn't prepare you for factories or slaughterhouses. We'd got used to going out a few days at a time, a week or two. Bring in a catch, go have a little fun for a few days, and start again. It was a loose kind of existence, and it suited me. I went and checked out the situation in Omaha. They had plenty of breweries, but of course they were about to be shut down. The Volstead Act.'

At that point there was silence for a while, with some muffled coughing, then Steve heard Wanda asking Pete if he was good to carry on. 'Maybe tomorrow,' he said.

Now Wanda glanced at Steve. 'You need a break?' she asked.

'I was gonna ask you the same thing.'

'I'm managing.'

So they continued listening to the tape. Wanda was reminding the old man where they'd got to the day before.

'Right,' he said, 'Lincoln. Well, I didn't stick around there too long. I mean, Marie was friendly enough. She told me that the mechanic guy was nothing much to her, but he could dance, and that was something she always loved. That and swimming. Roller skating too. She told me to write. I guess she was trying to ease the pain on me, but I reckon she could've tried harder. Wouldn't you say?'

Wanda gave a little laugh. 'Yeah. She could have. But maybe she was frightened of encouraging you.'

'Could be. Yeah, I can see that now. Well anyway, I was at a loose end by this time, and my money was running out. So I went back home, and there was a letter waiting for me.'

'Oh. From Mari?'

'No, not her. Jim. He was in North Platte, and he had something going. Wouldn't say what, but told me to get myself down there pronto.' Pete gave a quiet sort of chuckle. 'And that's how your law-abiding, tax-paying, Republican-voting papa became a wanted man.'

'Wanted? By who?'

Pete laughed, a proper warm laugh, something Steve

hadn't heard in fifty years. 'You never knew this, did you? Jim and me, we went into the liquor business.'

'Okay.' There was a pause, then Wanda said, 'But hey, that was illegal, wasn't it?'

'Well, of course it was. That was half the fun of it. Moonshine. Bootlegging. Paid pretty damned well.'

'Wow. No. I mean, the way Mom talked about you I thought you were just two regular railroad guys.'

'When she got to know us, we were. But that was a lot later, in the 1930s, after Prohibition was over. We'd had our fun by then - and paid the price.'

There was a long pause. Steve thought for a moment that the tape had seized up again, but it seemed Pete was just thinking.

'I tell you this,' the old man went on, 'serving time saved me from a criminal career. Although not Jim.'

'You were in prison?'

'Sure. Ninety days. That was enough for me. Jim seemed to take it in his stride. But boy, he made sure we got outta town fast.'

'What was the big hurry?'

'They wanted to deport him, and he wasn't sure the lawyer he hired was up to the job.'

'Hold on a moment, Dad. They wanted to deport your buddy? This is Jim you're talking about?'

'Sure. He was Mexican, see.'

Steve sat upright. Glanced at Wanda, whose eyes were closed. Mexican. The word sent a jolt through him. He wanted to stop the tape but couldn't.

'Yeah, name was Jimenez, but I called him Jim and it kinda stuck. His folk used to flit back and forth across the border, but he was born and raised on our side. Just never had any papers. Hell, nobody had papers. But if you looked

Mexican and spoke the language, they could treat you any way they pleased.'

'I never knew that. So he what, was on the run?'

'More or less. But once we were out of Lincoln he was in no danger.' There was a long pause, during which Steve found himself involuntarily holding his breath. Then Pete took it up again. 'But oh boy, you shoulda seen me and Jim in our prime. When they talk about the roaring twenties they ain't exaggerating.'

Pete was now more alive than Steve had heard him since those far distant days when they went from town to town together, to the auction sales, the livestock markets, the rodeos. Days when, for a few hours at least, Pete was everybody's best buddy, when he cracked jokes, told stories, slapped people on the back and was always invited to sit at their table in the diners they visited; when people stopped what they were doing and listened to what he had to say. And now Steve too sat and listened as this familiar voice described the adventures Pete had had, years before the man had ever thought of returning to his home place and raising a family; he described an entire other life that had remained obscured, barely even hinted at, in all the years of Steve's growing up. And here it was, served up fresh, vivid and sparkling with detail, told with a laugh that distorted Steve's face and twisted his gut.

It pained him to watch as scenes from this unknown life were re-enacted in the movie house of his mind. Pete described one adventure after another as two young men in double-breasted suits, homburg hats and co-respondent shoes accelerated away in a cloud of dust in their sleek roadster, leaving the Feds floundering in their wake; two young men holing up in hotel rooms across the Great Plains, counting out piles of dollar bills and sending down for champagne to melt the resistance of coy young flappers; two young men on a riverbank, fishing in their shirt-sleeves and laughing uncontrollably at all this easy money that came their way. Then two young men exchanging their neat suits for prison uniforms and thinking about whether it was all worth it.

Pete's final verdict? 'I wouldn't have missed any of it. You can say what you like about the good times and the bad, when we paid our debt to the law. But we were alive, living out our own dreams.'

THE TAPE HAD COME to end - the first side, at least. Steve sat and watched as his sister opened her eyes. Had she been listening to it all, or had she lapsed into semi-consciousness? She seemed dopy now, and her gestures in response to Lejla's questions when the young woman came to check on her were limp, compliant, weary.

'Time I was outa here,' Steve said.

'What you been doing to your sister, exhausting her?'

He couldn't be sure whether Lejla was joking or not. 'This thing ain't easy on either of us,' he said. 'Going over the past.' Steve waited, but Lejla didn't answer. She was busy preparing Wanda's medication, checking her pulse. 'Tell her I'll be back,' he said. 'In the morning.'

'Let's hope she's well enough,' Lejla said. 'I'm not sure this is good for her.'

21

Lyn's trawl through the Nebraska State Historical Society's newspaper collection was a slow process. Straining to read the decades-old typeface was hard on her eyes and made her shoulders ache. Around mid-morning she took a walk outside, strolling around the tree-lined streets of the Capitol area with the sun shining on the fat new buds.

As the day wore on she became less and less interested in her task. At times she asked herself what exactly she was hoping to find in these endless pages of news stories, most of which seemed less than earth-shattering. Was it enough just to steep herself in the period about which she would be writing? Did she really need to do that? She was acutely aware that she had come to Lincoln primarily in order to get over the unpleasantness with Steve. Chadron was where she really needed to be, searching for that missing manuscript. Perhaps it had been a mistake to drive all the way across the state.

She plodded on, gritting her teeth, eventually finding an occasional reference to Mari's circle of literary and artistic friends. But they didn't really tell her anything that she didn't already know from the biography. She did, however, establish a rapport with one of the archive staff, even to the extent of going to lunch with him in what was already her favorite part of town, the Haymarket.

Everett had studied Mari's work as an undergraduate and written a master's dissertation about her. As part of his researches he had spent a lot of time going through her papers in the University's special collections, in particular her personal correspondence. When Lyn brought up the subject of the missing manuscript he was quite firm in his opinion that it wasn't there.

'If it was, I would have found it. Trust me. I got to know that whole collection. And it's very well organized, everything neatly catalogued, and the curator there is extremely knowledgeable. Accommodating too. Always willing to help out.'

'Well, that's good to hear,' Lyn said. 'I'm planning on spending some time there later on. But what about the material at Caroline's place?'

'What do you mean?'

'I visited her one time - oh, this was way back in ninety-three - and she had just mounds of papers and books. I mean of Mari's.'

'Well, you know she moved out of there in the late nineties?'

'No, I didn't. I corresponded with her for a year or two, but in the end I managed to lose touch with her. I had a lot going on in my life around that time. Damn, I wish I'd managed to stay in touch.'

'Yes, that is a pity. Anyway, when she moved out they shipped a whole bunch of stuff to the Center. So I'd say that's where it ought to be.' Everett thought for a few moments, then said, 'But you know, I sometimes wonder whether Caroline didn't get a bit reckless and throw out more than she should have. It's just a hunch. I mean, there was such a lot of material, and she may have felt overwhelmed. Listen, when we get back I'll pull out an article for you. It's in one of the Sandoz Society's publications, *The Story-Catcher*. Just a short piece, but it might interest you. There's a little bit about her collection.'

Lyn was about to thank him when he added, 'A remarkable woman.'

'Mari?'

'I was thinking about Caroline. Good writer too, very good. Although she always compared herself to her sister and felt she didn't measure up.' He was quiet for a moment, then said, 'And when you think, there's her sister, dead and buried - what, forty-five years?'

'Exactly that,' Lyn said. 'It was 1966 she passed away.'

'And yet Caroline is still alive. Incredible, isn't it?'

'*No way!* Are you kidding?'

Everett shook his head and laughed. 'Didn't you know?'

'No, I didn't. I assumed she'd be long gone. I mean, what year was it she was born -1910?'

'That's right.'

'So she's like... a hundred!'

'And one.' He thought for a moment, then said, 'It was a very different world, wasn't it? Frontier period fresh in everybody's memory. Out there, I mean. You know, she was at one of the conferences I went to a few years ago, but I have to admit – same as you, I assumed she'd passed. Then last year she popped up in one of those smalltown newspapers, in Rushville or Gordon, I don't remember, but there she was, celebrating her hundredth birthday with the family. You want me to dig that out too? I should be able to find it easily enough.'

'Definitely. Wow, I never dreamed - I hadn't the faintest idea she was still going.'

'Well, I'm pretty sure she is or we would've read about it. I don't want to sound ghoulish or anything, but I keep a watch on the death notices. She hasn't featured yet.'

'Do you have any idea where she is?'

'Nope, but it'll most likely be in the newspaper piece if I can find it. Anyway, you'll be heading back to Chadron, won't you?'

'In a day or two.'

'Well, people there'll know.'

'I guess they will. Someone, at least.' Lyn sat shaking her head. 'Wouldn't that be something, if I could go talk to her again. I mean...'

'I guess it would, yes.' Everett smiled.

They walked back to the State Historical Society together and went up to Everett's office. It didn't take him long to find the *Story-Catcher* issue he'd mentioned. He left her with it and went back to his own office.

Lyn was intrigued to read that when Caroline left her beloved ranch in 1997 she sent no fewer than forty-four boxes and twenty-nine suitcases to the Center, as well as 'some furniture'. The collection, she read, included carbon copies of Mari's letters and 'multiple drafts of her books and short stories'. That tallied with what she had glimpsed in the basement that day in 1993.

As she cast her mind back she recalled asking Caroline about the time her sister decided she wasn't going to make it as a writer. She'd read about it in the biography. This was in 1933. Mari wasn't well, she was sick and tired of having her work rejected, she was bogged down in researching her father's life and she decided she was going to quit. The story went that she invited some friends round to her room, gathered up no fewer than seventy stories and burned the lot in a wash-tub in the back yard. Then she returned to the Sandhills.

When Lyn raised this story, Caroline looked at her as if she was being unspeakably naïve. 'My sister was always inclined to make dramatic gestures,' she said. 'Besides,' she added, 'she kept copies. It was all a performance.' So, Lyn wondered, was it possible that there was more than one copy of *Murky River*? Another draft? Maybe so. But leaving that aside, here was the clearest suggestion that the thing she was after would be up at the Center, somewhere in one of the unsorted boxes. That was where she really ought to be right now, not in Lincoln.

She decided she would pack up and go the very next morning.

22

'You're early!' Lejla looked surprised to see Steve, but her face lit up in one of her warmest smiles. 'It's good to see you. Wanda will be very happy.'

'You think so?' Steve was disconcerted at just how pleased he was to see this woman, the way she disarmed him, completely. The fact was, he was enchanted by her. She melted everything that was hard in him, instantly; everything that was cold, skeptical or bitter just started to peel away. There was a musicality to her voice, a warmth in her greeting, her unguarded pleasure in the happiness of others, that reminded him of only one other person in his life: Bonny. How had he let her get away? He actually shook his head as the question formed in his mind. And Lejla must have noticed the brief grimace of a man struggling to cloak himself anew in his protective armour.

Now the young woman frowned. 'She's not been good. The night staff have been worried about her.'

Steve stood there for a moment, unsure of himself. 'So . . . it okay to see her now?'

'Sure. She's a little more awake now. She told me about

yesterday, how you heard your father talking.' Your father. The smile again, like sunshine, even as the words slipped so easily from her tongue. 'That must be so wonderful for you both.'

'Yeah.' Steve could see that she genuinely believed that. He never knew how to handle the easy assumptions of people like her, that everyone loved their parents the way they might have done when they were three years old. Where did it come from? Surely from having received great gobs of uncomplicated love. Didn't they know that not everyone had that? Sometimes he felt contempt for their naivety, and sometimes pain, from having lost out on what for everyone else seemed to be a given, a universal experience of connection. In the case of someone like Lejla he felt particularly wretched. If things had been different, could he have shared his life with a sunny-tempered woman like her? Or still be with Bonny? Could he yet be bathing in the warmth of a perpetual smile such as the one that lit up Lejla's face, there in the reception area? It was a loss he preferred not to think about.

He found Wanda sitting with the cassette player at the ready. She looked a shadow of what she'd been the day before.

'How you feeling?' he asked.

'Not my best,' she said. 'Someone once told me old age isn't for wimps. I'd settle for being old ahead of this any day. But what about you?' She tapped a finger on the player. 'You want another dose of this?'

'I guess it's got me hooked. Jesus, Wanda, how much of all this did you know? I mean about the boot-legging - the time in jail? He ever mention that to you?'

'It was all new to me when we made the tapes. And there wasn't a lot of time left, as it turned out. I mean for discussing things. I never got to ask too many questions. He went downhill pretty fast.'

'Weren't you shocked?'

'Shocked?' Wanda let out a sort of 'pah' sound. 'When you're looking at a man the age he was, and he's talking about his two-tone shoes, about flappers and speakeasies, I didn't know whether to laugh or cry. It was like he was talking about some other guy, him and his plaid shirt and jeans, those black fingernails. When we played the tape yesterday, it brought it all home to me.'

'Brought what, exactly?'

'That he'd had this whole other life before he got together with Mom. Think about it. He was fifty when you were born. And he left home at – what, eighteen?'

'That's right.'

'It's a long time, Steve.'

'Thirty-two years.'

Wanda thought for a moment, closed her eyes, then said, 'Remember how he used to play those old records of his? Hank Williams?'

'Hell yes. I can still sing every damned word.'

'He sure loved old Hank, didn't he? And Hank lived quite a life. You know how old he was when he died?'

'Pretty young, I believe.'

'Twenty-nine. So Dad had plenty of time to live before he settled down.'

Steve looked at his sister. What was she doing, preparing him for more revelations? 'Let's play side two,' he said. 'Find out what else he got up to.'

'Go ahead,' Wanda said. 'But not too much. I get about an hour of feeling okay, if that. Then I'm done.'

'I can only take so much myself.' He had his finger poised over the machine. 'Okay to start?'

She nodded.

Pete took it up pretty much where he'd left off. He didn't say much about his short stay in jail. He talked instead about going home – and taking Jim with him.

'You mean to the ranch?' they heard Wanda ask. 'I thought you said you went to North Platte?'

'We did, after a few days. But first to the ranch. We needed to keep our heads down. There were people out there looking for us - particularly for Jim.'

'You mean the law?'

'Not the law so much. We weren't too worried about them. No, Jim had upset a bunch of folk all across the state, even a few over the Kansas line. He'd been creaming off more than his share. Y'know, the big operators may have been crooks but they ran a regular business. They had accountants and record-keepers. A shipment came in short, they'd wanna know why. And they soon figured out that Jim was someone to watch. Sure, he was a slick operator. Reliable, safe, one heck of a driver. He could be relied upon to bring home the bacon. Just that he liked to carve himself an extra slice, time to time. He said we deserved it. So yes, the heat was on. He knew his life was in danger.'

'And you?'

'Well yeah. I mean, Jim and me, we were a team. So I guessed I was in the firing line too. We'd been together a long time. We'd stood side by side, defending each other, especially in jail. Guys in there, they see a Mexican-looking guy and they want to pick a fight right away. I was all for keeping out of trouble, but Jim - he had this kinda devilish streak in him. Like he'd goad them. Fact is, without me he'd have got himself into a heap more trouble. He owed me a lot, and once in a while, after a few beers, he admitted it.'

'So you took him home with you.'

'Yeah, just till the heat died down, that was the plan. Then it was going to be business as usual. We still had the contacts, and we had a few bucks put away. Except that Congress had a change of heart. 1933, they scrapped Prohibition. Put a lot of folks out of work.'

'What did Grandpa make of it? Having Jim around?'

'He didn't like it. He made that plain from the get-go. Never did like Mexicans. Didn't want no "goddam wetback" around the place. He was happy to set him to work, of course. Same as he'd been happy to accept the money I sent him when we were bootlegging even though he knew where it came from. He chose to overlook that. Anyway, Jim always pulled his weight. He never ducked out of work. But then one day when Nadia was around he started getting fresh with her. She didn't object any, but your Grandpa, boy, he was through the roof.'

'Seriously?'

'Oh, when your Grandpa got mad people took notice. And then he told Jim he'd get the law on him. Said he was off to see that cousin of mine, the sheriff I told you about?'

'To get him deported?'

'Yeah. So Jim left, and I soon followed. Met up with him in North Platte. Like I said, we were close, a unit. He'd got family down there working on the railroad, said they could fix us up. His uncle was up from Houston. He remembered me from the first time we went down there. He liked me.'

'So that's how you got started on the Burlington.'

'Yep. And I was down there ten years. More than that. Right up until I married your mom.'

'Which was in 1945, right?'

'January forty-six.'

At this point, a long pause ensued on the tape. Steve had had his eyes closed but was now watching his sister, who returned his gaze as the tape rolled on.

'Let's go back, can we?' Wanda said on the tape.

'Back to where?' Pete grunted.

'North Platte, when you first met Mom.'

'That was way before this. Ten years. More than that. I knew her a long time before we got hitched.'

'Yes, that's what I thought. So, tell me about that. Like, how old were you? No, how old was she?'

'When we first met? She was just a kid. Very sassy, very good-looking, but to me just a kid. You could see right through her.'

'Oh. So not someone you'd have been interested in?'

Steve could hear Pete shifting in his chair, lighting another cigarette. 'Wanda,' Pete said, 'you sure you want to go down this road?'

'Don't worry, Dad. I've heard Mom's side of the story.'

'I'll just bet you have. Yeah, mother and daughter, I can see that. Listen, I'm gonna say one thing right now, and you're gonna have to believe me. All the time me and Jim hung out in that place, all the Saturday nights we spent there, I never laid a finger on Irena. Hell, I was forty-some years of age.'

'So was your buddy.'

'Jim had a different outlook on girls. Once they hit puberty they were fair game. I never saw it that way.'

'So didn't you ever argue with him - like, say "leave her alone she's too young"?'

'At first I did. And in fairness to him, he treated her different from his other women. And he had plenty, the years I knew him. But the fact is, he loved her.' Silence, and then in something close to a whisper, 'And I guess she loved him too.'

'But she ended up with you.'

Another silence, this one longer. While it lasted, Wanda and Steve sat staring at each other, Steve noticing how she seemed to shrink as the visit wore on. For the first time, he truly believed she could be dying. It was as if he could see it happening, the slow decline.

Pete spoke first. 'There was a reason for that.' It seemed to Steve that his father was about to reveal something important. Instead, he switched tack. 'And don't forget,' he said, 'there was a war in the middle of all this.'

'Okay. But you didn't serve, did you?'

'Serve? I don't like it when people use that word. I served my country, all right - just that I did it by keeping the railroad running. We were considered a special case, you know that. Exempt from the draft.'

'But what about Jim?'

'He was gone, way before Pearl Harbor even.'

'Gone where?'

'Jim didn't like the settled life. We were both working in the yards. Regular pay, overtime. We were doing okay, considering what the rest of the country was facing. But he missed the money he'd been used to - the big money. And I guess the excitement too. And he was a smart cookie. He could see a chance to make a few bucks. He got mixed up with some guys who were hijacking shipments from the freight cars. Tried to rope me in, but I wasn't playing. No way I was going to risk another spell in jail. And of course, he got caught.'

'What, he went back to jail?'

'No, this time they deported him.'

'Hadn't he been through this already? Proving he was a citizen?'

'I told you, people didn't have documentation then the way they do now. And these were county officials we're talking about. They did as they pleased. Way they saw it, if you looked Mexican that was good enough. Who was gonna complain? These people just came and went. Here for the harvest, and back home again. Or if they got a girl in trouble, they'd vamoose. And anyway, far as Jim was concerned, better to be shipped back to Mexico than do another spell in the joint.'

'So was that it? Did you ever see him again?'

'Not until after the war. By which time Irena and I were married.'

'How did that come about? I mean, whose idea was it?'

Before he could hear the answer, Steve became aware that Wanda was in trouble. Her head had slumped forward. Her breathing was deep but irregular, like a series of gasps with no rhythm to them. Steve switched off the machine and hurried down the corridor to fetch Lejla.

'What you been doing with her?' Lejla was running to Wanda's room, Steve trying to keep up with her.

'Just listening to her tapes,' he panted.

'Yes, and get her all emotional.' Lejla was at Wanda's side now, checking the line that fed pain relief into her arm. 'You knew about this. So why didn't you stop?'

'Look, I'm sorry. I asked her if it was okay to carry on.' He was torn between remorse at causing this to happen, and anger at Lejla for her sharp tone. 'She gonna be all right?'

'We'll see. You need to go.'

'Okay,' he said, 'I'll go. Come back this afternoon, see how she is.' He hesitated. 'I mean she will be all right, won't she?'

He watched as Lejla fixed the feed. She got Wanda into a more comfortable-looking posture, then beckoned Steve out into the corridor. 'Yes,' she said. 'Your sister will be all right for now. But remember, Mister Kaminski, she is dying. The sickness make her weak. The drugs help her, but they are exhausting. She cannot be excited. You must remember that. She likes to see you but you need to set a time limit on your visits. Otherwise . . .' She shrugged.

'Okay,' he said. 'I got it.' He went back into Wanda's room, picked up the cassette recorder and unplugged it. Before he left, he took a last look at his sister. She was breathing regularly again, but looking quite frail. He reached out and held her hand. It seemed small, and her skin delicate. He muttered a goodbye to her and left.

Outside, he sat in the truck for some minutes, thinking. Listening to these tapes was far harder than he'd imagined. It was disorientating, confusing. It was rocking his world. It wasn't good for him. Couldn't be good for his sister either. Maybe he should forget the damned things. Except that he knew he couldn't. You open a door like that and you have no choice but to step through and see what's there. This man Pete, who was and was not his father, he wasn't anything he had seemed to be. If Steve was going to make sense of the past that was disintegrating before his eyes, he needed to hear the whole damned story.

He fired up the engine and headed back towards the highway. At the junction he hesitated before turning west. Should he stay in town and check up on Wanda later on? Phone in first and get an update? No. He didn't want to be around Gordon. Never did like the damned town. Trouble was, he realized, he had nothing to do other than visit Wanda. How long could he keep that up, sitting by her bedside raking up memories as she got weaker and weaker? Maybe after all she had the right idea, that he should take her home and move in with her. Christ, he'd never foreseen all this. He'd been thinking of the future, about selling the ranch, settling his debts, then maybe buying a place on the Gulf Coast, or a big old RV and hitting the road. As he drove, his mind was in turmoil. All the years he'd resisted the idea of coming back here and now he was being sucked in . . .

He felt a sharp jolt as a blaring car horn sent a shock of adrenaline through him. His speed had dropped to a crawl, and he realized he was driving with one set of wheels on the shoulder. He responded sharply, almost over-compensating, and raised an apologetic hand as the other driver passed by, peering curiously at him and shaking his head. Christ, this was really getting to him. All these revelations about the past and the way they clashed with his own assumptions. The fact that there was only him and his sister left to figure it all out, and her getting ready to die. No wonder he was losing his grip. No wonder he was struggling to drive in a straight line. No wonder he was ready to lash out at anyone - like the way he'd given the woman Lyn such a hard time. He replayed that confrontation and saw once more the look of absolute uncomprehending shock on her face, and the way it contorted into pain. She didn't deserve that, and he knew it. Every time he thought about it he felt like shit. He glanced at his watch. Eleven-thirty. Okay, why not head back to Chadron and call in at the hotel? He'd be there in forty minutes. That was one positive thing he could do, go find her and see if she'd accept an apology. He refocussed on the road ahead, and pressed down on the accelerator.

THE DOOR to the Olde Main Street Inn was open, but the place appeared to be deserted. He walked in and took a seat under one of the front windows. Sooner or later Jeannie would come in and he could ask her where Lyn was. He had in his hand his copy of *Old Jules*. He'd been trying to get back to it for a couple days now and figured he might just sit and take it easy. He was pretty sure Jeannie wouldn't mind him hanging out. She ran a sociable kind of place - a home from home for one or two of the regulars, like Glenn and Tina. He looked around the bar, the antique spinning-wheel at one end with a skein of raw wool draped over it; the table covered with the kind of oil-cloth he remembered from his childhood; the lacy drapes at the windows; at the far end the old photographs in glazed frames. This place was home-like.

It wore its history like a well-worn coat. It was the perfect place to read about the old days. He settled in his chair and opened his book.

As he flipped through the pages to find his place, the one word that caught his eye was 'Niobrara'. And there it was again, in a chapter heading: *The Niobrara Feud*. It got him thinking about the moment, just a few days previously, when he and Lyn had stood on the old wooden bridge that spanned the infant river, up near the first Old Jules place. The surprise he'd felt then, at how small and insignificant it seemed, nothing more than a stream coursing gently through a meadow. He'd always remembered it as a much broader river that flowed in great sweeps below the limestone bluffs it had carved out of this undulating landscape. Sitting in the inn, he recalled places where he could wade on a summer day in almost tepid water, and then feel the cool current of some creek that came tumbling in from any one of a dozen deep, shaded ravines that joined the river at regular intervals like tributaries to an artery; groves of tall trees populated by herons and chewed by an occasional beaver. One time, he remembered, he had startled a doe. It was a face-to-face confrontation, a staring match under dark pines, the pair of them held in suspended animation, barely a dozen paces apart, until she appeared to shrug, then tiptoe away, daintily, silently, with two little kids trotting after her.

Steve was struggling now to recall just where and how he had accessed such places. It must have been after he had started driving one of the old trucks that were around the ranch, because where they lived was some way from the river. Or had he gone on horseback? That was possible. Grandpa had encouraged him in that. Said it was his right to roam the land. He wondered then whether such places still existed, and whether they would match up to his memories, the ones in which he seemed to recall being contented, if only momentarily.

From somewhere behind the bar he heard the sound of a door creaking open, then the *clack clack clack* of paws on a bare wooden floor. Looking up, he saw the old tan dog walking slowly towards him, head slightly to one side, tail wagging. Steve reached out and stroked its silky ears.

'Looks as though he's made up his mind about you.' Jeannie had come in, carrying a bunch of flowers which she placed beside a vase on the bar. 'And he's a good judge of character.'

'Always got along pretty well with dogs,' Steve said. 'Grew up with them.' He closed his book. 'Dogs and horses. Fact is, they're a lot less complicated than people.'

'You said it.' She picked up a pair of scissors and started trimming the stems. 'So how are you getting on at the State Park? Nice and quiet, I'll bet.'

'It is.'

'And your sister?'

'Good days and bad.' Steve didn't want to talk about Wanda. He was looking around the place once more, taking in the atmosphere, so welcoming and peaceful. 'This is quite a place you have,' he said. 'Unusual. You always been here?'

'Me personally? No, my mother ran it for many years. Then when it got to be a bit too much for her to manage on her own I quit my job in Denver and gradually took over.' She stepped back to take a look at the way she'd arranged the flowers and added, 'We've got a long history. Goes back over a hundred years.'

'That far, huh?'

'And further. It's about as old as this town, as old as the history of settlement in the Panhandle, give or take a few years.' She took the vase to the sink and filled it with water. 'I was always fascinated by history, and I heard this story that

General Miles had stayed here. He was in charge of the government troops - the time of the Ghost Dance troubles.'

'Oh. You mean - that ended up with Wounded Knee?'

'That's right. But he wasn't involved in the massacre. That was one of his subordinates, and boy, he really condemned him for it. He lobbied the government to pay compensation to the survivors, so we have no problem with celebrating the fact that he was here under our roof.'

'So he definitely did stay here?'

'Yes. It took us a while to verify it, but we turned up a newspaper report from 1890. And then once we realized just what a past we had, we started campaigning to get ourselves put on the Register of Historic Places.'

'And did you?'

'Eventually, yes. Which we were pretty darned pleased with.'

'I'll bet you were.'

Jeannie brought over a jug of coffee and a pair of mugs. 'Do you have time?' she asked.

Steve had been thinking about a beer, but he didn't want to deter her. He was interested to get to know this woman. 'Sure,' he said. 'I gotta few things to chew over, but . . .'

'Oh.' She had been about to sit down but changed her mind. 'If you need to be alone?'

Steve shook his head. 'No,' he said. 'Fact is, I was kinda hoping I'd run into Lyn - you know, the professor?'

Jeannie was pouring the coffee. 'Yes,' she said, 'interesting woman.' She gave a short laugh. 'She certainly got my regulars buzzing.' She looked at Steve with a steady gaze.

Steve stared at the cover of his book, moved it away across the table. 'Listen,' he said, then stopped. 'I don't know whether she said anything to you, but we had a . . . well, fact is I was pretty damned rough on her. I mean verbally. Brutal would be more like it.'

'Is this about when you dragged her out of the ditch?'

'No, we got over that. This was something else. Something quite different. She came to my room to tell me something - all she was doing was trying to help me. But you know how it gets when you're just not in the frame of mind to listen.'

'Oh yes,' Jeannie said. 'Sometimes you just don't feel as though you need help. Or advice.'

'Or advice. That's right. I was in a bad place and I guess I just took it as an intrusion. I - well, you could say I shot first and was planning to ask questions later.' He looked up at Jeannie, questioning her with his eyes. But at first she didn't answer and he added, as an afterthought, 'It's a habit of mine. Not a good one, but it goes back a long way. And I'd been drinking bourbon up there. Something else I'm inclined to do when I'm troubled.'

'If it's any help to you,' Jeannie said, 'she didn't say anything to me. And she seemed fine, although she did say she was going on a research trip.'

'So she's not here?'

'No. She's in Lincoln. At least, that's what she said when she checked out.'

'Right. Well, I guess it'll have to wait.' Steve took a drink from his mug and checked his watch. It was coming up to noon. 'Look, I got to go, but - do you have my cell-phone number?'

'Sure, it'll be in the register.'

'Okay, so could you do me a favor? Text me when she gets back?' He hesitated, then said, 'Unless you think she – well . . .'

'You mean if she comes in brandishing a shotgun and asking where you're holed up?' Jeannie smiled at him. 'Yes, of course I'll do that.' For a moment neither of them spoke. Then Jeannie said, 'Look, you're neither of you bad people.'

The remark surprised Steve. 'No?' he said.

'No. So maybe it's just a matter of one of you deciding to call a truce.'

'That'll be down to me. That's why I came by, to tell the truth. See if I could fix it up with her.' He got up from his seat. 'Well, thanks for that. But you will call me?'

'Just as soon as she comes back.'

'Thanks.'

Before the conversation with Jeannie Steve had no plan for the rest of the day. He wasn't going back to Wanda. Whatever Lejla had said, he was sure she was implying that Wanda wasn't up to it. And then there was Lejla herself. He wanted to be confident that, when he did go back, she would greet him the way she did those first few visits. There was something precious there that he didn't want to tarnish. He would leave it until tomorrow.

By the time he'd got in the truck he was quite certain how he was going to fill the day. He was going to look at the Niobrara, as he remembered it. He was going to find that spot where he used to swim. He was going to sit there, watch the water glide by as it used to when he was a youngster, the way it had done, broad and shallow and steady, winter and summer, since the beginning of time. He was going to find out whether it still had the power to make him feel good. If only for a moment. That was all.

To get there he had to drive east, beyond Hay Springs, past Rushville, and take one of the county roads south. That much he remembered. He just wasn't sure which road. Had it simply been a matter of reaching the river it wouldn't have mattered a great deal. In theory, any north-south road ought to get him there eventually - although that didn't take account of the fact that many of them had disappeared or fallen into disuse, terminating abruptly at a wire fence, or veering off to east or west. A hundred and more years after the government survey lines divided the land into neat mile-square sections, the gradual expansion of one ranch at the expense of another had reduced the grid-pattern to something more like a patchwork of remnants and loose ends.

It seemed at first that he'd got lucky with his choice. The road he'd taken was broad, straight and well maintained. Steve was watching his odometer as he drove, as well as the mile markers. So far, they were all there, in sequence, as they would have been when Grandpa Andrzej was looking for a place to settle, and at each one of them a county road or a farm track ran to east and west. He rolled along over an even surface, the gravel popping and pinging against the wheel arches, a cloud of dust billowing up behind him. Ahead, the sun was high in the sky. There were barely any clouds. It was already warm, a perfect spring day. Before long he could see the river, or at least its course, marked by a line of trees, gray, winter-bare cottonwoods mostly, with a tangle of underbrush, and running along a low valley just a few miles ahead.

Then, quite suddenly, the road veered off at ninety degrees towards the east. It was narrower now, and ran along the side of a rough slope, thinly grassed and dotted with cedars. He began driving much more slowly, steering cautiously around the hollows filled with muddy water, the occasional lump of limestone that had fallen across the trail, but all the time he was drawing closer to the river.

In the end he ceased to care about trying to find the particular spot he carried in his mind. He realized it was a dumb notion. Spotting a patch of rough grass that sloped gently to the water's edge, he stopped the truck. This now seemed the important thing, to be beside the water. He was never going to find the precise location. It was doubtful that it really existed. He'd visited the river many times as a youngster, sometimes with Pete, later with his buddies and, if they were lucky, their girls. So maybe it was a composite, pieced together from several different occasions. Besides, he knew that rivers change and evolve over the years, even this one. Facing him on the other bank was a bare wall of limestone, yet to be colonized by the plum-trees and vines, the sumacs and coarse weeds that grew elsewhere. The untidy pile of rock below it was evidence of the erosion that must have been happening all along its course for millennia. In midstream, low banks of gravel, sand-bars through which the water rippled and sparkled, marked the constant changes in the river's flow.

Taking *Old Jules* from the passenger seat, he opened the door and got out. Here was as good a place as any to sit and finish this extraordinary book, this study of a man both fascinating and repulsive, penned by a woman who - he couldn't shake off the thought - might in other circumstances have been his mother. What if she had agreed to marry Pete, her childhood sweetheart? What then? The idea clung to him, haunted him, and filled him with an acute sense of regret, even of loss.

By the water's edge he paused beside the trunk of a fallen cottonwood, its bark long gone and the wood bleached white. It had the look of a colossal bone. He wondered how long it had lain there. Could it have been upright forty-five, fifty years ago? Might he have sat leaning against its coarse bark with a girl on his arm and luxuriated in her embrace, the summer warmth? He slipped off his boots and socks and stepped slowly into the running water, shivering as a gust of wind came down from the bluffs opposite. He recalled now the time he and his buddies had come with tire-tubes and floated downstream, carrying them across the shallows. Enchanted by the sheer delight of the experience, they'd allowed themselves to drift and drift. They washed up, finally, under a bridge that crossed Highway 61, and had to send the youngest to a nearby ranch-house to use the phone and persuade his father to come pick them up. Across on the other bank was a stand of tall trees. He remembered now how he would come, spring-time, and hunt for morel mushrooms in such shady spots, how, when he took them home, Andrzej would reminisce about the fungi he himself used to bring home from the forest, and the way his mother would dry them, to be added to a stew the following winter. Steve stood in the water and let these memories wash over him.

As the wind eased, the warm sunshine and cold water offered a bracing contrast. He looked up into the sky and watched a pair of buzzards circling high above him. Reaching down, he cupped his hands and splashed water in his face. As he stood up it trickled down over his neck and made him shiver.

Slowly he made his way back to his tree-trunk, now warm to the touch. Sitting down, he pulled out his glasses from his shirt pocket and opened the book. He didn't have many pages to go now. He found it fascinating, the way the author had taken this coarse, dirty, violent man and now, subtly, deftly, was casting him as a man of vision, of intelligence, determination, an almost heroic figure.

Here, in the closing pages, she presented him as a man who, despite a lifetime pursuit of confrontation and resolute individualism, grew to relish his role at the center of the community he had indeed helped to establish. Here was a kind of elder statesman, a clan leader, opening up his barn for dances, running informal horseraces and rodeo events in the yard, a man who would put a notice in the newspaper inviting everyone in the neighborhood to come on over and enjoy the huge spread cooked by his diligent, put-upon wife, and take away sacks of fruit he had grown, against all the odds, in orchards that were talked about right across the state - fruit that he exhibited annually in the big show in Lincoln, the one event in the year that prompted him to shave and get his hair cut. These parties were lively events that lasted deep into the night. People would come prepared to sleep over and share in a big breakfast next morning. And still Steve remained perplexed. How come this daughter that Jules had so badly mistreated, so neglected in her young years, how come this author with the power of the pen at her command had resisted the temptation to slip a length of literary steel between the old bastard's ribs? How had she managed to bottle up the resentment she must have felt, to write, as she did in these latter pages, with admiration - even affection - for her erstwhile tormentor?

He looked out on the river, quietly going about its eternal business, nudging each bank in turn with a foam-flecked ripple, testing its boundaries, pushing a floating log into this or that backwater, constantly looking to linger a while before heading on, as it must, towards the east. He carried on reading, determined now to reach the end.

When he got there, he saw just what Mari had accomplished. To him it seemed very clever. She had started the book with a description of the land, of the Panhandle as her father had first seen it, at a time of year when it was 'shaking off the dullness of winter'. Spring was in the wind and Old Jules was making a fresh start in a new land, afire with the vigour of youth and the vision of the adventurer. Then, 425 pages later, she brought it to an end in late fall with a reference to the 'unalterable sameness of the somnolent land' as this man who had started more fires, aroused more passions than any dozen ordinary men might have experienced, passed quietly away. She had taken great pains, Steve felt, to portray Jules at the peak of his powers, a raging bear of a man determined to live out his life by his own rules and nobody else's. And now, in the aftermath of the emotional whirlwind she must surely have passed through, she showed him as a man who, like the storm that grows from a tiny cloud, 'to flash and thunder and roar and bring rain to the needy earth', was now about to 'disintegrate, to drift in a pale shred of nondescript cloud': to die, peacefully, in bed, with his daughter Mari sitting beside him.

Steve thought, naturally, of Pete. Of course, he had never seen him in decline. Grandpa Andrzej, yes; but not Pete. He had no idea what this man-who-was-not-his-father had become in old age. There might be a clue in the tapes, which he now knew he had to play to the end.

He closed the book and sat for some time looking at the river, constantly changing yet forever the same. Then he got up, put on his shoes and walked back to the truck. He had done enough for today.

23

Once Lyn made her mind up about something she generally acted fast. Having decided that she ought to return to Chadron and resume her quest for the missing manuscript, she checked out of her hotel and was on the road by seven next morning. Even taking into account the hour she would lose when she crossed to Mountain Time, and allowing for pit-stops, she was hoping to be there before evening. Just as she was leaving, downing a quick coffee in the hotel foyer, she paused under a TV and checked the weather forecast. High winds and driving rain were on their way late in the day. She shrugged. She'd arrived in Nebraska in the face of a blizzard, so what the heck? And besides, right now the sky was clear.

When she set off from downtown the city was looking its very best, the tree-tops lit up by the rays of the rising sun. Several miles out along I-80, glancing into her rear-view mirror, she could still see its light reflected from the gilded dome of the Capitol. She thought once more of Mari, standing at the end of J Street on an April day back in 1930 and watching *The Sower* being winched into place atop that very dome. The thought gave her a sudden shiver of delight.

She made good time along the interstate and took a short break outside Grand Island. The light was still good, the only clouds puffy and light. As she filled up with gas she remembered she had yet to call ahead to see whether Jeannie had a room free. Initially, after the unpleasantness with Steve, she had assumed she would look around for another place to stay, but she'd really enjoyed the Olde Main Street Inn, so why should she allow herself to be elbowed aside just because some alcoholic grouch didn't appreciate her attempts to be friendly? Screw him. It turned out there was a vacancy, which she took. She didn't ask Jeannie about Steve. Didn't want to hear herself speak his name.

On Highway 2, with little traffic on the road, she found herself relishing this part of the journey. She was on an adventure, once again crossing the Great Plains. She was alone, on a mission to complete a project that she'd lived with for years. And she was heading west. How romantic was that? Damn, it felt good. She was the heroine of her own private drama, and she felt no need to shout it out to the world, being content to cherish it in her breast, and glow with satisfaction at finally setting her dream in motion. She put on the radio, searching until she found a station that played classic rock. Then she sang along, full-throated, joyous, raucous, to a sequence of old favorites. It was a thing she rarely did, and never in company. She was no kind of singer, never had been. Maybe that was why she liked her music loud and full-on, aggressive songs that permitted you to scream out the words. She kept it up all the way to Broken Bow, pausing only to laugh at her own exuberance - and the sore throat she'd given herself.

Entering the Sandhills, she settled down to enjoy the meat of the journey. Nebraska had been described to her by so many people as flat, drab, empty - a stretch of barren land to be crossed on the way to more scenic places farther west - but here she was grinning with anticipation, mentally hugging to herself the knowledge of something much more varied, more meaningful. As the rolling grasslands unfurled before her and the horizons widened, she relaxed, deciding that she needed to intersperse her necessary research and reading, her writing too, with more days out in the country. Much as she preferred not to think about Steve, she had good memories of that trip around the Old Jules Trail. She would repeat it. Take picnics. Explore further, deeper. Maybe rent a four-wheel-drive and probe these gravel byways and two-tracks. Allow herself to find the essence of this extraordinary landscape, its *genius loci*. Just now the hills still wore their winter drabness: dun-colored grasses with occasional glimpses of orange or pink, and then the sudden emerald circle under a center pivot irrigator. She wondered just when the new season's grasses would emerge, and whether she'd still be around to watch the whole land turn green. And then she wondered how long that phase would last. If she was going to get to the heart of this Sandoz business then perhaps she should take time to observe these seasonal shifts, to engage with the land that had fuelled her heroine's creative impulse. She glanced up at the sky. Still no sign of that change in the weather.

As she headed west she grew hungry and pulled in at Mullen for a bite of lunch. Didn't linger. Just grabbed a BLT. Passing Alliance she could feel the tension leave her shoulders as she turned north on 285. Just one more hour and she'd be there. She was ready for that, weary now of the long hours at the wheel.

When she passed the State Park entrance she checked the time. Five o'clock. A stiff breeze was tossing the pines and the sun was now veiled by a thin layer of high cloud. Ten minutes later she was pulling up outside the hotel. She got out, stretched her arms above her head and crossed the sidewalk. The bar appeared to be empty, and that put her at her ease immediately. She wasn't ready to answer the kind of questions the regulars would be bound to fire at her.

'Well, you made good time.' Jeannie looked up from behind the register, where she was going through a pile of receipts. 'Welcome back.'

'Thanks.' Lyn pulled out a seat from the bar and sat down.

'How was the drive?'

'Oh, it was fine. No traffic to speak of. Just a long, long way, that's all.'

'That's the joy of Highway 2,' Jeannie said. 'So, how did it go in the big city?'

'Not so bad. But it's hard on the eyes, working with microfilm. And the back.' Lyn wriggled her shoulders and grimaced. 'I just got to where I'd had enough. If I'm honest, I mistimed the trip. I should have stayed here for now. But there you go . . .'

Jeannie brought the register across, got Lyn signed in and handed her a key. She looked at the clock and said, 'Well, it could be a very quiet evening. Tina and Seb are out of town, Glenn's staying home with a cold. Guess we'll just see who calls by. Can I get you a drink of anything?'

'That would be great, thanks.' Lyn took out her purse. 'Listen, it has to be my turn to treat you. Would you care to join me?'

'Well sure, that would be a pleasure.'

They sat for a while and carefully avoided the subject that was on both their minds. Gently prompted by Jeannie's questions, Lyn talked about herself: where she came from, what it was like growing up in Carbondale. 'People don't realize,' she said. 'You tell them you come from Illinois and they immediately think Chicago. But that's actually a very rural part of the world down there.'

'Oh, I know it,' Jeannie said. 'I've been that way more than once, in my biking days. You got Missouri one side of you, Kentucky the other.'

'Right. I mean, my mother's people came from there and they were very southern in outlook.'

'So your mom's people were what, farmers?'

'Yes. My grandmother, she was real country. Her folk were pioneers. In the 1860s, I believe. She was always coming out with quaint old sayings. If she wanted to say something happened real fast it was always "quicker than Grant took Richmond".'

Jeannie laughed. 'That's not one I've heard before.'

'Oh, there were lots. I wish I could remember them all. Should've written them down while she was still with us.' Lyn thought for a minute, then said, 'Here's one. You know when people say, "Does the Pope wear a funny hat?" As in, well of course, it's true?'

'Sure.'

'Grandma had her own version of that. Didn't care who was listening, she'd just come right out with it. "Is a pig's pecker pork?"'

'Whoa, that's one to remember.'

'I still use it when I want to make people take notice. When I started bringing friends home from college, oh man, they thought she was so quaint. They started calling her Granny Clampett.'

'Ha. From *The Beverly Hillbillies?*'

'That's it.' There was a moment's silence between them. Then Lyn asked, 'So what about your mom? She ran this place before you, didn't she?'

'She did. You know, if you're still around next week you'll get to meet her. Soon as the weather warms up she comes over from Arizona.' Jeannie paused to reflect, then said, 'Yes, she sort of ran the place as a boarding house for railroad workers for some years. And of course, being where we are she always had a few Native customers, down from Pine Ridge.'

'Oh, the reservation? That's quite near here, isn't it?'

'Just over the state line, in South Dakota. Yes, it was a point of pride with Mom that they always regarded her as a friend. You know, a lot of the young guys would come to town after they'd got paid, get drunk, wake up in the morning and find they'd spent all their wages or lost them. Had them stolen in some cases. Then of course they'd be in big trouble. Well, after a while they found they could come to town, give their wage packet to Mom, then go out and have their bit of fun.'

'Wow, and collect it in the morning? Your mom sounds like a pretty resourceful lady.'

'Oh, she is. And those guys, they trusted and respected her. She was well thought of by most people. Still is, by those old enough to remember her. Mind you, she could upset folks too.'

'Really? The way you describe her she sounds like a regular saint,' Lyn said.

Jeannie laughed. 'She had a bit of devil in her. Back in the 1970s she tried to bring this place up to date. She started putting on live music, which went down pretty well. Then she had this great idea. I remember her telling me on the phone, "I'm gonna get a couple of go-go dancers in. Liven the place up".'

'No way!'

'Oh, but she did - and boy, did that get the tongues wagging.'

'What are you saying, that Chadron wasn't quite ready?'

'Absolutely not. They wanted to close her down. Well, the

city did. Other people were loving it, of course. And her takings - oh, they were through the roof.' Jeannie looked at Lyn and said, 'You're a sort of historian, right?'

'Biographer really, but yeah, I do historical research.'

'Well you know, Mom kept some press cuttings from those days. Put them in one of her scrapbooks. I should hunt them out for you.'

'I'd love to see them.'

'She kept all kinds of things I've never gotten around to sorting out. Maybe they're old enough now to be interesting.'

'Sounds like my mom,' Lyn said.

'Old enough to be interesting?' Jeannie laughed.

'Ha. That's just the sort of thing she would say.'

'But maybe it's something we all end up doing,' Jeannie continued. 'Hanging onto the past. Every year when she comes home I try to get her to do a bit of sifting. She was always cutting things out of the newspaper. Never threw away a letter or the postcards people sent. You know, we get a lot of bikers stay here, older people mostly.'

'The only people who can afford a bike, right?'

'Tell me about it. So a lot of them will send a card from their next stop down the road.'

'And your mom just kept them?'

'Hundreds.'

'Sounds like you have a regular historical archive there,' Lyn said.

'Archive? More like a junk pile. There are books, magazines. Anything people left in their rooms, right down to a pair of shoes or an old sweater.'

'Shoes? Seriously?'

'Last time I looked, yes. And a couple of raincoats. I'm always trying to get her to have a clean-out, but she'll be . . . "well, you never know when the owner might come back".'

Jeannie got out of her seat. 'I wonder whether I can find those cuttings. Are you sure you'd like to see them?'

'You bet I am.'

Jeannie was already around behind the of the bar. 'Okay, back soon.'

In fact, she was gone some time. Lyn assumed she'd gotten distracted. Twice she heard a phone ring. It was easy to forget that Jeannie had a hotel to run. She finished her drink and went to the window. Cloudy, but still no rain. She walked out to the car to get her case. Back inside, she started to flip through the notes she'd made in Lincoln.

'Well, well, well.' Jeannie was back, and grinning from ear to ear. She was carrying a couple of large scrapbooks and a pile of old newspapers, all of which she now put on the table.

'You find them?' Lyn asked.

'Sure. I don't know how long it is since I went through that closet,' Jeannie said. 'Quite some years. So I got the cuttings, and the newspapers she took them from.' She dumped them on the table. 'And then take a look at what else I found.' She was holding out a large manila envelope with Lyn's name written on the cover in large capital letters.

'What on *earth* is this?' Lyn slid off her chair and took it from her, opened it and pulled out a yellow legal pad. 'My notebook! Whoa, I cannot freaking believe this!' She opened it up and started flipping the pages. 'Look! Look at the date. *July fourth, Hastings Nebraska. July fifth, Hyannis. July sixth* - here we are.' She held the notebook up for Jeannie to see. 'Look at the heading: *eight forty-five, Caroline Sandoz house.* 1993. July of ninety-three. Oh man, I can't take this in.' She folded back a page and showed Jeannie. 'See how fast I was writing. Look at the scrawl. Jeannie, you absolute doll. This is fantastic!' She threw her arms around the other woman's neck. 'How do I ever thank you?'

'Well, you're making a pretty good stab at it.'

'I don't know whether you can possibly imagine just what this means to me.' Lyn was struggling to get the words out as her eyes widened and her lips stretched into a manic grin. 'Just the notes,' she finally said, taking a deep slow breath. 'It's the Holy freaking Grail. I mean, these are the notes I made in Caroline Sandoz' house.' As she spoke she kept flipping through the pages. 'There's thirty, forty pages here. Oh man, do you realize I transcribed these verbatim from the very manuscript I've come all this way to find. Plus here's our interview. Look at this!' She kept flipping the pages over, jabbing a finger at the scribbled notes. 'Look, I got quotations, page references. Man, I'd given up, years ago. Never, *never* expected this to turn up.' She was still gasping as she read things she'd jotted down all that time ago. 'See, I interviewed a bunch of people that trip.' She was looking at Jeannie, shaking her head. 'And you – you found it, just like that.' She put on a sing-song voice. 'Oh, I think I'll go out back and see what I can find in the closet. And next thing it's *ker-ching*!'

'Quicker than Grant took Richmond,' Jeannie said, rocking with laughter.

'You got it.' Lyn stopped and opened her purse. 'Oh this is a real-life hold-the-front-page moment. *Read all about it. Ark of the Covenant discovered in Chadron Nebraska.* Lyn Collier's long-lost notebook is finally unearthed. Bonus material!' She waved the book in Jeannie's face again. 'This little book is the key to the whole damned project! I mean, sure I wanna find the missing manuscript I told you about, but here's most of the evidence I need, right here in your mom's collection of old post-cards.

'And old shoes,' Jeannie added, laughing. 'Coupla sweaters too.'

'Okay,' Lyn said, pulling out a twenty-dollar bill, 'time for a little judicious rule-breaking here. Gimme a glass of,' she looked along the shelf of the cold cabinet, 'yeah, let's make it sparkling white wine. And please pour one yourself. We're celebrating. Are you allowed to celebrate this time of day?'

'One thing about running your own business, Lyn. You're the one who makes the rules.'

'Well, come on. Start pouring. But I'm making you personally responsible for holding me to one glass. That's a whole half year's allocation. I want a clear head when I read these.'

As they sat there, just the two of them, Jeannie gently teased it out of Lyn, the full story. 'Because I only get to hear bits and pieces from behind the bar there,' she said. 'Tell you the truth, I never really understood what it was you were looking for. And I don't think I've ever heard you explain about this missing manuscript.'

Lyn found that it helped her, trying to boil the entire story down to its essence. Not that she doubted Jeannie's interest, rather that she had tried to make a practice over the years of distilling difficult ideas into single sentences. It came from the need to sell her idea for this book about Mari to publishers, academic and commercial, to come up with an 'elevator pitch' that neatly, and forcefully, encapsulated what it was all about. *Tell me your idea in twenty-five words or less.* That kind of challenge.

Quite what her hostess thought about it she never really found out, because no sooner had she mentioned Caroline's part in it all than Jeannie beamed and said, 'Oh yes, what a character!'

'You know her?' Lyn asked.

'Met her, many times.' Jeannie reminded Lyn that she provided rooms and food for many of the academics who converged on Chadron annually for the Mari Sandoz conference. And, yes, Caroline had attended until relatively recently.

'Oh, I feel such an idiot hearing you say that,' Lyn said. 'I mean, all these years when I should've come along, but . . .'

'Other things getting in the way, huh?'

Lyn nodded. 'Divorce. Changing jobs. Moving house. Teaching summer school to pay the bills.' She picked up her glass and swirled the contents around, watched the bubbles rise to the surface and disperse. 'And then I go to Lincoln and find out that guess what? She's still alive. I had no idea. I mean, she's turned a hundred now.'

'She must be. Yes, she battles on. Or so I'm told.'

'Do you have any idea where she is?'

Jeannie shook her head. 'What, are you thinking of calling in on her?'

'Wow, wouldn't that be something. But why not?'

'Well, I have a friend who'll know. Would you like me to call her?'

Lyn hesitated, but only briefly, before firing off her answer. 'Is a pig's pecker pork?'

24

As he was driving away from the river, heading north on the gravel, Steve reached into his coat pocket and took out his phone. Damned if he hadn't forgotten to check on his sister. When he'd left the care home that morning he'd said he would return some time in the afternoon, but it was already three o'clock, and the day was running away from him. The last thing he wanted right now was another round trip to Gordon. So he was relieved, if a little concerned, when Wanda didn't pick up. He tried the office instead and spoke to a woman called Carla. She told him that Wanda had slept a couple of hours and had been given morphine for her pain. Steve told her he would visit in the morning, and asked her to make sure she passed that on.

He set off along Highway 20. Jeez, it had been a strange afternoon. First the calmness he'd felt, sitting by the river, soaking up the spring sunshine, then a growing agitation triggered by what he'd read in the closing pages of Mari's book. With that came a feeling of vexation. He was still feeling cheated, that she should treat Old Jules so kindly. Like he was some kind of old-time western hero. Damn it, if a guy was a sonofabitch when he was living, why should the story change the moment he was laid in his coffin? Did he deserve to be treated so kindly? Okay, you're not supposed to speak ill of the dead, but you got to be respectful to the living, don't you? Here was a guy who'd been flat out abusive to his kids, and his wife. Wives, in fact. All four of them. It was like some politicians you hear about. They spend an entire career condemning their enemies, and as soon as one of them dies their opponents are lining up to tell the world what a fine person they were.

Steve's thoughts rolled around like distant thunder, clashing against each other. Lies. Pious bullshit. He wished now he'd read more of the biography he'd picked up in the hotel, and wondered what the woman Stauffer made of it all. He checked his watch. It wasn't even four o'clock yet. Screw it, he needed to fill up on gas, buy a few groceries. While he was in town, why not swing by the Center? They sold books there, didn't they? He was certain Jeannie had mentioned it.

He found the place easily enough, and parked out back. Walking around towards the main entrance he was stopped in his tracks, arrested by the statue of this woman who had become such a presence in his life these last few days. Here she was, the girl his father wanted to marry - and maybe should have. He stood and looked at her. He noted her demeanour, the optimism of her posture: head up and fearless. He studied the frank, honest expression on her face, a look accentuated by the way the sculptor had conjured up a prairie wind to push the brim of her hat clear of her luxuriant, full-bodied hair. Sure, it was only a likeness, but if the artist had truly captured the spirit of the woman, if he'd done his job, then he, Steve, was looking at the woman who might have been his mother. . . Even as he told himself not to be so dumb he could feel the pain inside, an anger with himself for still harboring that crazy thought. If the old man had indeed married her, he wouldn't be here now, would he? So why couldn't he rid himself of this corrosive fantasy? Some stubborn notion was telling him he might have been spared the pain the old man had caused him. Turning, he walked up the steps to the glazed door that led inside.

A few minutes later he emerged with a copy of the biography *Mari Sandoz: Story Catcher of the Plains*. He stopped in front of the statue and took another look at it. Then he flipped through the book to remind himself of the pictures he'd seen just a few days earlier. There were a dozen or so, and the difference between the young Mari and her mature self was striking. Even into her early thirties she looked gaunt, her face taut with worry. As a mature woman, buoyed by her success, she seemed confident, happy, vivacious. Better dressed too. And then there was the cover photo, the one that had caught his attention that first morning in the hotel room, her hat slanted over one eye, the other gazing steadily, seductively, at whoever was behind the camera. But none of them, it seemed to him, was quite like the barefoot figure in bronze. He stood there for a while, then made his way back to the truck.

At the campground he cracked open a beer. The wind had got up and the sky had clouded over, so he decided to get a fire going. He had another steak to fry. Sitting at a picnic table he skimmed through the book again, back and forth, not entirely sure what he was after. He kept returning to the photographs, fascinated by the changes that fulfilment had wrought on Mari's face, from awkward hesitation to radiant self-possession. And then he found himself reading about that time of her life that Lyn had spoken about, where the young Mari, just starting out on her literary career, wrote a first version of her upbringing, and so created this unpublished manuscript that Lyn herself was hunting for. Thinking about Lyn, he went back to the day they'd traveled the Old Jules Trail. He'd enjoyed her company, been intrigued by what she had to tell him about the Sandoz story. And then he'd screwed it up. He wondered whether there might be a way back.

Sitting there as the wind hushed through the tree-tops, Steve read what this Helen Stauffer had to say about *The Ungirt Runner*. It ran to no more than a couple of pages, which disappointed him. He read it a second time. Stauffer, it seemed, was in no doubt that what Mari had written was highly autobiographical, was fueled by a rage against her father's tyranny. That was interesting enough, but what stopped him in his tracks was the name Mari had adopted for the fictional character who represented her younger self in the story. Endor.

No sooner had he read it than he could hear the old man, way back when Pete and Mom started arguing. What did he call her? The witch of Endor. Steve never knew why. Why not the wicked witch of the west? More than once the whole family had sat around the TV over the Christmas holidays and watched *The Wizard of Oz*. It was a favorite, a rare thing they could all enjoy together. He had picked up on the name and learned to apply it to everybody he wanted to put down, from unpopular teachers to any woman who dared to reprimand him or his buddies, even girls in high school who had the misfortune to be plain or combative. Mom had adopted it too. It was like a standing joke. You cross me, you're the wicked witch of the west. It was common parlance. So how come Pete didn't use it? Where did this witch of Endor come from?

Years later Steve thought to check it out in an encyclopaedia. Endor, he found, was a Biblical character, a seer. She appears in the book of Samuel, when King Saul goes to her to hear what fate might await him in battle against the Philistines. It isn't good news. She tells him that he and his three sons are going to die. True to the prediction, the sons are cut down, whereupon Saul falls on his own sword. But that didn't explain why, whenever Pete was angry at Irena, the name would slip out as slick as a snake's tongue. 'Listen to the witch of Endor,' he'd scoff when she tried to tell him how to answer some letter from the bank. 'Go ask the witch of Endor,' when the kids wanted a special favor. Did he get it from Mari? Was it a name she was playing around with when they were teenaged sweethearts, some kind of alter ego she adopted?

Well, he could speculate all night long. Nevertheless, he couldn't resist going over the whole passage one more time. In Mari's portrayal of her father - she calls him 'Jock' - there was, according to Stauffer, 'no redeeming vision to offset his grossness'. And Mari, he read, depicted a mother who was 'unloving, often hostile'. She had a scene in which 'Jock' locks the eleven-year-old 'Endor' in a snake-infested cellar as punishment for having sent a short story to a newspaper. Jesus. No wonder she described him as a monster. That's what he was.

Steve put the book down. With the wind, his fire had burned through quickly and was already reduced to a mound of red-hot coals. He reached out a foot, raked them level, and threw a steak on the grille. He was just about to crack open another beer when he heard his phone ping. He opened it up and saw that Jeannie had texted him. *Lyn is back.* That was all it said. He snapped it shut and sat for a moment, thinking, before turning the steak. Was he going to make a stab at it? Apologize? Ask to be forgiven? It was all he had to offer. Thinking it through just made him tired, that and the cool evening air. As soon as he'd eaten, he was ready to turn in.

Despite what was going through his head, he still found comfort in the physical pleasure of crawling into his bed and lying under the rugs in his custom-made camper shell. Through his new windows he could watch the tree-tops swaying to and fro, then the first rain-drops splashing on the dusty glass. He'd always felt he was lucky in this, that no matter what else was going on in his life he could be calmed by a good meal and a comfortable bed. It seemed to suggest to him that there was something sound at his core. He'd talked to Bonny about it one time, and she'd said deep down he must love himself, and that was healthy. It was just other people that caused him problems. It was in that frame of mind that he decided he would, of course, make overtures to Lyn. All he had to do was hang onto that inner feeling of . . . what was it? Compassion? Remorse?

HE SLEPT in an awkward position and woke with an aching back. Then he sat too long with his coffee, which he brewed over the stove, waiting in vain for the sun to warm his bones and watching the clouds he breathed out unfold in the still air. Now, at last, the sky was clearing and the day was warming up. He wondered how much longer he could live like this. It was the way a lot of people managed these days, of course, in an RV or a converted truck, a VW bus, but that didn't make it any easier. It wasn't so long ago that he'd assumed he would be with Bonny until the end. Then he had to lose his temper and blow it all to hell. But could he face returning to the old place to watch his sister die? He slung his coffee grounds into the dying embers and got in the truck.

He arrived at Sunny Acres soon after ten. When he got out of the truck he was walking stiffly. He found Wanda looking pale, even haggard. She wore a robe over her night clothes. But she was awake. He sat down opposite her, shifting the seat around so that he could share the view over the gardens.

'How are you this morning?' she asked.

'That's what the visitor's supposed to ask the patient,' he said, then, 'Yeah, not so bad.'

'You still camping?'

'Yeah.'

'What's your big objection to sleeping in the house?'

'Leave it,' he said. 'I'm fine as I am.' Then he added, 'Memories, if you must know.'

'Okay,' she said, 'I get that. So what we going to do? Talk over old times again?'

'I need to hear what else you got on that damned tape.'

'I guess you do.' She motioned to her bag. 'Help yourself. There's not much left to hear.'

Steve took it from her and slotted it into the machine. He placed his finger on the PLAY button. 'You know what's on here, don't you?'

She nodded. 'I got a fair idea. But it's been a while.'

He pressed his finger down, then changed his mind and rewound for a second or so before starting it. And there were those familiar old voices again. A younger Wanda, and an aged Pete picking up where they'd left off the previous day.

'I told you, people didn't have documentation then the way they do now. And these were county officials we're talking about. They did as they pleased. As far as they were concerned if you looked Mexican that was good enough. Who was gonna complain? These people just came and went. Here for the harvest, and back home again. Or if they got a girl in trouble, they'd vamoose. As for as Jim, he reckoned it was better to be shipped back to Mexico than do another spell in the joint.'

'So was that it? Did you ever see him again?'

'Not until after the war. By which time Irena and I were married.'

'And whose idea was that?'

'Does it matter?'

'Yes, Dad, it does. I mean, the way she spoke later on I got the impression she wanted Jim, right?'

At that point, Pete all but exploded. 'Jim, Jim, Jim! Lemme tell you about fucking Jim. Everyone assumes it was me that got rid of him.'

'Do they?'

'Your brother does - you know that. But it wasn't, Wanda. And I wish you'd understand that. Jesus, if Steve would only come home I could explain it to him myself. Listen, how much tape you got left there?'

'Not a lot. Why?'

''Cos I'm gonna say this once and once only, and then we're gonna agree not to bring it up again. Ever. You got that?'

'Sure. I mean yeah. Whatever you say.' Wanda was sounding nervy, eager to comply.

'Okay.' Steve could hear Pete letting out a weary kind of sigh. 'Remember me saying how I never laid a hand on your mother, when we were down in North Platte?'

'Yes.'

'Well, that don't mean I didn't want her. Like I said to you, she was a very desirable woman. Just young. Too young. But man, she had this thing about her . . .'

'Okay, okay, I get what you're saying.'

'Maybe. Maybe you do. But just quit trying to control this, will you?' They could hear the match flare up as Pete lit another cigarette. 'But as the years went by...' He seemed about to say something, but checked himself. 'You remember how I said your grandpa threatened Jim? And how he took off?'

'This was after you'd been in jail, right?'

'Yeah, and I followed him to North Platte. And eventually we went our separate ways, and he got deported, okay?'

'Yes, we've covered all that.'

'Just listen, will you?' Pete spoke sharply. 'I'm trying to piece this together and it ain't easy. We're going back a long, long way here.'

'Sorry, Dad. Go ahead.'

'So the war ends, and I - wait a minute. I forgot to say about Irena, didn't I?'

'Yes, what did she do during the war?'

'It was her big chance to make a break, and she grabbed it. She up and left North Platte and went to work in a munitions factory. Out in California.'

'Whoa, like Rosie the Riveter?'

'Hell, I don't know. Just that by the time the war ended she was writing to me saying why don't we settle down and live on the old place?'

'What - the ranch?'

'Yeah, where else? She always said she wanted to live in the wide open spaces.' Pete was quiet for a while. The tape rolled on, giving out a rhythmic series of squeaks. Steve leaned forward and saw there wasn't far to go. Then Pete was speaking again. 'Kind of ironic, the way she ended up stopping in town after work every night. You'll remember that.'

'Sure I do. And the arguments when she came home. But when you say she was asking you to settle down with her, I mean, were you two an item by then? Were you - you know?'

'Had I been to bed with her? By this time, yeah. Did we imagine we'd get married? No. I was still writing to....'

'To the Sandoz gal, right?'

'Yeah, but by now my letters were getting bounced. *Return*

to sender. Guess she'd moved to Denver by this time. And after the war of course she went to New York City.'

'So if the letters were coming back, why'd you keep writing?'

'Why? Because I figured she was the one person who would understand. Damn it, Wanda, I'd been closer to her than I ever was or ever have been to another human being. When she stopped answering my letters it was like part of me had died, and I wouldn't have minded if it was the whole of me.'

'So you were suicidal?'

'I wouldn't use that word. Just that I didn't really give a shit. But I kept going to work. It's how we were raised. And of course, later on, when I came back here, you know how that is. Running a place like we had keeps you going. You can neglect your own self but you don't neglect livestock. I seen that in a lot of older men. Wives gone, kids gone, and nothing to live for, but they ain't gonna let the livestock starve. It's ingrained.'

Another suck on his cigarette and a cough, then: 'But me and Irena had stayed in touch throughout the war. We never did the proposal thing. I'd moved back when the war ended. Had enough of railroading, working through the night, and as soon as I got here I realized I needed someone around. So it was never a romance. It was practicality. She wanted to get away - from people, I guess, city life - and it just seemed natural to assume we could have a life together.'

'Which meant getting married.'

'Of course. We tied the knot in Gordon, twenty-six January 1946. And then a week or two later Jim came visiting. Just showed up. No money, no car. I guessed he'd been in the joint again. Hitched a ride with one of the neighbors. This would be February time - I remember it was Valentine's Day coming up, and your mother announced that she liked to get a card. I'd never sent one in my life to that point. But I did the right thing. Went to town and bought one. When it arrived it was Jim who picked it up from the mail-box, and he gave it to her. I saw him. Took her a moment to realize it was from her own damned husband. I swear to God she was disappointed. '

'Then what? I mean, how was it having Jim around?'

'It was tense, that's for sure. I mean, we'd been through a lot together, me and Jim. I still had feelings for the guy. She did too. Irena, I mean. Your grandpa wasn't too happy, of course. So there was an atmosphere. And sure enough, it blew up. Couple days later I was out in the yard and I heard a lot of shouting. Came into the kitchen and Jim's on the floor, Dad's kneeling on his chest with a knife in his hand. I tried to separate them, of course. But boy, the old man was fighting mad. Lashed out at me, and caught me in the eye. He never meant it. He was just trying to throw me off. '

'You always said you lost your eye in a barroom fight,' Wanda said.

'Well, now you know different. I had to tell you kids something. What was I gonna say, that my own father stabbed me when he was trying to kill my best friend?'

Pete was drawing on his cigarette again. There was no mistaking the sound. Steve could see him now, the way he used to hold the smoke in before letting it out, real slow. He gave a dry, humorless laugh. 'I'm sitting there holding my eye, shaking like a leaf, blood running down my wrist, and he's got a hand on my shoulder. "Thanks, old buddy." Those were the last words I heard him speak. Thanking me for saving his goddam life.'

'Do you know what they were fighting about? I mean, I know they didn't get along, but why then, why at that moment?'

So far, in the room where they were both listening to the

tape, Wanda appeared to have been dozing, the way she lay in her reclining chair, her eyes closed. Not now though. Now she was looking at Steve closely, and there was a strange sort of compassion in her gaze. He sighed and nodded, slowly.

'Yeah,' he said, 'I guess I got it figured now.'

Pete was talking again. 'He'd found Jim and your mother together, in a clinch. That's what he told me.' Pete sounded disgusted more than angry. 'That was when he was driving me to the hospital.'

'And then?'

'What do you mean, then?'

'What happened to Jim? He take off or what?'

'Okay, remember your cousin, the sheriff?'

'Yes.'

'Well, your grandpa calls him. Tells him Jim's raped Irena.'

'Raped? Wow. And what was her version?'

'Ha.' It was a bitter little laugh. 'That nothing ever happened: that was her story. She flat out denied that anything ever took place.' Another silence. A lengthy one this time. Then Pete spoke once more. 'I guess it was a month later she told me.'

'What? What did she tell you?'

'That she was pregnant.'

'With Steve?'

'Who else?'

'Yeah okay. But how did you find out that . . .'

'That Jim was the father?'

'Yes.'

'Well, she sure as hell didn't volunteer it.'

Another silence. In the room, Wanda was watching Steve, waiting for something. Some kind of reaction. But he was buttoned up tight, hands locked together over his knees, body leaning forward as the tape squeaked towards its end.

'No, I had to watch my son grow up and start to look

more and more like my best buddy. So you could say it dawned on me slowly. You imagine what that was like, Wanda? Does your brother have the faintest idea what that was like for me? All that anger I got from him - after I'd saved his father's life?'

'Course not. But listen, what about Jim? Did they press charges?'

'It just didn't matter in the end. With him getting killed.'

'I guess not. So how did he die?'

Steve was concentrating hard. He could have sworn he heard Pete sob. It was very faint, it was muffled, but there was no doubt that was what he was hearing. Then there was a loud CLICK as the tape came to an end.

Steve looked up, startled. 'Is that it?' He reached across to pick up the player. 'That all you got?'

'He wouldn't let me put another one in. Wouldn't speak about it again. Except to say that as soon as Jim heard the law was after him he got in Grandpa's car and took off.' Wanda was sounding desperately tired now.

Steve looked at her, slumped in her seat. He stood up. Maybe he should go fetch Lejla, except that he wasn't through yet. 'How much of this did you know?' he asked.

Wanda managed to open her eyes. 'Before we made the tape?'

'Yeah. How much had you figured out? I mean, by the time I left home?' Steve looked at her, not sure that she'd heard. Or had she had just about as much as she could take? Maybe he should leave it there, except that he couldn't.

Finally, she answered. 'I knew Dad wasn't your father, if that's what you mean. It seemed obvious. You never looked the slightest bit like him. But Jim? I never even knew he existed, not until we made the tape. It was years later that Mom started to talk about him, when I went to visit her in Colorado.'

'So why didn't you tell me?'

'Oh, Steve. Our one phone call a year? What was I gonna say? "Happy Thanksgiving, and by the way, your dad was a guy called Jim"?'

'But if I'd known . . .'

'You knew Dad wasn't your father. You told him so, when you hit him - the day you ran off.'

'Sure, I'd figured that out. Or thought I had. But what happened to Jim? How'd he get killed?'

'I never got that out of them. Just Mom hinting to me that somehow Dad . . .' She looked away, and closed her eyes once more. 'Look, they said he got killed. And that was it. Like it could've been a car wreck or something. But she hinted it was Dad's fault.'

'There's more to this, Wanda. Grandpa told me more than once that he had a hand in fixing him. Maybe he cut the brake-pipe or something. He was talking about some bootlegger and I never knew what he meant, but now - Jesus.'

'Well, that's not what Mom said. Or hinted at.'

'What are trying to tell me?'

'She seemed to reckon it was Dad's fault.'

'No way, Wanda. We just heard him say he saved the guy's life. Jesus Christ.' There was a rasping noise as Steve stood up and shoved his chair back on the polished floor. 'I need to get some air.'

Wanda was trying to get out of her seat, and the effort was making her gasp for breath. 'Don't be long.' She all but coughed the words out. 'We need to talk about this.'

'Do we?' he said. 'I think we should maybe put it back in its box, don't you?'

He was out in the corridor. He didn't have a plan. He didn't need one. He just had to go. Anywhere. Distance himself from the messenger and find a space for thought. His gut instinct was to get in the truck and drive. Out in the hills.

It's what he did when he was a kid. Take the horse and ride. Get away. Think. Later it was the pick-up. Even in Portland, if he had a bust-up with Bonny he'd get out of town, find a quiet spot in the woods. Sometimes he'd stay out the night. Calm himself down. It helped. Better than confronting his demons unprepared. He was already thinking about the spot by the river where he'd spent the afternoon, but he wasn't sure. He stood there in the doorway, trying to make up his mind.

25

First thing on the morning after finding the lost notebook, Jeannie called her friend and found out where Caroline was living. It was a care home in Gordon. Lyn still hadn't come down for her coffee, so Jeannie phoned the place to check that the old lady was receiving visitors. The woman she spoke to said that would be fine, so long as they understood that Caroline spent a lot of her day sleeping and wasn't always up to talking.

Lyn had been up late the previous night, going through the newly discovered notebook. She'd read the whole thing twice, and then found she was so excited that she couldn't sleep. Her mind was still racing, and she knew she would go through it again the first chance she had. By the time she came down to the bar, bleary-eyed and nursing a mild headache, it was past nine o'clock. Jeannie's news, however, galvanized her. She hurried her coffee, shoved a pile of papers into her shoulder-bag along with the notebook, and was on the road well before ten.

Within an hour she was in the nursing home, being escorted along a corridor by a bright, cheerful young woman who introduced herself as Lejla. She told Lyn that Caroline had not slept well, otherwise she would be in the day-room, or even outside, a beautiful sunny morning like this. She knocked on Caroline's door but didn't wait for an answer before entering, beckoning Lyn to follow.

There was no more than a sliver of light shining through the gap between the drapes which had been drawn across the window, floor to ceiling. But it was enough for Lyn to see her, sitting in an easy chair, wrapped in a rug, her head slightly to one side, eyes closed. As Lejla ushered her fully into the room Caroline, the sole remaining child of Old Jules Sandoz, blinked her eyes open and squinted at the two women.

'Well, looks like you had a nice little nap,' Lejla said, in that musical, joyous voice. 'You feeling better now? Ready to greet the day? It's a real pretty one.' She crossed the room and opened the drapes, allowing the sunlight to burst into the room and illuminate a vase of dark blue lupines that stood on a low table. Then she went across and eased the old lady upright. She placed a pillow behind her head and held a hand out to Lyn. 'See, I brought you a visitor.'

Lyn was nervy, hesitant. 'My name is Lyn - Lyn Collier. I'm writing a book about your sister Mari's work. I visited you back in 1993. We exchanged letters for a while.'

When Caroline didn't respond, Lyn turned to Lejla. Was she overwhelmed by the torrent of information? 'I brought something to show her,' she said in a half whisper.

'Go right ahead,' Lejla said.

Lyn reached into her shoulder-bag and pulled out a beige soft-cover book entitled *A Kinkaider's Child* by Caroline Sandoz Pifer. She opened it and held out the inside page, where it was inscribed *To Merilyn Collier for her enduring interest in my sister Mari Sandoz' work.* Underneath was the date, 6 July 1993. 'I kinda dropped in on you out of the blue,'

Lyn said. 'We spent the whole day together. You fed me lunch, and when I was leaving you gave me this.' She handed the book across. 'I loved it. You write so well about your life.'

Caroline took the book in her hand and looked down at it. Her mouth parted and she gave a faint smile. She caressed the book's cover with her thumb, slowly back and forth. She still didn't say anything, didn't even look up, just ran her forefinger slowly across the book's title, the way a child might who was still learning to read. Again Lyn gave Lejla a questioning look. She had no experience of dealing with a situation like this.

'Isn't it lovely, to see that?' Lejla said, leaning forward to look at the book. 'Yes,' she said, 'I thought so. It's one that you wrote, isn't it? That must be wonderful, to write a book. Such a lot of work. I think you have to be very clever.'

Caroline made a slight movement of her head. It might have signified agreement. Lyn couldn't see whether she had closed her eyes or was just looking down at the book in her lap. Whatever the case, there were no more words, just that one little gesture, which Lyn took to signify recognition. *Ah yes, this is my book*. She reached out a hand, thinking to reclaim it, then hesitated. Maybe this wasn't the moment.

Lejla broke the silence. 'I'll go fetch you a drink, yes?' She glanced at Lyn and said, 'Leave you two alone for a couple of minutes.'

Lyn nodded. It looked to her as though Caroline had fallen asleep again, and a part of her was relieved. Trying to make conversation was hard. She already feared that she would have sounded condescending. She sat back in her chair and watched Caroline, whose head was now drooping further down with each slow breath. The book was falling: Lyn caught it before it dropped to the floor. Was she going to gain anything at all from coming from here, she asked herself. Had it been worth the effort? Was it presumptuous of her - intrusive? She certainly wasn't going to learn anything in the sense of adding to her research material, was she? And yet. And yet. She knew she was right to have come. If nothing else, she had paid her respects to someone who had been a great help to her. And maybe it was enough just to be sitting here in the company of the old lady who was once, almost a hundred years ago, Mari's naughty little sister, a woman who, according to what Lyn had read last night, used to cheek Old Jules, laugh in the face of his threats and run away from him before he could come hobbling after her.

Going through the notebook had brought back so much that she had forgotten, so much that had been blown out of her mind by the tsunami of events that crashed over her when she called home that awful night in 1993. They would surely help her flesh out her book, these little details Caroline had given her about her father. How Jules would go to town in his dirty old brown coat using his rifle as a walking stick. How he always sat at the table facing the door, with sundry firearms, all loaded, lined up on either side during those days when they were at war with the cattlemen. How, when he got old and unpredictable, her brothers doctored his guns so that they only fired blanks, or sand.

'People say my father was crazy.' Lyn had noted down these words of Caroline verbatim. 'But he was crazy like a fox. He got by in this life and got what he wanted out of it. He was very bright, very talented and quite lazy. Physical labor was for *grobians*. A German word.' Lyn had looked it up right away. It meant boors or ruffians. Caroline had spoken too of how her father liked to hunt and read, and got everybody else to do the work around the place. How he made sure he married a hardworking woman, and a good cook. 'He was an interesting man,' Caroline told her, 'and always had something to say, and if he ran out of things to tell you about he'd go away and read until he found something.' As for the rages that so terrorized young Mari, they held far less terror for the younger siblings. 'Well,' Caroline said, 'he could swear magnificently in five languages, but we knew it was all bluff. And you know he never had heart trouble. Because he gave vent to his temper, and that's good for you. Course, he overdid it and that affected his liver. But people should give vent.'

Lyn had always assumed that the Sandoz sisters would have been close, but then Caroline reminded her of the age difference, of the fact that Mari was married when her little sister was four, had divorced and gone to Lincoln by the time she was eight. During that period, which coincided with the war, Mari was Caroline's school-teacher, a real disciplinarian.

'It was only after she died,' Caroline said, 'when I went to New York and gathered up her papers, that I really got to know what she was about.' She told Lyn that Mari didn't want her or Flora to get married, that when she won the *Atlantic Monthly* prize, in 1935, she offered to send Caroline money so that she could get divorced and go to college. 'Mari didn't like being married,' Caroline said. 'She came to that conclusion two weeks after hitching up with the Macumber fellow, and started saving for the day she could get divorced, buying war bonds.' As an after-thought she added, 'I didn't like being married either, but then I had the children, and they were bright, they were fun.'

Lyn's thoughts were interrupted by Lejla coming back into the room. 'Oh, she asleep again?' she said, and at that Caroline opened her eyes and smiled. 'Ah, you just fooling us. Here, I got you some coffee.'

Lyn looked at the old lady. She tried to imagine herself being a hundred years old, and wondered what she would have to look back on. Lejla was pulling up a seat next to her, and explaining that she would need to help with the drink.

It seemed to Lyn that this was a good time to withdraw. There was nothing to gain by staying any longer. She stood up. 'Well, Caroline, thank you so much for seeing me. It's been great to visit with you, but I think it's time for me to leave. I need to get back to my work.'

'You can stay if you like,' Lejla. 'I could fix you a drink too.'

'No, I'm good. I've done what I came to do. Thanks. And maybe I'll call in again some time.'

She took one last look at Caroline, then stepped out into the corridor.

26

'The hell you doing here?' Steve blurted out the words as Lyn emerged from the doorway and almost collided with him.

'And you?' A look of alarm erupted on her face as she stumbled, grabbing at her bag before it slipped right off her shoulder.

'Just visiting my sister,' Steve said. 'Listen, I wanted to say something.' He stepped closer, arms apart, grasping for the right words.

Lyn held up a hand in front of her. 'Whoa,' she said. 'You got something to say, just say it from there, will you?'

He opened his mouth to answer but the words wouldn't come. There wasn't room in his head for this, not on top of the conversation he'd just had with Wanda. He saw the wariness in Lyn's eyes, and something else. Maybe hurt as much as anger; he couldn't tell for certain.

'Okay,' he said. 'About the other night. I'd been drinking.'

'What - do you think I couldn't see that?' She made no attempt to disguise the contempt she was feeling.

He waited, expecting more, but that was it. She wasn't

going to make this easy for him. There was clear anger in her eyes.

He turned and gestured towards Wanda's room. 'Listen, my sister, she . . .' Oh Christ, why did Lyn have to show up now? Ever since it happened he'd been rehearsing an apology in his head, but he still hadn't explained his behavior to himself yet. He needed to say something, and here she was, prodding him again.

'She okay?'

'Pretty much the same,' he said. Looking at Lyn all he could see was the frown, the defensive posture. He was remembering how she had taken him in her arms that time in her room and how he'd backed away from the comfort she offered him. Why? Why had he let that moment pass? Why had he shrunk from crossing the space that separated them? What might he have from her right now if he'd only dared to let her in?

She was still holding his gaze, looking just a little less guarded. She seemed about to say something, then changed her mind.

'So,' he managed, 'you're here too.'

'Yes. Same as you. Visiting.'

His turn to frown. 'Visiting who?' he asked.

'An old lady. Mari Sandoz' sister Caroline.'

'I thought she was dead.'

'Yes, me too. But I was wrong.'

'So you came to interview her?'

'She's way past that. Far too frail. Look, I need to go.'

'No.' He glanced up and down the corridor. 'Look, I've just been with my sister. I - oh shoot, can we just sit down for a few minutes? There's something I need to say to you.'

A door creaked open and an old man shuffled from his room pushing a walker. He turned and headed off towards the communal lounge.

'What?' Lyn said. 'What is it you need to say?'

'There's a bunch of things.' He could see the uncertainty in her, the way she kept glancing over her shoulder towards the exit. 'I mean, if it's okay with you. If not, hey.'

She was deliberating over her every response, cranking up the tension in him. Finally she pointed to a bench seat, bathed in sunlight. 'How about there?' she said.

Behind the seat was a plant trough full of ferns. They'd just been watered. Steve could smell the moist warmth of the soil, see the droplets sparkling on the leaves. He waited for Lyn to sit down but she remained where she was, waiting.

He lowered himself slowly onto the seat. He needed to tell her about the tape he'd just been listening to. Tell her what he'd just found out. About the fight. Except that he'd had no time to process that. And looking at her, the way she finally parked herself at the far end of the seat, arms crossed in front of her, could he risk it?

'Listen,' he said, 'I'm real sorry for what happened.' The way her eyes met him, so direct and unblinking, made him turn away. 'No,' he said, 'let's get that right. I'm sorry for what I did. It was flat out wrong, okay? And you didn't deserve it.' Still she didn't say anything. 'There were reasons for the way I acted, but no excuses. You're a good person, Lyn, you've been a friend to me. And if it makes you feel any better I'm feeling like a piece of crap right now.'

He realized he was looking at his hands as he spoke, not at her. He remembered how Bonny had chided him one time for doing just that. She accused him of being evasive, and told him you should damned well look at a person when you got something to say. He took a breath, adjusted his position on the seat and looked right into Lyn's face. It wasn't easy, seeing someone who had trusted and liked him and was now reduced to peering at him through narrowed eyes, deliberately distancing herself. And her silence, that was unnerving.

'Okay,' he said. 'So I'm telling you I was wrong, and I'm sorry. Real sorry. Will you accept that?'

Again the pause. And he understood that. It was okay.

'I can accept it,' she said, at last. 'Sure.' Then she added, 'You know, I used to be married to a guy who turned to the bottle when things got rough. Did it myself, time to time, if you must know. It seemed to help with the pain.' She watched as a middle-aged man pushed an elderly woman past them in a wheelchair. Then she turned back to Steve and added, 'He said it helped him cope with his feelings. I think if you asked him now he'd say he was wrong about that.'

Steve nodded. 'Yeah. Point taken.'

Lyn didn't smile exactly, but her face did soften. She blinked, so slowly that for a moment he thought she was closing her eyes. 'Anyway,' she said. 'Yes, apology accepted.' Then there was a flash of something that might indeed have been a smile. 'I've had some good news,' she said, nodding her head.

Steve waited. Just a few days ago whatever she had to tell him would have burst out unannounced. Now she was weighing her words, every inch of the way, with little of that animation in her voice. There was damage to repair here, bridges to be built. 'Well, you gonna risk it?' he asked.

That did make her smile. 'You aren't going to believe this, but when I came out here in ninety-three and went to Caroline's house that time, I ended up staying the night at Jeannie's. Did I mention that?'

He shook his head. 'I don't think so. Maybe. But then I got a lot on my mind.'

'But I must've told you about losing my research notes.'

'Yeah, of course.'

'Well, guess what? They showed up.'

'That's good. Where?'

'Jeannie's place. In a closet. With a bunch of lost and found that her mom had collected over the years. She dug them out yesterday morning.'

'I guess that's a pretty big deal for you, isn't it?'

'About as big as it gets. Not like finding the actual manuscript, but I have twenty, thirty pages I transcribed from it, key passages. As well as my interview notes. This is a young Mari writing about her family, but as fiction.' She paused and let out a breath. 'Boy, it's revealing. There's some dynamite material in there. She really got some rage out of her system.' Lyn then muttered, almost to herself, 'Catharsis at work.' Then she looked at Steve. 'I should show you some of it.'

'Me?' he said. 'Why?'

'For a lot of reasons.' She looked at her watch. 'Listen, I never had any breakfast this morning. Do you wanna go find a place?'

'Sure, I could do with something.'

They drove downtown, each in their own vehicle. He followed her into a place just off the highway. They entered, and took a table by the window.

The waitress brought them their silverware and iced water. As soon as they'd ordered Lyn took the notebook from her bag.

'So everything in here is what I wrote when I was at Caroline's, eighteen years ago.' She was turning the pages. Steve could see that each one was filled with notes written in a small, cramped hand. There were bright yellow marker tags scattered through it. 'There's a couple passages here I was going to read you,' she said, stifling a yawn. 'Excuse me. I was up way too late going through this. But can you imagine what that felt like, after all this time?'

Steve was watching as she thumbed through the pages. 'Must mean a lot to you.'

'Such a relief, apart from anything else.' To his surprise she closed the notebook and turned it over, face down. 'But listen,' she said, 'this can wait. You have things to tell me. Am I right?'

The door was opening and he was backing off, instinctively. 'Nothing important,' he said. 'No. '

The waitress arrived with their coffee. 'I'll have your order in just a couple minutes,' she said.

Lyn was looking into his eyes. 'Nothing? Come on, Steve. The words don't match.'

'Match what?'

'They don't tally with what I'm seeing. The look on your face, your body language. Everything else you've told me about your family.' She reached out a hand across the Formica table-top and touched his. He felt his resistance ebb as she urged, 'Tell me about it.'

'Jeez.' He looked away. Outside, a large truck cruised slowly by, hauling a pair of trailers, both full of cattle. Green streaks of shit ran down the aluminum sides. A swirl of dust followed it along the highway.

'Where do I start?' he said. 'Okay, hard facts. I knew the man we called Dad wasn't my true father. There was a seed of doubt, but I only figured it out when I was about sixteen, seventeen. I swamped it in anger. It was "screw him, screw everybody".' He looked up at her. 'And you know how that goes. You end up screwing yourself, right?'

'Precisely,' she said.

'And eventually I got this idea, from my sister, I guess, that he'd gotten rid of my real father.'

'Whoa, you don't mean . . .?'

'"Got rid of" is what I heard.'

'But you didn't even know who he was, did you?'

'No, except looking back, years later, I remembered that my grandfather spoke about this guy that Mom was in love with, I guess. Called him the boot-legger. And of course, the letter you saw, that bore him out, I guess.'

'Okay. And what else?'

'Coupla times my grandfather said things, when I was young, before all this crap blew up, implied that he'd fixed him. He actually said that. "We fixed him. Pete and me." No explanation.'

'So you were angry with your father, I mean with Wanda's father?'

'Hell yes. Came to hate him. And part of why I left was this feeling that I should get out before I acted on that.' He returned Lyn's shocked stare. 'Yeah, like kill him. Because that's what was in my heart. Hatred, and anger. You ever felt that way about someone?'

Lyn made a short, nervy sound, a little like a laugh. 'Briefly, yes. Yeah, I can see why you'd want to get away.' Then she held up a hand. 'Just hold on a minute,' she said, and reached into her shoulder-bag. 'I got some more dope on your father in here. I mean Pete.' She looked at Steve and he saw the same empathy she'd revealed, that time she hugged him in her room. 'You're lucky I still have these. I was in such a "to hell with him" mood with you that I nearly destroyed them. But here you are.' She placed several sheets of paper on the table between them.

'What are they?' Steve asked, trying to read the slightly blurred newsprint upside down.

'The archivist in Valentine ran them off for me.' Lyn slid along the bench seat towards the wall. 'Why don't you come sit round here, make it easier for me.'

He was next to her now, watching as she flipped through the photo-copied pages. 'You know,' she said, 'this is the material I came bounding up to your room to show you the other night, when you blew up on me.'

'I'm sorry,' Steve said. 'If I'd known . . .'

'Well, we've covered all that, but it's hard to recall just how excited I was for you.' She pulled out a single sheet of paper. 'I'd found a few items about Pete, about when he and this guy Jimenez went to jail, made sure I got copies of all that. Soon as the curator spotted the name she dug out this other story for me. And this is the one you want right now. Here.'

What she handed him was a short report from February 1946, headlined *Fatal Auto Wreck*. It detailed a high-speed collision between a car and a truck in Sheridan County. There was a second account, from a later edition, which cited a police report shedding more light on the incident. The deceased driver, it stated, was Diego Jimenez, native of Brownville, Texas. The truck driver, who was uninjured, told police that the car approached him at high speed, the driver appearing to lose control on a curve. From the side-on collision it was thrown down an embankment and caught fire.

Steve read it, and shook his head. 'So there's my father,' he said. 'Dead in a ditch. Probably leaving town one step ahead of the law. And all because someone accused him of something he never did.' He thought for a moment. 'I guess that's what Grandpa meant when he said he "fixed" him: just that he put the law on him, frightened him enough to make him run. I'd been wondering whether he'd cut a brake-pipe or something, but no way he'd do that on his own car.'

Lyn laid a hand on his but said nothing. The waitress was putting their food on the table. Steve had only ordered toast. He thanked her, then shoved the plate to one side. Lyn already had her knife and fork in her hands. 'You'll have to excuse me,' she said, 'but I haven't eaten since yesterday.'

'Sure, go ahead,' Steve said. 'You know, you dig around for the truth, and eventually you find it. And then you wish you hadn't. Jim didn't need to die, did he? But if he knew Grandpa had called the sheriff... I mean, a Mexican accused of rape? Jim wasn't going to stick around and argue his corner, was he?'

Steve was silent for a long time, toying with a slice of toast while Lyn finished her breakfast. 'So,' he said, 'I guess it was a big deal getting your notebook back.'

'It certainly was.'

'And you wanted to show me something?'

Lyn sighed. 'I may be trying too hard to make a point,' she said, 'but I see parallels between the way you reacted to your supposed father and the way Mari reacted to Old Jules.' She stopped and looked him in the eyes, the question unspoken. 'But maybe you don't want to go there.'

'Don't worry,' he said. 'I trust you. Maybe that's why I wanted you to back off the other night. Maybe I realized you know me better than I know myself - in regards all this family crap, I mean.'

'Oh sure,' Lyn said. 'Other people's problems. I can solve them any time you care to ask. Ain't that the way of things?'

'I guess it is.'

'So, shall I give it a go?'

'Sure.'

'Okay. I'd say you got mad, justifiably mad, at Pete. I mean, when you were in your teens. Something was going on that hadn't been acknowledged. You figured out he couldn't be your real dad, and that was your moment of realization - that adults are fallible.' She smiled at him. 'Been making young kids mad since the dawn of time. Hasn't it?'

'I guess it's part of growing up,' Steve said.

'Yes, exactly, a necessary part. But the anger needs to be directed - outward, not inward. What I wanted to share with you was some of the ways Mari Sandoz expressed her anger towards what you might call her father's dark side.' The waitress arrived with more coffee. Lyn waited till she'd done the refills, then opened the notebook.

'So this is from the draft novel that she never published. This piece grabbed me, soon as I read it. She's writing about a guy she calls Palin. He's a convict, out on parole. Old Jules would take in people like that. Goodness knows why, but they had at least one jailbird lodging with them when Mari was a kid. Her mother wasn't happy about it, as you can imagine. And this one, in the story here, had been locked up for, quote, *a mysterious crime committed long ago, called Rape.* Capital R. *That made Jock laugh until his face turned fiery red. When Endor asked what rape was, her father supplied the short ugly word that she understood. Awful, of course, but why lock him up for that?*'

'Kinda near the knuckle, isn't it?' Steve said.

'Yes, but she's getting things off her chest. Trying to portray her father at his worst. Giving voice to her experience, and her feelings. Validating them, as we'd say now. I mean, she wrote way darker stuff than this. There was a novel, *Slogum House*. Boy, that was seriously murky. Based on an actual road-house not so far from their place.'

Steve was sitting with his elbows on the table, hands pressed into his eyes. 'Road-house?' he said. 'Mom was in a road-house, in her teens. Did I tell you that?'

'No, you didn't. But that would give any person problems. This one Mari wrote about, there was rape, incest, a kid gets castrated. It's genuinely shocking. A lot of places banned the book. But what intrigues me is that she wanted to express these powerful feelings, and she does it so vividly. It's like she's exorcising a whole lot of bad vibes.'

Steve nodded. Then he said, 'Course, she could have

decided to keep it under wraps. Like, protect the family name.'

Lyn gave it a few moments' thought before answering. 'But she did, to a great extent. I mean, this has never gone out. And there's a note in it - I copied it out, verbatim - that expressly states it was never to be published.'

'For the family's sake?'

'Hm. She doesn't say that. I think it's more that she felt it was embarrassingly badly written. Anyway, I got a couple more passages. Yes?'

'Go ahead.'

Before she read, Lyn glanced around the café. It was almost empty, just a couple of farmers in a far corner near the men's room.

'Right, listen to this.

'Her bed was just one thin board wall from that of her parents' . . . All winter she was reminded of what went on in her father's bed. She dared scarcely look at her mother, yet watched her constantly. And then it happened again.'

Lyn looked at Steve. 'She makes it plain that her mother's flat out horrified at yet another pregnancy. She has her mother lamenting she'd, quote, *'give five years of my life if this hadn't happened. All this time anger seethed and boiled in Endor's breast. They had no business - as if there weren't enough of them now! And then to hate each other for it afterwards! Never would she get married . . . Endor watched her mother's thickening figure in repulsion. Ugly, ugly.* And she adds in pencil, *why must everything be so ugly?* Then she has to help deliver the child. Can you imagine? *Somehow they got through the night. Not for years did the mother's screams die from the girl's ears, an audible echo every time she saw a pregnant woman.'*

Lyn put the notebook down, took a drink of coffee. 'I think she's describing the process of growing older, tougher, worldly wise. Of rebelling, in spirit at least. There's a whole catalogue of run-ins with her father. It's as if she's re-living every argument they ever had. And it does get seriously unpleasant. When she needs to pay the fee for her school-teacher exam, Jock tells her to get it herself. "*You got a way of making money with so many young bucks around*," he says. "*Why don't you make it?*"

'I think she's feeling very vulnerable, sexually. Like all men are playing the same game, all after the same thing. She goes to this dance where some young guy takes her outside and tries to force himself on her. She really fears the worst, she's about to give in. But then she imagines getting pregnant, the life of drudgery she would face, and she dredges up some deep inner power and fights him off. She turns on him, threatens him, quote, "*I'll kill you so dead you'll stink in an hour*".' Lyn looked up. 'Sounds familiar?'

Steve nodded. 'I guess she's her father's daughter, that what you mean?'

'Isn't she just.' Lyn picked up the notebook. 'Okay, just one more. After this near-rape there was a whole page missing; it had been torn out. I found it later, tucked away at the end of the book, except it's a photocopy of the original. Can't figure out what happened there. Maybe she ripped it out, then decided to re-insert it. Anyway, this is what it says. She's reflecting on the way she fought off the would-be rapist. And I think it's a key passage.

'*Often she had wondered . . . what she would do in a case like this, something not so unusual if the papers and the gossip could be believed. And now she knew. A sense of power coursed through her arms. Men? Strong men? They were afraid of her, afraid of her tongue, of her courage, the steel in her eyes, the iron in her will, the cruelty in her heart. Never again would she worry about them! For they were weak, she was strong!*'

'Yeah, that's powerful stuff,' Steve said. 'Sure it is, but...?'

'But why am I reading it to you? Instinct, primarily.

Because my first thought was that it seems relevant to your situation. And then I have to stop and ask myself why that's the case.'

'Well?'

'I'm not sure I've worked it out yet, but I'll think about it.'

Steve closed his eyes and thought for some time. 'Maybe,' he said finally, 'maybe I can answer my own question.'

'You mean about the significance of Mari's rage?'

'I guess, yeah. I mean, I know about rage.'

'I can believe that,' Lyn said. Then, 'Sorry. Cheap shot.'

'That's okay. I got a lot of anger. Always have had. I left home in a rage. Punched my old man on the mouth. Like I said, I'd figured out he wasn't my father, but I had no idea who was. Then I wondered whether Pete had got rid of him somehow. Wanda had stirred up my doubts, before I left home. That's what made me blow up, and then I was outa there. Except now I'm hearing maybe it was Grandpa who was responsible. And I'm remembering him telling me how he'd fixed the bootlegger. This was when I was a kid. I'd forgotten it, but it came back to me the other night in a dream. I didn't want to hear that. Because whenever I looked back - and I did, many times - I remembered being close to Grandpa in a way I never really was with Pete. And this morning . . .' He put his head in his hands. 'This morning . . .'

'What? What happened this morning?'

'I went to see Wanda and we played the last of the tapes. She's talking to Pete and it turns out he actually *saved* my father's life.'

'Seriously? How?'

'Grandpa knew that Jim and my mother were lovers and he pulled a knife on him. Probably wanted to scare him off. Pete jumped in to protect his buddy, and in the struggle Grandpa stabbed him in the eye. It was an accident, but . . .

Christ.' His head was in his hands again, bowed towards the table, eyes closed.

'Tell me,' Lyn began, then waited until he raised his head and their eyes met. 'This guy Jim, what kind of guy was he?'

'Hell, if you listen to Mom on the tape . . .' He checked himself, and started again. 'Y'know, that's the weird thing. She was plainly in love with him but she knew what he was.'

'What? What was he?'

'Kinda wild. Preferred living outside the law to having a settled job; and reckless with women. But, like I say, she fell for him. It's an old story, isn't it?'

'Suppose you met him now - I don't mean as a father and son reunion, I mean suppose you met him in a bar and were watching him. What would you think of him? If you can imagine that.'

'That's not a bad question. He sounds like he was a pretty rambunctious guy.'

'That can be attractive, or not.'

'True. I mean, you could say he led Pete astray, but when I heard about Pete's adventures - you know, bootlegging and all - I gotta say I found it exciting. If only he'd shared that with us. Does it sound crazy to say I wish I'd been there and lived it with him?'

'No. I can understand that.'

'Thing is, what I'm getting from what you're reading to me, and from reading *Old Jules*, is that Mari did it all.'

'Meaning?'

'Well, she had her outbursts in this book. She got it off her chest. Put her old man in a story and stripped him bare, I guess. Exposed him. Kicked the crap out of him. And then when he was old and weak she could afford to . . . Jeez, I'm running out of steam here, Lyn.'

Lyn took up the thread. 'She was able to see the other side of him, that what you're saying?'

'Yes. It was like she'd had an explosion, and the smoke had cleared and it was, "Right, that's that dealt with." In fact, it opened up another possibility for her, that she could feel tenderly towards him. Does that make sense? Taken him apart and exposed the bits worth salvaging.'

'Yes. It's the very thing I plan to write about. And where does that put you? How does your situation compare?'

Steve exhaled, a long slow release of breath. 'I'd say I never got to beat the old man and express my anger. Not fully. Just one wild swing, when I all but busted my wrist, and I was out the door. I never offloaded my anger, just carried it with me. I've carried it around ever since, and a lot of people who don't deserve it have had to feel it.'

He stopped abruptly. Lyn was looking at him. She was expecting more, but he'd stopped. All he said next was, 'Let's get outa here, can we?'

They settled up and left. Outside he said, 'Would you take another little trip with me, down memory lane?'

'Sure,' she said. She knew this was no time to quiz him. It was too important a moment to be complicated by questions.

'Do you mind leaving your car here?' he asked. 'We're heading out to the back roads again.'

'Where else?' she said, her voice light in tone.

27

They were bumping along a two-track, snaking their way between the hills that pressed in on either side. A stiff wind was stirring up the dust, and ragged white clouds trailed shadows that caressed every contour of the bare landscape. Here and there a group of black heifers, with their calves huddling close by, stood and watched them pass.

'This your family's land we're on?' Lyn asked.

'Used to be,' Steve said. 'There was a time when Pete had all of this. Some fifteen thousand acres, I believe. Then in the mid-eighties when things were real tough, he sold off a couple of parcels: half his entire holding, according to Wanda. Ever since he died she's been renting out the rest of it.'

They were out of the hills now, into a broad level expanse, almost featureless. Steve pointed to a lone tree, leaning to the east, its skeletal branches reaching out as if to grab hold of the sky. 'Used to be a big old place there, when I was a kid. Four bedrooms, a few barns. It was abandoned even then, but me and Wanda used to hang out there. Just a couple of farm kids playing house.'

They came to a stretch of chain-link fence that ran alongside the track for fifty yards or more. Steve braked, pulling up beside a metal gate. Above it a weathered board swayed in the wind.

'*Polish cemetery, 1909.*' Lyn read the words aloud. 'So where's the church?'

'There never was one,' Steve said, 'at least not in my lifetime.' He unfastened his seat-belt and opened the door. 'You gonna come in with me?'

The gates weren't locked. Just a chain, loosely threaded between the metal bars, held the two together. Steve opened up and had already walked several paces into the plot when he thought to go back and kick a rock against the open gate to stop it swinging.

'Come take a look around,' he said, and waited as Lyn came towards him. He saw her half stumble and realized she was still wearing her city shoes. 'Woulda warned you,' he said. 'If I'd known we were coming out here.' He grabbed at his feed-cap to stop it flying away.

'So who does this place serve?' Lyn asked, pulling out a bright blue scrunchy to tie her hair back. Looking around she could see no more than a dozen, perhaps fifteen gravestones.

'Family mostly. Grandpa fenced it off when Grandma died. That was shortly after he built his house, remember?'

'Right. 1910?'

'You got it.' He looked around the lot. 'Plenty of room. I guess he was still expecting the family to join him from Europe.' He walked on a few paces and stopped at a simple granite marker set in rough grass. Beside it was a fake stone vase containing a spray of faded plastic flowers. 'Here she is, right beside her husband. Gabriela and Andrzej.' Lyn looked at the simple inscription. In both cases there was nothing more than a name and their dates.

'I guess Pete should be around here someplace.'

'Here.' Lyn was standing over a simple stone slab set in the ground with a brass plate fixed to it.' There was no more information than on the others. Steve stood and looked at it for some time. Lyn zipped up her coat and hunched her shoulders. Glorious day as it was, the wind was making her feel chilly. She wanted to ask questions, but managed not to.

Pretty soon Steve said, 'Somewhere over there are my two aunts. And after that you're looking at neighbors, folk who lived on this land or adjoining it. But that's about it. Course, Wanda will be buried here. She told me that already.'

'What about you?' It slipped out before Lyn could stop herself.

Steve walked back towards the gate and she turned to follow. As he re-threaded the chain he said, 'Yeah, I been thinking about that.'

He lingered a moment, then looked back at the little plot, far too big for its handful of occupants, the short, dry grasses nodding in the wind.

'How can you talk of good people and bad?' he said. 'We're born knowing nothing, we're raised by people who were too busy surviving to figure out where they went wrong. All we can do is...' He sighed, deeply. 'I guess all we can do is understand what causes the bad, then find the good in each other and cherish that.' He turned towards the truck, and seemed to nod his head in agreement with his sentiments.

They drove on. The land rose very gently, then fell away, and there below them were the dark cedars and bare cottonwoods that surrounded the place he'd once called home. Steve was still silent as they approached the two houses. When they got out of the truck he walked across to the old house. Lyn followed, watched as he leaned back and looked up at the roof, then the second-floor windows. He took out his phone and snapped a couple of pictures. She waited, but he said nothing.

He led her right around the outside, paying careful attention to the bits of debris that were scattered around among the weeds. 'You gotta tread carefully,' he said, pointing out a loop of wire here, a jag of metal there. At each side of the house he seemed to be making the same checks. And he kept snapping. When they returned to the front he said, 'Shall we go inside?'

'Yes, let's.'

In the old kitchen Steve took out a knife and probed the bottom of the windows where the paint had flaked off. 'Still sound,' he noted. 'Grandpa hated spending money unless it was for timber. He always bought the best. He said long-term it made better economic sense.' He stood back and pointed at the decorative wooden trim around the window-frames. 'Made all that himself. Then he taught Pete, and Pete taught me.' He turned to Lyn and said, 'Did I tell you I made my living as a handyman?'

'No,' she said. 'You never told me a great deal about your past.'

'Had a decent little business for twenty years,' he said. 'Then I started drinking.' He stood there, remembering. 'To ease the pressure. I got the kinda contract you'd die for. Big old house in the Northwest Heights. People with money to burn. And other properties that needed fixing. Enough work to keep me in clover for years. But I screwed up. Still owe money around town.'

'Ouch. That why you're planning to sell this place, when your sister – I mean, when it comes to you?'

He didn't answer her question. Instead he said, 'Yeah, all we can do is look at everything we picked up from them and feed the good things, starve the bad. I guess that would work, wouldn't it?'

'I think so,' Lyn said. 'I reckon it worked for Mari. Got her out of a rut and let her produce her best work.'

'Sounds like it.' He went to the window and wiped the glass, peered out at the yard. 'And as for this piece of real estate,' he said, 'I got a proposition for my little sis.' He looked at Lyn. 'Okay if I run it past you?'

'Of course.'

'I'm gonna ask her to sell off some of the land. Just enough acreage to pay my debts.'

'D'you think she would do that?'

'If I agreed to bring her back home she would.' He looked around the room, went to the workbench and placed a hand on the vise. 'I can look after her. I'm not a bad cook. I can give medication. Had to in Nam, time to time. Then, in between caring for her I'll start on this place.' His tone was brighter now. 'It's basically sound. Just needs a new roof, new glass in the windows, wiring and plumbing. But it's what I do. Taught by a man who was taught by the guy who built it.'

'Wow. But that's still a project, and a half.' Lyn looked around, trying to imagine what it would take. 'And long-term?'

'Long-term? Just . . . live here.' He looked at Lyn and added, 'Wouldn't you, in my place?'

'It sounds as good a plan as any.'

He looked at her. He didn't smile, just held her eyes in his. 'And if some researcher wanted to come and hang out while she finishes her book, or just vacation here, she'd be more than welcome.'

He didn't wait for Lyn to respond. 'C'mon, let's get you back to your vehicle. Then I'm gonna go make the pitch to my sister.'

'In twenty-five words or less,' Lyn said.

'How's that?'

'Nothing,' she said as she followed him back to the truck.

Printed in Great Britain
by Amazon

78243879R00171